ERLE STANLEY GARDNER

- Cited by the *Guinness Book of World Records* as the #1 bestselling writer of all time!

- Author of more than 150 clever, authentic, and sophisticated mystery novels!

- Creator of the amazing Perry Mason, the savvy Della Street, and dynamite detective Paul Drake!

- THE ONLY AUTHOR WHO OUTSELLS AGATHA CHRISTIE, HAROLD ROBBINS, BARBARA CARTLAND, AND LOUIS L'AMOUR *COMBINED*!

Why?
Because he writes the best, most fascinating whodunits of all!

You'll want to read every one of them,
from
BALLANTINE BOOKS

THE CASE OF THE BORROWED BRUNETTE
THE CASE OF THE BURIED CLOCK
THE CASE OF THE FOOTLOOSE DOLL
THE CASE OF THE SHOPLIFTER'S SHOE
THE CASE OF THE FABULOUS FAKE
THE CASE OF THE CROOKED CANDLE
THE CASE OF THE HOWLING DOG
THE CASE OF THE MYTHICAL MONKEYS
THE CASE OF THE DEADLY TOY
THE CASE OF THE DUBIOUS BRIDEGROOM
THE CASE OF THE LONELY HEIRESS
THE CASE OF THE EMPTY TIN
THE CASE OF THE GLAMOROUS GHOST
THE CASE OF THE LAME CANARY
THE CASE OF THE CARETAKER'S CAT
THE CASE OF THE GILDED LILY
THE CASE OF THE ROLLING BONES
THE CASE OF THE SILENT PARTNER
THE CASE OF THE VELVET CLAWS
THE CASE OF THE BAITED HOOK
THE CASE OF THE COUNTERFEIT EYE
THE CASE OF THE PHANTOM FORTUNE
THE CASE OF THE WORRIED WAITRESS
THE CASE OF THE CALENDAR GIRL
THE CASE OF THE TERRIFIED TYPIST
THE CASE OF THE CAUTIOUS COQUETTE
THE CASE OF THE SPURIOUS SPINSTER
THE CASE OF THE DUPLICATE DAUGHTER
THE CASE OF THE STUTTERING BISHOP
THE CASE OF THE ICE-COLD HANDS
THE CASE OF THE MISCHIEVOUS DOLL
THE CASE OF THE DARING DECOY
THE CASE OF THE STEPDAUGHTER'S SECRET
THE CASE OF THE CURIOUS BRIDE
THE CASE OF THE CARELESS KITTEN
THE CASE OF THE LUCKY LOSER
THE CASE OF THE RUNAWAY CORPSE
THE CASE OF THE RELUCTANT MODEL
THE CASE OF THE WAYLAID WOLF
THE CASE OF THE MOTH-EATEN MINK
THE CASE OF THE LUCKY LEGS
THE CASE OF THE HALF-WAKENED WIFE
THE CASE OF THE DEMURE DEFENDANT
THE CASE OF THE SLEEPWALKER'S NIECE
THE CASE OF THE SULKY GIRL
THE CASE OF THE SINGING SKIRT
THE CASE OF THE SUBSTITUTE FACE
THE CASE OF THE NERVOUS ACCOMPLICE
THE CASE OF THE FUGITIVE NURSE
THE CASE OF THE GREEN-EYED SISTER

The Case of the

Hesitant Hostess

Erle Stanley Gardner

BALLANTINE BOOKS • NEW YORK

Copyright © 1953 by Erle Stanley Gardner
Copyright renewed 1981 by Jean Bethell Gardner and Grace Naso

All rights reserved under International and Pan-American Copyright Conventions. Published in the United States of America by Ballantine Books, a division of Random House, Inc., New York, and simultaneously in Canada by Random House of Canada Limited, Toronto.

Library of Congress Catalog Card Number: 53-5336

ISBN 0-345-37871-7

This edition published by arrangement with William Morrow & Company

Manufactured in the United States of America

First Ballantine Books Edition: August 1993

Foreword

There is something about the appearance of Dr. Milton Helpern that is strongly reminiscent of a big, cheerful English squire.

Even a pretty shrewd observer experienced in cataloguing the characters and occupations of men whom he meets would be likely to misinterpret Dr. Helpern and associate him with a country estate somewhere, with flower gardens, hedges and pastures.

Actually the man knows as much about murder as anyone in the United States, and behind his genial, easygoing demeanor is a shrewd, remorseless brain.

The attorney who wants to cite a list of authorities that will dispose of a question in the field of forensic medicine will be apt to top his list with a reference to *Legal Medicine and Toxicology* by Gonzales, Vance and Helpern.

Twice each year Dr. Helpern takes a train from New York to Boston and comes ambling into the lecture hall at Harvard University's School of Medicine, where Captain Frances G. Lee is holding one of her seminars on homicide investigation. There Dr. Helpern lectures for an hour or an hour and a half on some important aspect of homicide investigation. He speaks in an amiable, conversational manner, but his talk fairly bristles with bits of knowledge that are completely unknown to the average investigator.

At these times the eighteen law enforcement officers, who have been carefully selected as being worthy to attend one of Captain Lee's seminars, will be participants in a spectacle of the greatest incongruity.

Standing up in front of the class, lecturing them, will be a man who looks more like a human mastiff than a human bloodhound. It is difficult to associate him with murder.

At the rear of the room is the fabulous Captain Frances G. Lee, whom I have mentioned before from time to time. A woman in her seventies, she was brought up in the formal mid-Victorian surroundings of a wealthy New England family, and according to tradition should have retired to a life of coupon clipping.

However, some fifteen years ago, Captain Lee took an interest in legal medicine, donated a fortune to establish a school of legal medicine at Harvard University, then became interested in police science and is now everywhere recognized as one of the outstanding figures in police science and homicide investigation.

To attend one of these seminars, where a handpicked group of the keenest officers in this country rub elbows with men who have been sent over from Scotland Yard, from Canada, and even at times from India, is a rare privilege. It is a privilege that is only available to men who have for the most part (if they live in the States) been cleared by the state police and the governors of the states where the men live.

The lecturers at these classes are even more carefully selected. They are the cream of the crop. To be invited to so appear is a recognition of high merit and professional standing.

Dr. Helpern appears regularly, always smiling, always good-natured, as precisely accurate as a delicate surveying instrument.

Having finished his lecture, Dr. Helpern takes the train back to New York and there resumes his profession of examining dead bodies, ferreting out the cause of death, making deductions which would be a credit to Sherlock Holmes, and doing it all so casually and unostentatiously that only those who are familiar with legal medicine realize that he is one of the outstanding figures in the United States.

Talking with Dr. Helpern, going through the long rows of specimens which have been collected in the course of thousands of autopsies, one begins to realize the importance of the work of a thoroughly skilled medical examiner.

Dr. Helpern will prowl around among these bottled specimens with the air of an enthusiastic gardener showing off some choice flowers. "Now here," he will say, "is a collection of excellent examples of spontaneous subarachnoid hemorrhage." Dr. Helpern will indicate an assortment of carefully dissected brains, many of them proof that an innocent man could well have been convicted of murder if it hadn't been for competent medical work.

"The spontaneous subarachnoid hemorrhage," Dr. Helpern will point out, "is more frequently encountered than many people realize. Too often the inexperienced autopsy physician will certify death as being due to a hemorrhage caused by external violence. Actually it is nothing of the sort. But the peculiar circumstances under which such hemorrhages occur and the confusing symptoms which they produce may lead to an erroneous suspicion of violent death and to the conviction of innocent people.

"Most subarachnoid hemorrhages arise from the unexpected bursting of a small aneurysm, which is a thin sac-like protrusion, in some cases no larger than a match head, of one of the blood vessels at the base of the brain. Such aneurysms of the arteries of the brain develop at points of weakness in the blood vessel wall and eventually blow out or rupture, causing a more or less rapid hemorrhage to spread out on the undersurface of the brain. Death may occur within a few minutes or be delayed. Some individuals recover after the first hemorrhage to have a second episode of bleeding. If the aneurysm is embedded in and bolstered by brain tissue, as it often is, the hemorrhage is at first slow and affects only a small part of the brain without producing loss of consciousness.

"It frequently happens that this localized bleeding causes

the individual to become disturbed and aggressive, and at the same time to lose orientation and mental perspective.

"Perhaps an usher in a theater will be called to quiet a man who has suddenly become obstreperous. The usher suggests that the man leave the theater. The man makes an ineffectual swing at the usher, mutters something that is completely unintelligible, and the usher, warding off the blow, grabs the man around the shoulders and rushes him toward the theater exit.

"Halfway to the exit the man collapses. An ambulance is called and the victim is dead on arrival at the hospital.

"An incautious and inexperienced medical examiner, learning the history of the case and encountering an area of cerebral hemorrhage, and overlooking the small aneurysm from which it arose, is very likely to jump to the conclusion that the hemorrhage resulted from injury and that the usher had roughed the man up a bit. Sometimes a person in the audience will describe the altercation in terms sufficiently vivid to indicate that a blow was struck by the usher and that the victim fell to the floor.

"The usher finds himself facing a charge of involuntary manslaughter and the theater faces a huge suit for damages."

That is, incidentally, one case which actually happened and which Dr. Helpern likes to talk about as he pauses before the section on spontaneous cerebral and subarachnoid hemorrhage.

Modesty keeps Dr. Helpern from telling about the part he has played in a whole series of cases where death, apparently from natural causes, was, by his careful work, proven to be murder.

He will, however, on occasion show one of his close friends the evidence in one of the most remarkable cases of circumstantial evidence in the United States.

A man engaged in an altercation with another received a blow on the side of the head. He went on fighting and won the fight. He went home, and after a while began to feel ill.
viii

He went to bed, got up, wandered around in something of a daze, and, finally, was sent to a hospital where in due course he died. There was no conspicuous wound on the head and no one suspected the cause of death, but Dr. Helpern, in performing a routine but thorough autopsy, found a hemorrhage, which had resulted from a stab wound of the skull and brain. The blade of the weapon had penetrated the skull and had broken off flush with the scalp, part of it embedded in the brain.

Dr. Helpern inquired into the man's history, learned of the altercation, had the police pick up the other combatant and search him, whereupon they found in the prisoner's possession a penknife with the blade broken off.

Dr. Helpern fitted the segment of the blade found in the head of the dead man to the broken stub of the blade of the knife found in the possession of the defendant, and the two parts fitted together into a perfect whole.

Dr. Helpern, who received his early training from the late Dr. Charles Norris, the first Chief Medical Examiner in New York City, and has been closely associated with Dr. Thomas A. Gonzales, Dr. B. Morgan Vance, Dr. Harrison S. Martland and Dr. Alexander O. Gettler, in the Office of the Chief Medical Examiner in New York City and in the Department of Forensic Medicine at the New York University Post Graduate Medical School, was, with his distinguished colleagues, among the first to pioneer the field of the Medical Examiner. He has been largely instrumental in establishing consistently higher standards in the field of the medicolegal necropsy. His innate modesty and good-natured, retiring disposition have kept the public from learning the extent of its indebtedness to him. Only in the field of the professional investigator is his eminence known, and this is a shame because people generally should know something of what he has done.

Therefore it gives me great pleasure to tell my readers

about his invaluable work and to dedicate this book to my friend,

DR. MILTON HELPERN.

Erle Stanley Gardner

Chapter 1

For the past fifteen minutes it had been apparent that Harry Fritch, the assistant district attorney, was marking time. He fumbled through papers, asked repetitious questions, and from time to time surreptitiously glanced at the clock on the wall of the courtroom.

Abruptly he straightened. "That is all," he said, and, turning to Perry Mason with a bow of official courtesy, added, "You may cross-examine, Mr. Mason."

Mason got to his feet, realizing the trap into which he had been led.

"If the Court please," he said affably, "it is twenty minutes to five on a Friday afternoon."

"What of it?" Judge Egan asked in his most irate manner.

"Merely this," Mason added, smiling. "It occurs to me that the Court might not care to interrupt the cross-examination of this witness with an adjournment. My cross-examination will, I feel, be rather protracted, and perhaps if we postponed it until Monday morning . . ."

Judge Egan was courtesy itself in a routine case which was tried without a jury, but when the courtroom was filled with spectators, when a jury was present, Judge Egan made it a point to be rude. A shrewd politician, he had long since learned the popular appeal of dominating his courtroom and bullying the lawyers. He was hated by the lawyers but idolized by the voters.

"Court will adjourn at the usual time, Mr. Mason," the judge said. "Court adjourns at the hour of adjournment, not at the convenience of Counsel. You have some twenty min-

1

utes. The jurors want to get this case over with and get back to their business. Proceed with your cross-examination."

"Very well, Your Honor," Mason said, and, ostensibly turning to sort through some papers on the counsel table, gained a few precious seconds in which to study his strategy.

The woman on the witness stand was deadly clever. Unless he could shake her testimony the defendant was going to be found guilty. Mason had one surprise, and only one surprise. He hoped it would be a bombshell.

There was hardly time to spring that surprise and capitalize on the confusion it would cause before five o'clock, yet if he floundered around for twenty minutes with an aimless cross-examination the jury would retire for the week end firmly convinced that the woman's testimony should be taken at face value.

Mason reached a decision.

"Mrs. Lavina," he said, smiling courteously.

The well-tailored, good-looking woman on the witness stand smiled right back at him, a smile which seemed to indicate she was only too glad to face the most searching cross-examination he could give her.

"You have," Mason said, "identified the defendant in this case as the man who perpetrated the holdup."

"Yes, Mr. Mason,"

"When was the first time you saw this defendant? When was the first time you ever saw him in your life?"

"The night of the holdup. Mr. Archer had stopped the car for a traffic light. The defendant sprang up seemingly from nowhere, jerked open the door of the car, thrust a revolver almost directly into Mr. Archer's face, calmly proceeded to take his wallet, his diamond stickpin and my purse. It was all done so rapidly I hardly knew what was going on until the man sprinted back to the curb, jumped in a car that was pointed in the other direction and took off."

"And Mr. Archer tried to follow him?"

"Indeed not. Mr. Archer did nothing so foolish. The man

was armed. Mr. Archer was unarmed. Mr. Archer drove across the intersection, stopped at a drugstore and telephoned the police."

"And what did you do?"

"I waited in the car," she said, "until I realized I could wait no longer."

"How long did you wait?"

"I would say a good five minutes. Then a radio patrol car showed up."

"Then what happened?"

She said, "While Mr. Archer was talking with the police, a young woman whom I know drove past, recognized me sitting in the car, drove ahead and parked her car. I called a bystander and told him to tell Mr. Archer that I would be available in case the police wanted a statement, but that I was going on to The Villa."

"Why didn't you wait and talk with the police?"

"Mr. Archer could tell them everything the police needed to know. I had some very important matters to attend to. The police are hired by the taxpayers for the convenience of the taxpayers. If there was anything they wanted from me it would be an easy matter for them to come and find me."

"You were with Mr. Archer at the time of the holdup?"

"Certainly, Mr. Mason. I have said so several times."

"And where did you go after you left Mr. Archer?"

"To The Villa."

"Now, by The Villa, you are referring to The Villa Lavina?"

"If you wish to be specific, Mr. Mason, The Villa Lavina Number Two."

"That is owned by you?"

"The property is not owned by me. I lease the property, but The Villa itself is owned by me, perhaps I should say it is operated by me."

"You were en route to The Villa with Mr. Archer at the time of the holdup?"

"Yes."

"And who was it who came along in the automobile and picked you up—the young woman whom you said you knew?"

"Miss Kaylor."

"Miss Kaylor, I believe, is more than an acquaintance?"

"She is an acquaintance, a friend and an employee."

"She works for you?"

"I take it you wish to know if she worked for me at the time of the holdup?"

"Yes."

"Yes, she was a hostess."

"And she picked you up at the scene of the holdup?" Mason asked.

Mrs. Lavina smiled sweetly. "No," she said.

Mason raised his eyebrows. "I understood you to say . . ."

"I don't know whether you are trying to trap me, Mr. Mason, but I said very distinctly that after the holdup Mr. Archer drove on through the intersection and parked his car at the drugstore. The place where Inez picked me up was a distance of perhaps one hundred and twenty-five to one hundred and fifty feet from the scene of the holdup."

She smiled smugly, and one or two of the jurors grinned.

"I didn't mean to trap you," Mason said. "I was speaking generally."

"I cannot afford to speak generally. You see, Mr. Mason, *I* am under oath."

A distinct rustle of merriment rippled the courtroom.

With a dramatic gesture Mason turned from the witness. "Mr. Paul Drake," he called.

Paul Drake, head of the Drake Detective Agency, straightened into lanky height. The curious eyes of the spectators turned toward him.

"Will you," Mason said, "please step into the law library and bring Inez Kaylor into the courtroom?"

Drake nodded and walked down the aisle and through the double swinging doors.

"Now," Mason said, whirling to confront Mrs. Lavina, "I want the truth. Are you absolutely certain that Inez Kaylor drove by and picked you up?"

The witness, frozen into immobility, controlled her facial expression so that by not so much as the flicker of an eyelash or the quiver of a lip was it possible to tell her thoughts.

"Well," Mason said, "can you answer that question?"

The witness slowly averted her eyes, frowning rather thoughtfully. "I am *quite* certain it was Inez Kaylor. Of course, Mr. Mason, it was some time ago, and . . ."

"How long have you known Inez Kaylor?"

"For approximately eight months."

"How long had you known her before this holdup took place?"

"About two months I believe."

"You are the proprietress of the chain of night clubs known as The Villa Lavina?"

"Not a chain, Mr. Mason. There are only three."

"All right. You operate them?"

"Yes."

"You employ hostesses?"

"Yes."

"How many?"

"Eighteen in all."

"You are a good businesswoman?"

"I try to be."

"You are in touch with your various night clubs every night?"

"Yes."

"You go from one to the other?"

"Yes."

"You keep a check on who is working and who is not working?"

"I try to."

"At the time of the holdup you had known Inez Kaylor for about two months?"

"Yes."

"You had seen her every night during that period?"

"I don't think she worked *every* night."

"Nearly every night?"

"Yes."

"Up to that time, however, you had never seen the defendant before?"

"No."

"Never in your life?"

"No."

"Yet from that one fleeting glimpse which you had of the defendant, a glimpse . . ."

"It wasn't a fleeting glimpse. I was looking right into his face."

"The holdup was done very quickly?"

She was unable to keep the venom out of her voice as she said triumphantly, "Very quickly. It was done with the skill of long experience, Mr. Mason."

"The comment of the witness will be stricken," Judge Egan said in a bored monotone. "The witness will refrain from making any comments. The jury will disregard the statement of the witness, that is, that much of the statement as relates to the skill of long experience."

Mason's jaw tightened. The damage done by the remark of the witness had only been intensified by the judge's admonition to the jury. Anything Mason could do would only add to the injury.

"You only saw him for a relatively short period of time?" Mason asked, his voice casual.

"It depends on what you mean by a relatively short period of time."

"Not as much as a minute?"

"Perhaps."

"Perhaps only thirty seconds?"

"Perhaps."

"You had known Miss Kaylor for two months. You got in the car with her and rode all the way to The Villa Lavina Number Two."

"A distance of not more than half a mile."

"That took you how long?"

"A few minutes."

"Four times as long as it took for the defendant to stage the holdup?"

"Possibly."

"Five times as long?"

"Perhaps."

"Six times as long?"

"I really don't know, Mr. Mason."

"Yet you now want this jury to believe that from that one glimpse you recognized the defendant as the man who staged the holdup, but that you are not sure that it was Inez Kaylor who gave you the ride to The Villa Lavina?"

Suddenly Mason saw a look of triumph in her eyes. She said, "I didn't say I wasn't sure it was Inez who gave me the ride. I said I was *quite* certain it was she. I mean by that I am *quite* certain."

Mason turned to look over his shoulder.

Paul Drake was standing alone in the doorway. He caught Mason's eye and slowly shook his head.

Mason matched the witness' affability. He turned to Paul Drake. "Never mind having Inez Kaylor step into the courtroom. If Mrs. Lavina is positive I'll take her word for it."

"Thank you," Mrs. Lavina said sweetly and her eyes held an expression of mocking triumph.

Mason glanced hurriedly at the clock.

There was no time now to try and figure how he had been double-crossed. The exigencies of the situation required that he be debonair, suave, poised for the next thirteen minutes, thirteen minutes during which he must match wits with a clever woman who knew that he was now powerless to disprove anything she might say. She held all the trumps and knew that she held them.

"You saw the defendant a second time," Mason said.

"Yes, Mr. Mason."

"Where was that?"

"In a line-up at police headquarters."

"And you picked the defendant from the line-up?" Mason said.

"Unhesitatingly."

"And you are absolutely positive that you hadn't seen him from the time of the holdup until you saw him at police headquarters?"

"That is right."

Mason paused for a moment, studying the witness. "Who was with you at the time of the identification at police headquarters, Mrs. Lavina?"

"Mr. Archer."

"You were both there together?"

"Naturally."

"Why do you say naturally?"

"Because we were both held up together and I assume the police wanted us both to make an identification."

"Then why not have you make an identification one at a time if they wanted to be absolutely certain?"

"You'll have to ask the police about that, Mr. Mason."

"Did the police advance any reason for having you there together?"

"Yes."

"What was it?"

"That, of course, is hearsay," Judge Egan interrupted.

"No objection, no objection, Your Honor," Harry Fritch said, smiling. "Let him go right ahead."

"It's cluttering up the record," Judge Egan said irritably. "The Court won't permit hearsay. And," he added, "the Court doesn't want any stalling for time or any fishing expeditions in cross-examination. Now go ahead, Mr. Mason.''

"Who identified him first—you or Mr. Archer?" Mason asked.

"It was a simultaneous identification."

"As soon as you saw him, you pointed him out as being the man?"

"Definitely, positively and absolutely, Mr. Mason."

"And Mr. Archer did the same, there in your presence?"

"Yes, Mr. Mason."

"How did you designate him?"

"By pointing."

"And what did Mr. Archer do?"

"He pointed."

"And you extended your fingers simultaneously?"

"At almost exactly the same split second, Mr. Mason."

"And you hadn't seen the defendant from the time of the holdup until the time of that identification?"

"No, sir."

Mason frowned. "Had you seen his photograph?" he asked.

She hesitated.

"Had you?" Mason asked, suddenly alert.

"Well, yes."

"And when had you seen that, with reference to the identification in the line-up?"

"The day before."

"Indeed! And who showed you the defendant's photograph?"

"Mr. Archer."

"And who was with Mr. Archer at the time?"

"A police officer."

"So when you identified the defendant in the line-up you had previously been studying his photograph?"

"I had seen his photograph, yes."

"Can you describe the circumstances under which you saw that photograph?"

"I was at The Villa Lavina Number Three. Mr. Archer, accompanied by a police detective in plain clothes, whose name I don't remember, came to me and said, 'Martha, they've caught the man who held us up. They found my wallet and your purse. They didn't recover any of the money, or the stickpin. Your purse had been cut and the lining ripped, but there's no question about it being your purse.'"

"Did the officer say anything?" Mason asked.

"He said that there was no use asking us to inconvenience ourselves to go down and look at a line-up unless he felt pretty certain he had the right man."

"And so he showed you a photograph of the man?"

"Yes."

"And this was a photograph that had been taken by the police?"

"Yes."

"Then Mr. Archer had seen the photograph before you saw it?"

"Naturally. He must have."

"And you identified the photograph?"

"I said that looked very much like the man, yes."

"So then an engagement was made for you to be at police headquarters the next morning?"

"At ten o'clock, yes."

"Were you positive of your identification when you saw the photograph?"

"Fairly positive."

"Was Mr. Archer positive?"

"Yes."

"How do you know?"

"He told me so."

"And he was the one who showed you the photograph?"

"Yes."

"So Mr. Archer handed you the photograph, said, 'Martha, this is the man that held us up,' or words to that effect."

"Well, he wasn't that crude about it."

"He told you that this was the man who had held you up?"

"Well, he said that he had identified him as the man who had held us up and he wanted me to take a look at him and see what I thought."

"So," Mason said, "before you went to this line-up, you had carefully familiarized yourself with the features of this defendant by studying a photograph?"

"I wouldn't put it that way, Mr. Mason."

"I'm putting it that way," Mason snapped. "Answer the question."

"I had looked at a photograph."

"You'd studied it, hadn't you?"

"I suppose so."

"And had become familiar with the man's features from looking at the picture?"

"Yes."

"So before you went to headquarters to identify the defendant, you had identified the defendant?"

"No."

"You identified his photograph, didn't you?"

"That's not the defendant."

"But you did make that identification?"

"Yes."

"Not a qualified identification, but an absolute identification?"

"Absolutely."

"You were certain?"

"I was certain."

"And you told the police you were certain?"

"Yes."

"Then, if you were certain of your identification from the photograph, why was it necessary for you to go to police

11

headquarters the next day to make a personal identification?''

"Because . . . I believe they said that was required in court as a matter of evidence."

"In other words, the sole reason that you went to that lineup was to manufacture evidence that could be used in court?"

"Oh, Your Honor, I object to the use of the word 'manufacture,' " the deputy district attorney stated.

"Sustained."

"The only purpose that you had in going to police headquarters the next day to make an identification of the defendant was to furnish evidence?"

"Isn't that the sole purpose of any identification, Mr. Mason?"

Mason said angrily, "I am asking you, wasn't the sole purpose of your trip to police headquarters to look at the defendant in a line-up?"

"I . . . well, I suppose so, yes."

"And you already knew that one of the persons in that line-up was going to be the defendant?"

"Yes."

"And you had already identified that person from the picture?"

"Yes."

"When Mr. Archer gave you the photograph of the defendant, he didn't show you photographs of different people and ask you if you saw anyone in that collection of photographs whose face looked familiar?"

"Certainly not. We were friends. He simply said, 'Martha, the police have the man that stuck us up. They haven't recovered the money, but they have the man. Here's his picture.' "

"First he told you that this was the man, and then he asked you if that was the man?"

"He asked me."

12

"And the officer then asked you if you thought you could identify the defendant in a line-up?"

"Yes."

"And what did you tell him?"

"I told him certainly."

"Were you still holding the photograph when you told him that?"

"No, I had given it back to him."

"Did you give it back to Mr. Archer or back to the officer?"

"Back to the officer."

"And after he told you that he wanted you to go to headquarters and pick the defendant out of a line-up, did you look at the picture again?"

"Yes."

"Why?"

"I wanted to make certain."

"Make certain of what?"

"That he was the man."

"Then you weren't certain when you first saw the photograph?"

"Yes, I was certain."

"But you have just said you looked at the photograph the second time so as to make certain."

"I mean in order to make certain that I could pick him out of the line-up."

"Then you were picking him out of the line-up not from your recollection of having seen him the night of the holdup but from your recollection of the photograph."

"Well, from both."

Mason glanced desperately at the clock. "Why did you ask to study the photograph the second time?"

"Oh, Your Honor, I object to that as having been already asked and answered," the deputy district attorney said.

"Sustained," Judge Egan snapped. "I suggest that Counsel has already exhausted this phase of the cross-examination and should move along to some other point."

Mason said, "Now I would like to ask you one or two more questions about just what happened at the time of the holdup, Mrs. Lavina. You were en route to The Villa Lavina Number Two?"

"Yes."

"How were you dressed?"

"I was wearing the same outfit that I am wearing now."

"And I take it," Mason said casually, "that you must have had the same purse that you are now holding in your lap?"

"Yes."

Suddenly she bit her lip. "No, I was mistaken. I had another purse at the time of the holdup. Naturally, the holdup man took my purse, Mr. Mason."

"You remember the circumstances of the holdup distinctly?"

"Yes."

"Mr. Archer is a friend of long standing?"

"I have known him for some time."

"He smokes?"

"I believe so, yes."

"Was he smoking a cigarette at the time of the holdup?"

Her eyes slithered away from Mason's. She placed a gloved hand against her cheek and said, "Let me think . . . I am not certain."

"Isn't it a fact," Mason said, "that when Mr. Archer stopped the car for a traffic light he placed a cigarette in his mouth and was leaning forward to press the cigarette lighter in the dashboard when the holdup man approached the left-hand side of the automobile, and that is the reason you didn't see him until he had jerked the door open?"

There was a period of silence.

Judge Egan glanced at the clock and stirred restlessly on the bench.

"Answer the question," Mason said.

"Oh, I'm sorry. I was, for the moment, thinking of something else."

"What were you thinking of?" Mason asked.

She smiled. "I'm quite certain it wouldn't be relevant."

"Then answer the question."

"I . . . I'm sorry but I am afraid I have forgotten the question. Something popped into my mind."

She smiled at the jury, and one or two of the fascinated male jurors returned her smile.

The court reporter read the question in a monotone,

" 'Isn't it a fact that when Mr. Archer stopped the car for a traffic light he placed a cigarette in his mouth and was leaning forward to press the cigarette lighter in the dashboard when the holdup man approached the left-hand side of the automobile, and that is the reason you didn't see him until he had jerked the door open?' "

"I . . . I'm not certain."

"Isn't it a fact that it was just as Mr. Archer straightened back, holding the cigarette lighter in his right hand, that the defendant pushed the gun in his face, and that when Mr. Archer elevated his hands the cigarette lighter dropped from his hands and scorched a hole in the upholstery of the car?

"You may look at this photograph of Mr. Archer's car if you wish, Mrs. Lavina. You will notice the round hole in the upholstery of the front seat."

"I . . . come to think of it, Mr. Mason, I believe that *is* what happened."

"It certainly should have made an impression on your mind," Mason said. "A cigarette lighter burning a hole in the upholstery of the car would make quite a bit of smoke."

"I suggest you ask Mr. Archer about that, Mr. Mason."

"Thank you for your suggestion, but I am asking you."

"I don't feel that I can really answer the question."

"Why not?"

"Good heavens, Mr. Mason, I am not a block of wood or stone. I am a human being with emotions. You can't expect

15

a woman to sit through a holdup and recall every minute detail.''

"You recall every minute detail of the defendant's features?''

"Not the minute details, no.''

"The general features?''

"In a way.''

"What color are his eyes? No, no, don't look—just tell the color of his eyes.''

"I don't know.''

"What color clothes was he wearing that night—the night of the holdup?''

"The same he's wearing now.''

"What clothes was he wearing when you saw him in the line-up?''

"The same—I'm sorry, I can't be certain.''

"As Mr. Archer approached the intersection where the holdup took place, what lane was he in? The one that was near the curb or the one that was over nearer the center of the road?''

"The . . . the center of the road.''

"Then,'' Mason said, "if the defendant opened the door on the left-hand side he must have been standing in the . . .''

"No,'' she said, "pardon me. It was my mistake. I remember now. It was the lane on the right-hand side, the one nearest the curb.''

"Exactly what time did this holdup take place?'' Mason asked.

"Why, on the 13th of September . . .''

"No, I mean what time of night?''

"It was . . . oh, along in the evening.''

"Nine o'clock?''

"I didn't look at my watch, Mr. Mason.''

"Ten o'clock?''

"I tell you I didn't look at my watch.''

"Eleven o'clock?''

"I'm sorry, Mr. Mason, I . . . no, it was before eleven because the drugstore closes at eleven."

Judge Egan cleared his throat, said, "It has now reached the hour of five o'clock. Court will take a recess until Monday morning at ten o'clock. During the recess the jurors are admonished not to discuss the case among yourselves and not to permit anyone to discuss it in your presence, nor are you to form or express any opinion until the case has been finally submitted to you for your decision. Court's adjourned."

Drake pushed his way through the stream of outgoing spectators to Mason's side.

"Well?" Mason asked.

Drake shook his head. "She skipped out."

"Hang it," Mason said. "You should have guarded against that."

"Perry, I swear I . . . well, I just can't understand it. I'd have sworn that that girl would have stayed with us. She wanted to testify. She swears that the only time she drove Mrs. Lavina any place was once when she drove her up town shopping, and that was in the afternoon."

"What about the night of the holdup, Paul? Where was Inez Kaylor then?"

"She doesn't know. She thinks she was in Villa Lavina Number One. She can't fix the date absolutely."

"Do you mean to say that she doesn't remember discussing the holdup with Mrs. Lavina? Didn't Mrs. Lavina tell her that she'd been robbed and . . ."

"Nope," Drake interrupted, "Mrs. Lavina never mentioned having been held up until a week or so later. That's why Inez Kaylor is positive she didn't give Mrs. Lavina a ride from the scene of the holdup."

"I'll be damned," Mason said, and then after a moment asked, "She's positive?"

"Absolutely positive."

"Then we've got to find her, Paul. It means a lot."

"We'll try," Drake said. "I told her to wait until I came for her. She must have crossed us up, but I never thought she would. She seemed to be a square shooter, and she came from Las Vegas with me without the slightest objection."

"Well," Mason said, "we've got a brand new lead to go to work on now, Paul. Don't let the jurors see you standing around talking as though we are dubious about the outcome."

Mason clapped Paul Drake triumphantly on the shoulder, said, "Splendid, Paul. That's fine work!"

Some of the jurors filing out of the jury box regarded Mason with friendly curiosity.

Martha Lavina swept by, a trim figure of a woman in the middle thirties, a poised, deadly dangerous individual who couldn't resist showing some measure of triumph before members of the jury who were listening.

"Good afternoon, Mr. Mason," she said with syrupy sweetness.

"Good afternoon, Mrs. Lavina," Mason said with equal courtesy, and then added with barbed significance, "I'll see you Monday morning."

Something in his tone stopped her in her tracks. She turned to look at him, the careful appraisal with which one measures a dangerous antagonist. Then, with just that brief instant of hesitation, she moved on out of the courtroom, her figure showing to advantage, the motions of her hips indicating she was well aware of that fact.

"The female cobra," Drake said in an undertone.

Mason's nod was preoccupied.

Mason and Paul Drake left the courtroom, shouldered their way through departing spectators, and then Mason guided Paul Drake over toward the stairs. "Wait until the crowd thins out, Paul," Mason said. "I don't like to be packed into the elevators and take a chance on having some member of the jury in there. Almost invariably someone recognizes me and asks me some question about the case, and . . ."

"Why don't they keep the jury shut up?" Drake asked.

"Sometimes they do in murder cases," Mason said. "Not in cases of this sort. We have a penniless defendant and an assigned case. If you shut the jury up they'd yell their heads off. A judge . . ."

A heavy hand clapped Mason on the shoulder.

"Mr. Mason!" a booming voice said.

Mason turned to confront the broad-shouldered, bushy-browned individual who was glowering at him with ill-concealed irritation.

"Hello, Mr. Archer, how are you?" Mason said.

"I'm angry," Archer said, smiling however as he spoke.

"Indeed?" Mason asked.

"What's this damn business of cooping me up in that room? My gosh, I'm going crazy in there."

"The witnesses," Mason told him, "are put under the rule by the Court. That means they aren't allowed to hear the testimony of the other witnesses. They're excluded from the courtroom. In that way we have an opportunity to test the independent recollection of each witness without having that recollection colored by the testimony of other witnesses."

"Oh, poppycock!" Archer said. "Bosh and nonsense! I'm a man of action. Good Lord, I've got business stacked up, people waiting to see me, and I have to drop everything and come up to court. It wouldn't be so bad if I could sit in the courtroom and hear what's going on, but to sit in that damn witness room is an imposition."

"It won't be much longer," Mason said reassuringly.

"Well, it's been too damn long already. I've talked with the deputy district attorney about it, and he said that it's up to you. I've already given my testimony in the case. I told what happened. Why can't I sit in the courtroom?"

"Because they may want to recall you."

"Well, that's what the deputy D.A. said, but he said it was up to you. He said if you wanted to stipulate that after wit-

19

nesses had given their testimony they could remain in court, that it was all right and the judge would let me stay in court."

"But," Mason said, smiling, "I don't want to make that stipulation."

"Why not?"

"Because I'm trying to represent the defendant in this case. I think it's in his best interests to have the rule of court strictly enforced."

"Now you look here," Archer said. "You're representing that defendant, a penniless drifter, a ne'er-do-well, a crook, a holdup man. I'm an important businessman in this community. I'm influential. I can do an attorney a lot of good or I can do him a lot of harm. I don't like this, Mason. I don't like the way you're doing this."

"I'm sorry, Mr. Archer."

"Well, I'm going to see that you *are* sorry."

"Is that a threat?"

"No, that isn't a threat . . . yes, dammit, it is! I think your action is unreasonable. It's bad enough to be stuck up. I lost four or five hundred dollars out of my wallet and a diamond pin that's worth twelve hundred bucks. I had to go to police headquarters to make a report, then they dragged me back to police headquarters to make an identification from a line-up. Then I had to come to court and testify. Why, the time I've lost today is worth more than the money I've lost, and before the case gets done I'd have been a damn sight better off to have kissed the whole thing good-by."

"I'm sorry," Mason said. "It is, of course, unfortunate where a man's time is valuable . . ."

"Well, I'm not kicking about the time," Archer said, somewhat mollified, "but I don't like to be stuck there in that witness room. I want to be out where I can hear what's going on. At least I want to keep my mind occupied."

"I'm sorry," Mason said. "You might get a good book and read it."

"A book!" Archer snorted. "I can't sit in there reading a

book. And those uncomfortable chairs that are furnished by the county—I'm wearing myself out sitting on those damn chairs. I get up and walk around, then I go look out the window. Then I go back and sit in one of those damn hard wooden chairs. I'd rather dismiss the whole case than have to go through with that much longer."

"I'm sorry," Mason laughed, "but *I* have to do what *I* think is in the best interests of the defendant."

"And you aren't getting a cent for defending him, either," Archer said.

"That's right."

Archer shook his head. "I can't figure it. Why, you're one of the most prominent attorneys in this part of the country. Here you are defending a man for nothing. Here I am with an enormous earning capacity sitting in there, cooling my heels, waiting for some damn lawyer to call me. Look here, Mason, suppose we dismiss the case?"

Mason smiled. "That would be up to the district attorney. I'm afraid he wouldn't appreciate having you go to him with the suggestion that he dismiss the case because your time was too valuable to waste in prosecution, and I'm quite certain that he wouldn't appreciate the suggestion if he thought you had discussed it with me."

Archer glared at him for a moment, then said, "Oh, all right. You damn long-winded lawyers have to have things your own way. No wonder citizens hate to go to court. Now you look here, Mason, you let me sit in court Monday morning—if I have to be there. I'm going to see if I can't get excused."

Mason smiled, shook his head and turned away. "Come on, Paul, we can get the elevator now."

Archer stood watching them, his bushy brows drawn together, his eyes angry, yet containing a certain amount of reluctant respect.

Chapter 2

Mason, accompanied by Paul Drake, unlocked the door to his private office.

Della Street, Mason's confidential secretary, looked up from the mail she was sorting, and asked eagerly, "How did you come out?"

"Through the front door," Mason said, grinning.

"How much longer will the case take?"

"We should go to the jury Monday," Mason told her.

"How did Inez Kaylor do?"

"Not so good."

"How come?"

"She skipped out," Drake said.

"What?" Della Street exclaimed incredulously.

Mason walked over to the bust of Blackstone and placed his hat on the marble head at a rakish angle. He stepped back to survey the effect, then, moving up, adjusted the hat so that it was sloping backward.

"That does it," he said.

"Kid stuff," Drake observed, grinning.

"Darned if it isn't," Mason admitted, "but I always feel sorry for the old boy. He presides over the law office with an air of beetle-browed solemnity and never has any fun. He and his thousands of replicas have been doomed to an austere, unsmiling contemplation of the present, a grim-faced appraisal of the future. Let's liven his life."

"Please tell me about that Kaylor girl," Della Street implored.

"I'm afraid it was a plant of some kind," Mason said.

"I can't figure it," Drake blurted. "I sat next to her on the airplane from Las Vegas. She certainly seemed a darn good scout. Of course, she wasn't the sort you'd pick for a Sunday school teacher. She'd been around and she didn't try to kid me about that. She wasn't kidding anyone, herself included. She was just a good scout."

"Did you talk with her, Chief?" Della Street asked Perry Mason.

"No. The plane didn't get in until after court had started. I'd told Paul what to do—to take her to the law library. So when Paul signaled me it was all fixed, I thought I had an ace in the hole—well, my ace was trumped."

"You'd never have known it the way you acted, Perry," Paul Drake said.

"Was he good?" Della Street asked.

"He was perfect, Della. He made her swear to all kinds of things."

"Such as what?" Della Street asked.

"Tell her, Perry," Drake said.

Mason grinned. "Archer's car had a round hole burned in the upholstery of the seat. I made her think that hole was caused by Archer dropping a cigarette lighter during the holdup. That rattled her."

Della Street watched Mason as he seated himself at the desk. Paul Drake slid into his favorite position in the big, overstuffed leather chair, sliding around so that his knees hung over one of the rounded arms, the other supporting the small of his back.

"What I can't understand," Drake exclaimed petulantly, "is what happened to that Kaylor girl."

"Don't mind me," Della Street said, "just keep on talking. After you've made enough comments I'll be able to put the thing together in kind of a crazy quilt conversational pattern. I don't mind it at all. In fact, I'm getting so I rather like it."

Mason grinned. "Well, Della, things worked out just about

23

as we expected, except that when we went to pull our ace card out of the hole and confront Mrs. Lavina with Inez Kaylor—well, there wasn't any Inez Kaylor, that's all.''

"That's the thing I just can't understand," Paul Drake said. "When you asked me to look up that hostess, Perry, I had some trouble locating her, but once I located her she seemed only too anxious to do the right thing. Good Lord, she didn't need to come here at all. She could have simply stayed in Las Vegas, Nevada, but she came voluntarily and seemed anxious to do whatever she could to straighten things out.''

"And she just walked out?" Della Street asked.

"That's right. I had her staked out in the law library, reading law books, so that anyone who looked in casually would think she was a woman lawyer looking up a point of pleading. I impressed on her that Perry would probably call her during the last hour of the afternoon session, and that she was to be right at that table no matter what happened.''

"And she wasn't there when you went for her?" Della Street asked.

"That's right.''

"What do *you* think happened?''

"I don't know.''

"What's that going to do to the case?''

Paul Drake shrugged. "That's up to Perry.''

"Well," Mason said, "I have been kicking myself ever since I got out of court.''

"Why?''

"Because I departed from good, basic, sound, common sense cross-examination.''

"The heck you did," Paul Drake said. "You got her all mixed up on routine stuff. What the deuce do *you* suppose happened, Perry?''

"It's too early to make a positive statement, but don't be too surprised if Mrs. Lavina wasn't in that car at the time of the holdup, Paul.''

Drake snapped his legs around so he could sit upright in the chair. "Wasn't in the car! Oh, you mean she wasn't in Inez Kaylor's car?"

"I mean she wasn't in Rodney Archer's car."

"Oh, but she *must* have been, Perry. You're making things up out of whole cloth."

Mason frowned, his face thoughtful. "Rodney Archer could have had some other woman in the car with him. Let's suppose it was some woman whom he didn't dare to let anyone know he was with. While he was in telephoning for the police he telephoned first to The Villa Number Two. He knew Martha Lavina pretty well. He told her he was in a jam and asked her to back up his play and say that she'd been in the car with him. He told her he'd give her the details later. Then he called the police, in the meantime making arrangements to get rid of the woman who was actually in the car with him."

"What principle of cross-examination did you almost overlook?" Della Street asked Mason.

The lawyer pushed his swivel chair back from the desk, shook his head deprecatingly.

"*I'm* curious on that," Paul Drake said.

"Never, never, never cross-examine a witness by following the pattern that the witness expects," Mason said. "This woman was all prepared to throw a harpoon into me whenever I gave her half an opening. She's quick-witted, diabolically clever, and she's attractive. She turned every one of my questions so she could crucify my client."

"Why would she be so bitter against your client?" Della Street asked.

"That's the point," Mason said. "She wasn't."

"I thought you said she was."

"Not against my client," Mason said. "She was trying to give me the worst of every exchange so I'd back off and quit my cross-examination."

"Why?"

"Because she was vulnerable."

"In what way?"

"That's the point. She was vulnerable and the only way I can figure it is that she wasn't there."

"But why on earth . . . ?"

"She's trying to keep the woman who really was there out of the picture," Mason said.

"And you trapped her?"

"I think I have her frightened," Mason admitted. "The first basic principle of cross-examination is to start asking a witness conversationally, affably and in a friendly way about some of the minor points that the witness hasn't thought over quite so much, and on which he doesn't expect cross-examination. As long as you're friendly and affable, if you get adverse answers it doesn't hurt your case in the least, but if you do uncover a weak point then you can move in on it swiftly and capitalize on the advantage.

"In that way you can cross-examine a witness with everything to gain and nothing to lose.

"Human memory is a tricky thing. If a person actually experiences a holdup, or sees a murder, or something of that sort, he keeps recalling the dramatic high lights of that occurrence perhaps a thousand times an hour. Whenever he starts thinking about the happening, he doesn't pay much attention to the connecting links which bridge the gaps between the dramatic high lights. The more routine matters are dwarfed in his mind by the spectacular.

"For instance, if a person witnesses a shooting, he keeps seeing the assailant level the gun and pull the trigger. He recalls seeing the victim stagger and fall a thousand times, but where the car was parked, whether the sun was shining or if it was cloudy, he may recall some forty or fifty times, or perhaps not at all. There is, in short, a mental unbalance as far as the memory is concerned. When a person gets on the witness stand and tries to connect up all the events in his mind he's quite likely to rationalize certain things which he thinks *must* have happened. Those things may not have happened at all.''

"But that wasn't the case with Mrs. Lavina."

"No," Mason said, "but if I'd followed a really skillful pattern of cross-examination with her I'd have uncovered the joker a little sooner."

"Does she know what you suspect about her?"

"I rather think she does," Mason said thoughtfully. "She's clever."

"Why did Perry have to be assigned this client, anyway?" Drake asked Della irritably.

"Perry just happened to be in court at the time of his arraignment, the man just happened to state he had no funds to hire a lawyer, and that he was not guilty, so the judge appointed Perry as an officer of the court to handle the case for him," she told him.

"Has he ever been in trouble before?" Drake asked.

"No," Mason said. "He has no criminal record. In fact his past record is good. He's retired and lives in a trailer park. He has a little pension and lives on that."

"How old is he?"

"Fifty-one or -two."

"Retired sort of early, didn't he?"

"He was a salesman. He had a nervous breakdown, got smashed up in an auto accident and never could get back into his stride. He'd been overworking and the accident touched off a complete collapse."

"How did he become involved in the case, Perry?"

"Apparently the man who ran the trailer park was dumping the rubbish from the cans that are assigned to the different trailers when he noticed a man's wallet and a woman's purse in the refuse. He took them to the police. It was Archer's wallet, and Mrs. Lavina identified the purse. The police came out, talked with the defendant, and picked him up."

"And you sent me all the way to Las Vegas, Nevada, to

hunt up that Kaylor girl in an assigned case, out of which you don't make a dime?'' Drake asked.

"Sure I did," Mason told him. "When I represent a man I try to fight his case."

"Even if it comes to putting up money out of your own pocket?"

Mason grinned. "A lawyer shouldn't meter his fighting ability or his services by the size of his fee. Now then, Paul, I want you to find Inez Kaylor. She walked out of that law library within the last two hours. She only has that much of a head start on you. You know what she looks like. You have photographs of her. Hire whatever men you need and get busy."

"That might be pretty damned expensive," Drake warned.

"I didn't ask you how much it was going to cost," Mason told him. "I want Inez Kaylor, and I'm going to have to have her before Monday morning. I've started this fight and now I'm going to finish it."

Chapter 3

At 9:45 that evening Perry Mason dropped into Paul Drake's office, nodded to the operator at the switchboard and asked, "Is Paul in?"

"Yes, Mr. Mason. He's been trying to get in touch with you."

"I told him I'd drop in," Mason said.

"I know, but he thought he might be able to reach you with information you would like to have before that."

Mason slid his fingers over the trick lock in the back of the gate which led to the corridor and said, "Okay, I'll go down and see him."

The operator nodded, plugged in Drake's line, and said, "Mr. Mason on his way to see you."

Mason, walking down the corridor between a rabbit warren of small offices, came to the door marked *Mr. Drake* at the end of the corridor and pushed it open just as Drake had finished hanging up the telephone.

"Gosh, Perry, I've been trying to get hold of you!"

"What happened?"

"We've located Inez Kaylor."

"The deuce you have! What happened to her? Why did she walk out?"

"Sit down, Perry. Things don't look good."

"How come?"

"I'm afraid she sold out."

Mason considered the matter in thoughtful silence for a moment, then said, "If she sold out, Paul, there's nothing we can do about it."

"We might get her to reconsider."

"If she's the type who would sell out, her testimony wouldn't do us any good. Where is she, Paul?"

"Right back in The Villa Lavina."

"Number Two?"

"No, Number Three."

"What's she doing?"

"Acting as hostess."

"How did you find her?"

"Just routine. We knew she was in that business. We had a pretty fair photograph and a darned good description. I started a bunch of men on the job, checking with B girls and some of the entertainers. They all stick together pretty close, you know."

"And received a tip that she was at The Villa Lavina Number Three?" Mason asked.

"No," Drake said, "that's the funny part of it. One of my men went into The Villa Lavina Number Three in order to contact some of the girls there and see if they knew anything about Inez, and darned if Inez wasn't working there."

"You're sure?"

"He saw her," Drake said. "Her name's Kaylor. The picture and the description match. My operative says he's sure. Of course, those hostesses use phony names as far as the trade is concerned. This girl is going under the first name of Petty, and no one cares about her last name, but it's the Kaylor girl all right. He telephoned in half an hour ago. I've been trying to reach you ever since."

"I took Della to dinner," Mason said. "I told you I'd be in around nine o'clock."

Drake glanced significantly at his watch.

Mason grinned. "All right, Paul," he said, "it was a good dinner and it had been a hard day. I think I'll go talk with this girl myself. Where's Mrs. Lavina?"

"Probably at one of the other places. She isn't out at Number Three. That is, she wasn't when I asked my operative the last time he telephoned."

"You have an extra picture of that girl," Mason asked, "so I can pick her up?"

"Yes. My operative's still out there."

"Well, tell him to stay on the job," Mason said, "but it **might be better if he didn't try to get in contact with me when** I walk in. Who is he? Anyone I know?"

"I don't think he is. He's relatively new, but I took the precaution of having every man working on the case wear a red carnation. That was in case I wanted to consolidate forces in a hurry in order to do a shadow job. In that way the operatives could recognize each other."

"Good idea," Mason told him. "How soon will you be in touch with your man again?"

"He's telephoning in every half hour."

"Tell him I'm on my way out there. Tell him not to make any contact. If she should leave, keep an eye on her."

"I should have two men for a shadowing job," Drake said.

"That's right. Get one of your other operatives out there. Keep two men on the job until I tell you different. Does this Kaylor girl know who I am?"

"She knows your name, of course, and she's probably seen pictures."

"But she didn't see me in court?"

"No. I brought her in from Las Vegas, then took her up to the law library. I parked her there and went into court to await your signal. She told me she'd never seen you."

Mason said, "When I got your signal that everything was okay and the girl was available I sure thought I had things coming my way. It just shows how easy it is to get fooled. Okay, Paul, give me a picture of her. I'm going out and have a talk with her."

"And I'm to shadow her when she leaves there?"

"That's right. Keep two men on the job. Three if you need them. Keep her shadowed until I tell you to stop."

"Do you care if she knows she's being followed?"

"Very much. I want it done surreptitiously."

"That's all I wanted to know. It costs more that way."

"And it works better," Mason told him. "Be seeing you, Paul."

"What kind of an approach are you going to make?" Drake asked. "Are you going to put it right up to her?"

"Not for a while," Mason said. "I'm going in as a rich sucker with money to spend. I'm going to try to eat another dinner. The way I feel I guess I can do it. I get ravenous after a day in court."

"After you've contacted her you won't want her shadowed, will you?"

"I can't tell. Let your men stay on the job until I call them off. If she leaves with me, shadow both of us."

Mason left Drake's office, took the elevator down to the street, climbed in his car and drove rapidly through night traffic until he reached the through boulevard running north. Here he pushed the throttle down until the speedometer needle was quivering at a speed ten miles in excess of the legal limit.

The congested district dropped behind, and after a few miles Mason turned in at the flaming red neon sign *VILLA LAVINA NUMBER THREE.*

A doorman parked Mason's car and gave him a numbered slip of pasteboard. Mason walked in, checked his hat and coat, and gave a headwaiter five dollars for a choice table. It was then 10:21 by Mason's wrist watch.

The headwaiter regarded Mason with that deference which is the universal recognition of generosity.

"Are you alone?" he asked.

Mason nodded.

The headwaiter made a little grimace. "That's a shame."

"Isn't it."

"It's a matter which *could* be remedied."

"I'll give you a signal if I need anything," Mason said.

"Any time you give me a signal I'll be on the job," the headwaiter promised, and escorted Mason to a table adjoining the dance floor and within a few feet of a little raised platform which served as the stage.

Everything about the night club indicated Martha Lavina's ability to create that intangible something known as "atmosphere."

One night club will spend thousands of dollars upon fixtures, entertainment and advertising, yet somehow manage to lack the distinction that is a drawing card for customers. People simply don't care to go there.

Another night club, with the expenditure of far less money, will somehow create an atmosphere. Celebrities will come to the place. People of character will drop in to spend the evening, ordering half a dozen rounds of drinks on which the management can make a tidy profit. The place fairly radiates vivid color and individuality. It becomes smart to be seen at the tables.

There is no magic formula by which this atmosphere can be achieved. Some authorities insist it is the result of a gradual growth, and is as unplanned as is the individuality of a person. Yet there are those who insist such an atmosphere can be the result of good planning.

Martha Lavina had managed to create this highly profitable atmosphere in all three of The Villa Lavina resorts. Villa Lavina Number One catered to a racing crowd. Villa Lavina Number Two managed to get a literary and motion picture crowd. Villa Lavina Number Three appealed to a Bohemian type of artist and the working newspaperman. There was a rumor that artists and writers who became regular patrons enjoyed a substantial discount on checks and were encouraged to loiter for long periods at tables which were specially reserved for them. In return these artists achieved a measure of distinction and contributed to the atmosphere of the place by bawdy paintings on the walls, risqué cartoons, caricatures and sexy quips which combined the appeal of the pin-up with an element of risqué humor.

Each of the three night clubs was careful to cater to its regular trade. The tourist, the sight-seer, the party that somewhat timidly ventured into the environs of Bohemia to look around with gawky curiosity at the "celebrities" received careful, courteous treatment, but were kept severely segregated.

Such people could look at the well-known figures. In fact, the waiters had a habit of whispering the names and identities of these celebrities, a procedure which not only interested the casual diner but was by no means distasteful to the celebrities who found themselves under the more or less constant surveillance of respectfully curious eyes.

Many an artist owed much of his reputation to the careful, conscientious plugging of waiters at The Villa Lavina Number Three. When such an artist had contributed a choice bit of art to the walls of the night club, or perhaps a particularly humorous bit for one of the rest rooms, the waiters would carefully point out that artist to diners who had been attracted to the place largely through curiosity and a desire to soak up "atmosphere."

Above all, however, Martha Lavina owed her success to the manner in which she created just the right impression of naughtiness without ever letting the affair get out of hand.

Less respectable honky-tonks had entertainers who appeared as strip-tease performers and then mingled with the audience, seeking an opportunity to fasten themselves upon some prowling group of wolves, promoting drinks on a commission basis.

Martha Lavina would have none of this. Her performers were performers. Her hostesses were demure of countenance, startlingly seductive of figure and dress.

Martha was reported at one time to have said, "There are three requirements for a good hostess, an innocent face, a wicked body and nothing under a seductive gown except curves.''

Martha operated within the limits of suburban cities in choice locations carefully selected.

Seated at his table in The Villa Lavina Number Three, Mason sized up the people in the dining room.

Some twenty regular patrons seated at a long table were engaged in a vigorous, somewhat alcoholic discussion. The people had evidently finished their dinner some time earlier and were now drinking coffee, liqueurs, and had settled down for an evening of sociability. The waiters left this table severely alone, coming to take orders only when one of the diners would gesture for attention.

The sharp contrast between the way these diners were treated, and the manner in which waiters politely impressed upon ordinary patrons the value of the space they were occupying, indicated that this group was part of the atmosphere which Martha Lavina strove so hard to maintain, and which was paying off in such good measure.

There were a few vacant tables, but for the most part the place was filled, and Mason knew it would remain filled until well after midnight.

It was difficult to spot the professional hostesses. They were unobtrusive and definitely not making overtures to the customers.

However, when the dance music started, Mason, watching the couples on the floor, saw two men, who had been dining together at a table, each dancing with a young, attractive girl. When the dance was over Mason watched these girls join the men at their table. They were cordial, attractive, discreet and could hardly be distinguished from any of the attractive young women in the place.

Mason caught the eye of the headwaiter. The man hurried over to Mason's table.

''Is Petty here tonight?'' the lawyer asked.

35

The headwaiter's eyebrows raised slightly. "You know Petty?"

"I know someone who knows Petty."

"She's not around at the moment, but I might be able to find her," the headwaiter said, keeping his eyes carefully fixed on the tablecloth.

"I'd like to buy her a drink if she'd care to join me," Mason said, and pushed another five dollars into the man's hand. "The first was for the table. This is for getting Petty."

"I'll scout around and see what the situation is," the headwaiter promised. "It may take a little time."

Mason ordered a carefully selected meal indicating that he desired the best and was not particularly concerned about cost.

The food was served and the lawyer dined at a leisurely pace, watching the couples on the dance floor speculatively but not too intently. He sat through a floor show which was definitely better than the average run of night club floor shows.

So quietly that he was hardly aware of her approach, Mason realized a young woman with willowy figure, eyes so dark brown it was difficult to distinguish the pupil from the iris, was watching him with just the faintest indication of a half-smile. When she realized that Mason was looking at her she moved toward his table, walking slowly so that every line of her figure showed through the clinging dress she was wearing.

Mason pushed back his chair. "Petty?"

She smiled, gave him her hand. "How do you do?" she said. "It's a pleasure to see you. Have I met you before?"

Mason moved around the table to seat her. Almost immediately an attentive waiter hovered over them and Petty ordered Scotch and soda, specifying a brand of Scotch that was twelve years old.

Mason seated himself, toyed with his coffee cup, aware that the young woman was sizing him up carefully.

"I'm certainly glad you took pity on me," Mason told her. "I was rather lonely tonight. It's not a pleasant experience to dine by yourself."

She smiled at him. "Well, you're not by yourself any longer."

"I am very favored," Mason agreed. "The good fortune which has come my way entirely compensates for the lonely hours of the first part of the evening."

"You asked for me by name?"

"Yes."

"How come?"

"I had heard about you," Mason said. "You were busy?"

She shook her head quickly, then, after a moment, said, "No, I wasn't here. I was . . . I'd gone home."

Mason said nothing.

"Alone," she added.

Mason's face refrained from showing any expression.

Somewhat mollified, she added, "I wonder how you knew about me?"

"A friend of mine knew about you."

"I haven't been here that long."

"That's what I was given to understand."

She smiled. "You certainly are garrulous, aren't you?"

The waiter brought her drink. Mason bowed to her, and her eyes glanced at him over the rim of the glass, appraising eyes that smoldered with some emotion which for the moment defied detection.

She was tall and graceful with long dark lashes and hair so brown it showed only a reddish glint in the highlights. Her mouth had been carefully touched with lipstick so that it seemed always about to break into a smile even when the eyes indicated cautious appraisal.

The floor show was now over and the band struck up a dance.

Mason raised his eyebrows in silent interrogation.

Her nod was almost imperceptible.

37

Mason pushed back his chair, and a moment later she was in his arms, gliding out over the floor.

They danced silently for several seconds, then she said, "You certainly *are* a dancer!"

"I was just thinking," Mason told her, "that I seem to be gliding over the floor with thistledown in my arms."

She laughed, and for a moment moved closer to him. Mason could feel every vibrant bit of her body beneath the folds of the gown. It was quite apparent that the gown, the dancing pumps and her stockings were all that she had on.

"You like to dance, don't you?" Mason said.

"I love it," she said, and then added somewhat wistfully, "with some people . . . I . . . I don't like to dance with everyone."

Once more she was silent, but there was that in the rhythm of her body which showed she had at least for the moment lost herself in the music.

Back at the table, her eyes studied Mason thoughtfully.

"Well?" Mason asked.

"You're different," she said.

Mason laughed. "Isn't that what men usually tell *you*?"

She made a little impatient gesture. "Let's not hand each other a line."

"Okay by me," Mason told her.

"You're different. You're strong and rugged and virile, and yet you're not a wolf."

"Is that supposed to be flattering?"

"It is, the way I mean it."

"Go on," Mason invited.

But she became silent.

Mason caught the eye of the waiter and beckoned for another drink.

"That's not necessary," she said. "We're not B girls here."

The waiter bent over Petty. "The same?" he asked.

She nodded, said, "Make it light, Charlie."

The waiter turned to Mason. Mason ordered a double twenty-five-year-old brandy in a snifter glass.

When the waiter had left she said, "We don't hustle drinks here. We don't work on a commission basis."

"It's very interesting," Mason told her. "Just how do you work?"

"Not in the way most people think."

Mason remained silent.

She said, "We're atmosphere. We're *really* hostesses."

"How many of you?" Mason asked.

"It varies," she said, smiling, and then added, "for the most part we're available by appointment, but when people drop in, if they're lonely and . . . and nice, they can have dancing partners and someone to talk with. Mrs. Lavina feels that a lonely man is a wet blanket under any circumstances, and The Villa Lavina doesn't encourage wet blankets any more than it does wolves."

"It evidently doesn't encourage hilarity either."

"She wants people to be natural. She wants them to have a good time, but she doesn't like loud people. She wants them to . . . she's something of a genius."

"Go on," Mason said.

Petty's face lit up as she started talking about Mrs. Lavina. "They're watching her. They'd close her up in a minute if she stepped over the line. That is, if she stepped *too* far over the line."

Mason nodded, and the corners of his lips twitched in a fleeting smile.

"Of course it's no Sunday school picnic here either," Petty went on hurriedly. "Martha Lavina has atmosphere, lots of atmosphere. The people who want to come in to see celebrities can see them.

"The people over at that long table are very, very interesting. That man with the dark hair and the horn-rimmed glasses at the head of the table, the one who's talking now and motioning with his hands, is a brilliant artist. He's the one who did the picture of the girl and the barbed wire fence. The girl next to him is a very attractive model who's very popular. They say she's living with . . ."

"You don't need to run through the catalog for me," Mason told her. "I'm not interested in atmosphere."

"Just what *are* you interested in?"

"You, at the moment."

She shook her head and said, "I'm not available."

"You're here, aren't you?"

"I'm not available."

"I didn't ask that," Mason said. "I'm quite content."

She let her eyes study him once more and said, "You *are* different . . . and you're nice."

Again the orchestra started up, and again she danced with Mason. This time there was a natural warmth in her dancing. She permitted Mason to hold her closer and he could feel the thrust of strong, youthful thighs, the lithe muscles rippling beneath the slender waist of the gown.

"All right," she said when the music ended, "I'm going to like you. I do like you."

"And I take it," Mason said, "that makes quite a difference."

She met his eyes, and said, "With me it makes all the difference in the world. I am not much good at this job. I never join people until after I've sized them up carefully."

"You were looking me over before you came out?" Mason asked.

"Of course."

"I'm flattered."

"What'll I call you?"

"Perry."

She knitted her forehead. "That's rather an unusual name."

Mason met her eyes. "It happens to be my real name. Moreover, I'm unmarried. I'm interested in people, and I'm not a small-time sport trying to make a big splash."

"You're interested in *people*?"

"In you at the moment."

"I like to dance with you."

"You dance divinely," Mason said. "You have that something, that deft touch that . . ."

"I'm a professional," she said as though that disposed of
the matter, and then added after a moment, significantly,
"dancer."

"Do you like it?" Mason asked.

"Dancing, yes," she said, and then added after a moment, "being a professional, no."

"Why?"

"Too many things go with it."

"Such as?"

"Do I have to tell you?"

"I was just wondering how much you had to put up with."

"Plenty."

Mason smiled. "Well, quite obviously you have to make
a living, and I suppose you receive some sort of a percentage
compensation . . ." He raised his hand to attract the attention of the waiter.

She motioned with her hand. "Don't order another drink."

"Why?"

"I don't want it."

"What do you want?"

"I want to dance again."

They had two more dances. She danced close to him, at
times looking up at him, at times holding her head so that
her forehead rested against the angle of his chin. During the
last dance she seemed thoughtful.

As Mason escorted her back to the table he said, "My
conscience hurts. So far you've been wasting your time with
me."

"I'm enjoying myself."

"You certainly must have *some* arrangement with The

Villa Lavina by which you receive compensation for your time and . . ."

"You want to go some place?" she asked.

"Where?"

"Where we can have some action and fun."

Mason regarded her searchingly. "It took you a long while to come to that point, didn't it, Petty?"

She met his eyes, and said, "Yes."

"Are you always that hesitant?"

"Yes. But when I go, I go all the way."

"And so?" Mason asked.

"So the invitation still holds."

"Let's go," Mason told her.

He beckoned to the waiter and paid his check, tipped the hat check girl for his topcoat and hat, and escorted Petty out to the driveway, caught the eye of the parking attendant and nodded.

The girl rejected the implied order with a shake of her head. "You don't want your car. You're going in mine."

Mason raised his eyebrows.

"It's all right," she said. "Eddie! The car, please."

The parking attendant nodded. A huge black limousine glided up to the entrance. A uniformed chauffeur jumped out smartly, opened the door.

Petty thanked him with a smile. Mason handed her into the car and followed. The heavy door swung shut.

"Now what?" Mason asked, his expression quizzical.

"We're going places."

"I take it," Mason said, looking at his wrist watch, "that by this time you know who I am and that this is something in the nature of a special reception that . . ."

"No," she said. "I don't care who you are. You're just nice."

She grasped a black silk cord and pulled. Dark curtains slid over the windows so that they were completely enclosed in privacy. The glass between the driver's compartment and the rear of the car was opaque. The rear window of the car was covered with a curtain. The side curtains which had slid across the windows when the girl had pulled the cord completely shut off all view.

"What's the idea?" Mason asked.

She moved over and snuggled up to him with a lithe motion, fitting her body close to his. "Don't you want privacy?" she asked.

Mason laughed and put his arm around her shoulders. Then, after a moment, he put his other arm around her waist.

She moved closer to him, and Mason drew his hand along the smooth surface of the dress, searching to see if a small weapon might be concealed within the garment.

There was, he realized, hardly opportunity to conceal a postage stamp beneath the satin smoothness of the single garment.

The car moved out into traffic, rolling smoothly.

"Where," Mason asked, "are we going?"

"Places. Don't you like me?"

"Yes."

"Well, why did you stop?"

Mason laughed. "I was looking for a gun or knife."

"That was only one side," she said. "Try the other side."

She shifted her position. "Go on," she invited, "try this side."

"No," Mason said, "the only weapon you have is the one nature gave you."

She laughed and moved closer to him for a moment, then put her head on his shoulder. "Why did you ask for me?"

"I heard you were a good scout."

"Who told you?"

"A friend."

"I don't go out like this with many people. Usually I just dance and that's all."

"Do you like your job?"

"Not too well."

"You like Martha Lavina?"

"She's a dear. Wonderfully understanding and considerate. She makes the job worth while."

"You meet many people?"

"Some."

There was a long period of silence.

Petty wriggled her body. "You're different."

Mason merely laughed.

"You *are* different."

"Just where are we going, Petty?"

"Places."

"What sort of places?"

"You'll see."

Mason moved slightly. His arm held her in such a position that her side was close to his. She asked finally, "Is that all?"

"Yes," Mason said.

She stiffened for a moment, then relaxed and remained motionless for so long Mason felt she might have gone to sleep.

Abruptly the big limousine slowed, made a sharp turn, crawled along what was evidently a narrow passageway, turned into a wider space, stopped, went back a few feet, then forward again and stopped.

The girl reached up and again pulled the silk cord. The curtains slid back. Mason could see that they were in a parking place evidently in the back of a building. There was the damp smell of untended back yards, a faint smell of onions frying. There were no lights.

Mason glanced at his wrist watch. They had taken twenty-two minutes to get where they were going.

The driver opened the door, stood at attention. Mason stepped out and helped Petty to the ground.

"Now what?" he asked.

"Leave your hat and top coat in the car," she instructed.

She led the way up three steps to an unlighted porch, pulled open a screendoor, fitted a key to a back door, unlocked it and pushed it open.

A small fifteen-watt light furnished weak illumination, disclosing a flight of stairs which led upward.

Petty motioned Mason to close the door, and placed her hand on the wooden rail. For a moment her fingers slid around the rail and gripped firmly, then she was climbing the stairs.

Mason followed.

"You live here?" he asked.

She made no answer, but continued to climb.

There was another door at the head of the stairs. She pushed this open and entered a long corridor, walked down this corridor, then opened a door on the right and smiled invitingly over her shoulder at Mason.

The lawyer followed her into the room.

It was a fairly large room equipped with the most simple type of furnishings. A long mahogany bar ran across one side. Movable stools were in front of the bar, and a few folding chairs were scattered around the room. A man was mixing drinks at the bar and several persons were sitting on the stools.

A door leading to an inner room opened. A man wearing black tie and dinner jacket stepped out, pulling the door shut behind him.

For a moment Mason heard the distinctive *whir-r-r-r* made by an ivory roulette ball as it finishes its run and clatters to a stop in one of the pockets.

The man came toward them, smiling affably. He was tall, dark, slender, and looked to be in the middle thirties. He had cold, gray eyes and smooth black hair which had been slicked back from his forehead so that it seemed like patent leather.

"Good evening, Petty," he said. "Do you know who's with you?"

She smiled. "He'll introduce himself."

"He doesn't need to," the man said. "He's Perry Mason, the lawyer."

Petty suddenly stiffened and said, *"Oh!"* It was an exclamation of utter consternation.

"I trust, Mr. Mason, that you're not on business?" the man in the tuxedo inquired.

"And if I am?" Mason asked.

"It wouldn't make any great difference, Mr. Mason, unless the business concerned us."

"I'm not in the employ of the district attorney, if that's what you mean," Mason said, smiling.

"Would you care to come in?"

"I take it," Mason said, "I was escorted here for that purpose."

The other smiled. "It would, of course, be a waste of time to attempt to pull the usual line on a person in your profession, Mr. Mason. If you care to try your luck we'd be only too glad to receive some of your money."

"And Petty?" Mason asked.

"Gets a flat fee for bringing you here and a small commission on the amount of your losses."

"And suppose I should win?"

"There is always that possibility," the man with the gray eyes conceded. "And in that event the hostesses have to look out for themselves. It is a situation they do not exactly deplore."

"I think we'll go in," Mason said.

"Step right this way."

"Perry Mason, the lawyer!" Petty exclaimed. "I should have known when you told me your name was Perry. I knew there was something about you, something . . . And I had to go and fall for *you!*"

"I'll try," Mason said, "to see that you are compensated in either event—whether I lose or win."

The man opened the door. Mason stepped into a room which was bare of all furnishings except folding chairs, two roulette tables, a crab table and two tables where games of twenty-one were in progress.

The man in evening clothes was exceedingly apologetic. "I'm very sorry, Mr. Mason, that we can't offer you more luxurious surroundings, but I can assure you the games are active and on the square.

"Unfortunately, owing to a narrow-minded attitude on the part of the authorities it becomes necessary to move our games from time to time and place to place."

"And then you advise the hostesses?" Mason asked.

"Not the hostesses. The drivers who pilot the cars."

"I see," Mason said. "That makes for a certain amount of safety."

"A certain amount," the man admitted. "We'll be only too glad to cash your check for any amount, Mr. Mason."

"It won't be necessary," Mason said, taking a roll of currency from his pocket and peeling off two hundred-dollar bills.

"Right over this way to the cashier, if you will, please, Mr. Mason. You can receive chips for your money, either one-dollar chips or five-dollar chips, or, if you prefer, we have some twenty-dollar chips."

"I think we'll start with five-dollar chips," Mason told him. "And I think Petty will want a few chips as well."

Mason received forty chips for the two one-hundred dollar bills, and handed Petty ten of the chips.

"What game do you prefer, Petty?"

"Roulette."

They moved over to the roulette table. Mason, somewhat quizzical, keenly observant, watched the play around the table, making a few small plays on the group of twelve numbers, on the colors and occasionally playing the corners. For a while he broke even, then started to lose. Placing his last chip on number seven, he was surprised to see the ball settle in the seven compartment.

The croupier paid off with an expressionless face. Mason

picked up his winnings, leaving one on the seven, putting one on the thirty, one on the five.

The ball settled in the nine.

Again Mason played the seven, the thirty and the five, and the five came up.

Once more he raked in winnings.

Petty, standing watching him, had, as yet, made no play.

"Well?" Mason asked her.

She placed a chip on the seven, the thirty and the five.

The ball settled on twenty-four.

With an exclamation of disgust she played ten dollars on the red. The black came up. She put five dollars on the red. Again the black came. She pushed her last remaining chips on the red and the ball dropped in the double o.

"All right," she said, "I'm broke."

Mason counted out ten more five-dollar chips. "Try those," he said.

The lawyer moved away from her, started playing with indifferent success, noted that Petty had a winning streak. Her face became flushed, her eyes gleamed with excitement as she raked in the chips.

Mason won for a while, then lost steadily. When he was back to his original capital of two hundred dollars he walked over to the cashier's desk and cashed in his chips.

The cashier smiled at him. "Didn't do yourself any good, Mr. Mason?"

"I didn't do myself any harm," Mason told him.

Mason walked over to the roulette table. Petty was stacking chips.

"How are you doing?"

"All right up to a minute ago. Now I can't seem to win anything."

"Cash in," Mason told her. "I want to go."

"Now?"

"Now."

"But we've just got here."

Mason shrugged his shoulders.

"I feel lucky tonight. I feel as though I could break the bank."

"I don't think you can," Mason told her.

She made three more bets, then turned to him with a little grimace. "You've caused my luck to fly out of the window."

"Then cash in."

"All right," she said suddenly, "I will."

Mason helped her carry her chips over to the cashier's window. She received six hundred and twenty dollars.

"That much?" she exclaimed. "Gosh, I didn't realize those chips mounted up so."

"I'm sorry to be taking your profits out with us," Mason told the cashier.

"Don't worry, we'll get them back." The cashier smiled affably.

"I take it this is a new angle," Mason said, "the sucker neither wins nor loses, the hostess cleans up."

"Damned if it isn't," the cashier admitted.

Mason escorted Petty out through the door. They paused at the bar for a drink. The man with the black tie said, "I hope we see you again, Mr. Mason."

"Thank you," Mason remarked politely.

They went down the stairs, and, as though by some pre-arranged signal, the limousine was waiting for them in front of the door.

Mason handed Petty in.

She pulled the silken cord once more, snuggled up against Mason. "I think you're wonderful," she said. "I'm so glad you made me quit. When I start gambling I always plunge until I'm broke. They get you sooner or later up there."

"Well, you're doing all right now."

"I've never had so much money at one time . . . gosh, if I can only keep from doing any more gambling until I've had a chance to use this money."

"Do they let you get away with winnings?"

"When somebody gives me chips, yes."

"Then don't go back until you've spent all this money," Mason said. "Stay away from the tables. What are you planning to spend it for?"

She was too excited now to try to tempt him.

"Gosh, Mr. Mason, if you only knew what this money means to me. Tell me, why did you go to The Villa Lavina and ask for me"

"Don't you know?"

"No."

"You walked out on me earlier today."

"*I* did?" she exclaimed.

"Yes."

"I never saw you before in my life."

"What about Paul Drake?"

"Who's he?"

"He works for me sometimes."

"I . . ." Abruptly she became silent.

"Well?" Mason asked.

Mason could hear the rustle of her skirt. "Don't disturb me," she said. "I'm putting my money down my stocking."

Then, abruptly, she was snuggling against him in the warm, dark interior of the limousine.

"You like me?" she asked.

"What about Paul Drake?" Mason asked.

"I'm not talking about Paul Drake. I'm talking about *us*. Do you like me?"

"Yes."

She slid her hand along the back of the seat. Her fingers pressed a concealed light switch. A light above the ash tray glowed into subdued brilliance, furnishing a soft illumination.

Her right hand slid along Mason's shoulders, stole up the collar of his coat, the fingertips caressed the short hairs at the back of his neck.

"Relax," she said, laughing. "I'm not going to bite you."

Mason looked down at her.

Her eyes were looking up into his. Her vivid red lips were parted, disclosing pearly teeth.

"I *like* you," she repeated.

Her fingertips moved in slow rhythm up and down the back of his head. "Do you like me?"

"Of course."

"You don't show signs of being overly enthusiastic."

"Did you want me to be *overly* enthusiastic?" Mason asked.

"Well, you might start in being enthusiastic, and we can carry on from there."

She let her left hand move along his coat until her fingers clutched the left lapel of the garment, gently tugging, pulling him toward her.

Mason said, "Do you remember the night Rodney Archer was held up, Petty?"

She stiffened into rigid, motionless attention.

"What about it?" she asked, her voice coldly cautious.

"Did you see Martha Lavina that night?"

Abruptly she pushed back from him, said, "All right, go ahead and be a stuffy old lawyer if you want to. I like you. But all *you* want to do is to ask a bunch of questions. I'm a human being but you're never going to find it out. You only think of me as a witness."

"All I'm asking," Mason said, "is whether you saw Martha Lavina that night."

She abruptly flipped the light switch which plunged the inside of the car into total darkness.

"Well?" Mason asked after a few seconds. "Are you going to answer my question?"

There was no answer, and then Mason could hear a peculiar sequence of rhythmic sounds, the sounds of a woman sobbing.

Mason groped to find her in the darkness.

"Get away from me. Don't touch me!" she said, as his fingers reached her shoulder.

"After all," Mason said, "let's invest this scene with a little touch of reality. I only asked you . . ."

He could feel her shoulder shudder in a convulsive sob, then she shook herself free.

Almost immediately the car braked to a stop.

"What's this?" Mason asked.

She didn't answer.

The door of the limousine opened. The driver slid the black curtain back along the rod which held it in place.

"Villa Lavina," he said.

Mason glanced at his wrist watch. The return trip had taken exactly six and one-half minutes.

Mason got out of the car. The hostess sat inside with her back turned to Mason, her head down, a handkerchief at her eyes.

"Coming?" Mason asked.

Her answer was muffled. "No," she said.

The driver closed the door, glancing accusingly at Mason.

"Are there any charges?" Mason asked.

"None, sir."

Mason walked up the steps to the porch of The Villa Lavina.

"You want your car now?" the man at the door asked.

"In a minute," Mason told him.

Mason entered the night club, once more checking his hat and coat. The headwaiter who had been so deferential before seemed a little dubious now. "I'm afraid we're pretty well filled up," he apologized.

Mason looked around for the red carnation which marked Paul Drake's detectives. He saw none.

"I don't think we have a table," the headwaiter said again, this time with a complete lack of cordiality.

"I'm just going to the men's room," Mason told him, and, skirting the dance floor, walked on back to the rear of the restaurant, his eyes making a quick survey of the place. There was no sign of anyone wearing a red carnation.

Mason detoured the rest room, walked through a door in the back which led to a passageway. The passageway in turn led to a back door. Mason opened the door which disclosed a small service porch, on which a dozen huge garbage cans were stacked.

Out behind the lighted service porch was an area of darkness. To the left was a parking space in which the cars of the diners at The Villa Lavina were standing in orderly array. To the right was a high board fence.

The smell of cooking onions permeated the atmosphere.

Mason turned back, re-entered The Villa Lavina, moved down the corridor, noticed a door on the right and tried it.

The door led to a flight of steps.

Mason carefully closed the door behind him, climbed the stairs, emerged into a second floor corridor, walked down the corridor, pushed open a door on the right and entered the same room he had been in a few minutes earlier, the room with the bar, the portable stools, the folding chairs.

The same man in a tuxedo came forward smiling, then suddenly the smile froze on his face. The eyes were cold and hard.

"Forget something, Mr. Mason?"

"Thought I'd try my luck again," Mason said affably.

"May I ask how you got here?"

"I climbed the stairs."

"What stairs?"

"The stairs from the corridor of The Villa Lavina."

The man in the tuxedo said, "You shouldn't have done that, Mr. Mason."

"Why not?" Mason asked innocently.

"We have no connection with The Villa Lavina."

"I didn't say you had. I said I climbed the stairs from The Villa Lavina and arrived here. You asked me and I told you."

Another man who had been at the end of the bar, a thick-necked individual, with the build of a wrestler, moved around from the bar, walked toward Mason, keeping between the lawyer and the door, then stopped to light a cigarette, standing about three feet behind the lawyer.

The man in the dinner jacket said, "You know, you're a pretty big man, Mr. Mason. You draw a lot of weight, but there are some things that it's unwise for *anyone* to do, even you."

"Such as what?" Mason asked.

"I'm not here to answer questions."

"What *are* you here for?"

"To maintain order."

"I'm being orderly, am I not?"

The man in the black tie reached a sudden decision. "Certainly, Mr. Mason," he said. "Would you care to step into the other room again?"

He stepped back and held the door open. For a moment Mason hesitated, then walked through the door and into the room where the gaming tables were located.

Mason walked over to the cashier's cage, took two hundred dollars from his pocket.

The cashier looked at him in astonishment. "Change your mind, Mr. Mason?"

"Yes."

The cashier hesitated. "You seem to be alone now."

Mason made an exaggerated gesture of being startled, looked at his right side, then at his left side. "Damned if I'm not!" he exclaimed in surprise.

The cashier looked up over Mason's shoulder, caught a signal from someone standing behind the lawyer, and became silently efficient, passing out forty five-dollar chips.

Mason turned back to the roulette tables.

For ten or fifteen minutes the lawyer played aimlessly, looking the patrons over, placing his bets on the color for the most part and losing every bet he placed.

At the end of fifteen minutes, Mason shrugged his shoulders, gathered his chips, and made one last bet on the twenty-seven.

The ball dropped into the number three pocket.

A woman's voice behind him said, "Tough luck, Mr. Mason, but you can't win all the time."

Mason turned to confront the appraising eyes of Martha Lavina.

"Good evening," he said.

"I hardly expected to find *you* here," she observed.

Mason laughed politely.

"How did you happen to find this place?" she asked, ignoring his skepticism.

Mason said, "That's the second time I've been asked that question within the last twenty minutes."

She said, "I think I want to talk with you, Mr. Mason."

"Where? When?"

"As you are doubtless aware, my Villa Lavina Number Three is downstairs in the adjoining building. I have an office where we can have complete privacy."

Mason bowed. "I am at your service."

He followed Martha Lavina down the stairway, through the door into the corridor of The Villa Lavina, and took her arm as they walked the length of the night club, through a curtained doorway into a small reception room, then through a heavy mahogany door into an office.

The decor of the office indicated a decided feminine influence. The desk was subordinated by several comfortable overstuffed chairs furnished in rich red leather, and the place was illuminated by an indirect lighting system which gave a soft light having the restful quality of summer moonlight.

Martha Lavina motioned Mason to a seat and seated herself, not behind the desk, but in a red leather chair. She crossed her knees and adjusted her skirt at just the right level. An expanse of sheer nylon showed graceful legs and neatly shod feet.

She opened her purse, took out a silver cigarette case with

a built-in lighter, selected a cigarette, snapped the lighter into flame, sucked in a deep drag on the first inhalation and let the smoke seep out in twin streams from slightly widened nostrils as she surveyed Perry Mason in wordless appraisal.

The lawyer casually reached for one of his own cigarettes, scraped a match into flame and returned her silent scrutiny.

"Well?" she asked at length.

Mason shrugged his shoulders, smiled, said nothing.

"What do you want?" she demanded.

"Nothing at the moment."

"I'm afraid you can be a rather difficult person, Mr. Mason."

"I'm quite certain I can."

"Why be difficult with me?"

"I'm representing a client."

"Pouf!" she observed, making a gesture of dismissal. "A down-and-out derelict of humanity."

"Nevertheless a client."

"He'd be just as well off in prison as where he is. Don't be silly. The man's just a barnacle."

"He's my client."

"He's guilty."

"That remains to be seen."

"All right, what do you want? What's your price? What are you leading up to?"

"I haven't any price."

"You seem to be taking quite an interest in my life."

"I am taking quite an interest in your testimony."

"What's wrong with my testimony?"

Mason met her eyes. "You weren't with Rodney Archer when he was held up."

"Who says I wasn't?"

"I think the jury will before we get done."

"And would that help you?"

"It might help my client."

"I don't see how."

56

"At the moment," Mason told her, "I am acting on the assumption the truth will help my client."

"What's your price?"

"I haven't any."

"All right, I'll put it this way. What's your client's price?"

"I don't think he has any."

"Don't be silly, Mr. Mason. Everyone has a price. Not perhaps to sell out their integrity, but there's a price for everything in the world. You're a lawyer. Everything you have is for sale."

"And you?" Mason asked.

She met his eyes. "And everything I have is for sale—at a price."

"Is that a comforting philosophy?"

"It's a practical philosophy. Everyone sells what he has to sell. Some women ask for a cash price. Some women want security. They settle for marriage in order to get security. Every woman who has a mirror appraises her bargaining position a dozen times a day.

"Now let's quit beating around the bush, Mr. Mason. You're a practical man. I'm a practical woman. I am perfectly willing to concede your personal and professional integrity. You're representing a client. Personally I don't know why you should be so stuffy about it. He's an insignificant drifter, who has probably been guilty of a dozen holdups. You aren't even getting a dime out of defending him."

"I was appointed by the court to defend him. The man is my client."

"All right, don't tell me that again! Good Lord, I know the man is your client. You keep harping on it. 'He's my client. He's my client. He's my client!' My God, I *know* he's your client. Now then, what do you want?"

"Justice."

"What's justice?"

"An acquittal."

"That's asking too much."

"What's your suggestion?"

"Suppose the district attorney lets him plead guilty to some misdemeanor charge, petty larceny, or vagrancy?"

"My client wants vindication, an acquittal."

"He can't have it."

"Why not?"

"Because that would make a monkey out of the deputy D.A. who's prosecuting the case. It would be a black mark on the D.A.'s batting average and would get the police in bad."

"How does it happen you are so certain about how they'd feel?"

"What do you think?"

"I was wondering if you'd ask them."

"Don't be silly. I've been around."

"I've been around myself."

"It's a good deal. One way your client gets a jolt in the pen. This way he cops a plea. I'll even give it all to you on a silver platter. The case will be continued for sentence. He can apply for probation. He'll draw probation. You can't beat that."

"An acquittal would beat that."

"You can't get an acquittal—not now."

"Who's going to stop me?"

"I am, for one."

"You might get fooled."

"Not me."

Mason said, "You've sworn you were present at the holdup."

"I was. I can tell you definitely, positively, absolutely and finally that I was with Rodney Archer at the time of the holdup, and that this client you keep talking about was the man who held him up."

"That, of course," Mason said, "is a matter for the jury to decide. I see no reason to debate the matter now."

"When are you going to debate it?"

"Monday morning when you return to the stand for further cross-examination."

Abruptly she asked, "What are you doing prowling around here?"

"I wanted to talk with Miss Kaylor. I heard she was here."

"Miss Kaylor will back up my testimony."

"That wasn't the way I heard it a few days ago."

"Ask her the way it is now."

"She told Paul Drake that you . . ."

"Who's Paul Drake?"

"A private detective I employ."

"All right, what did she tell him?"

"That she didn't pick you up and give you a ride on the night of the holdup."

"She wasn't under oath then. Put her on the witness stand and she'll be on oath. And she'll be *your* witness, Mr. Mason."

"Yes?" Mason asked.

"She'll be your witness," Martha Lavina repeated, smiling coldly, "and I happen to know that a lawyer can't impeach his own witness. You put her on the stand and ask her if she gave me a ride on the night in question and she'll swear that she did. You'll be bound by that answer. You'll be stuck with her testimony. You can't question it."

"It would be unfortunate for her if she testified to something that wasn't true."

"It would be true."

"That wouldn't be what she told Paul Drake."

"May I repeat, Mr. Mason, that she was not under oath when she was talking with your Mr. Drake."

"All right," Mason said, getting to his feet, "where does that leave us?"

"Sit down. Don't be in such a hurry. It leaves us right here. Why did you go back to the gambling place?"

"Because I was interested."

"In what?"

"Finding out how it operated."

"Why? Did you want to try to blackmail me?"

"No. Just curiosity."

"And may I ask what aroused your curiosity?"

Mason said, "It took twenty-two minutes to drive from the front door of The Villa Lavina here to the back door of the gambling establishment. It took six and a half minutes to return."

"Well?"

Mason said, "That impressed me as being strange. We were going at about the same rate of speed all the time. I noticed the odor of frying onions in the back of the gambling place, and when I returned here I went back by the kitchen just to check up. When I noticed the odor of frying onions I felt rather certain of my deductions."

"I'll have to check that," she said, frowning.

"And," Mason told her, "there was, of course, the discrepancy in the time element."

"If you'd behaved yourself, the return trip would have taken just as long as the trip going out."

"What do you mean by behaving myself?" Mason asked.

"Had acted biologically normal and hadn't started cross-examining the hostess."

"I see," Mason said. "I take it that there is a system of signals between the hostess and the driver so that . . ."

"No signals," she said. "There's a microphone which connects with the driver's compartment so he can hear what's going on. He is a man of discretion and he's expected to use that discretion."

"The possibilities," Mason said, "are most interesting."

"You don't even know the half of them."

"I take it," Mason went on, "that if the customer has lost money and is a poor loser, the ride home is very short. In that event the hostess collects her entire compensation from the percentage of the sucker's losings. If, on the other hand, the man has won and is in an expansive and generous mood, the ride is prolonged until the hostess has been able

60

to make certain his generosity has found a tangible means of expression.''

''You express that last very delicately, Mr. Mason.''

''And, I trust, accurately.''

''If you want to find out about that you'll have to do more field work,'' she said. ''I don't discuss these matters with the drivers, and, believe it or not, Mr. Mason, I have nothing to do with the operation of that gambling house. The Villa Lavina is an entirely separate institution. The only connecting link is the opportunity it gives the hostesses to pick up a little side money and still be respectable.''

''They insist on respectability, I take it,'' Mason said dryly.

''You might be surprised. Some of them do.''

''Well,'' Mason told her, ''I'll be going.''

''You haven't give me any answer yet.''

''About what?''

''About what is going to happen Monday morning in connection with that case.''

''As far as I'm concerned,'' Mason said, ''on Monday morning the Court is going to call the case. You are going to be on the witness stand and I'm going to continue my cross-examination.''

She met his eyes. ''Mr. Mason,'' she said, ''let's not mince matters. If you try to continue cross-examining me, you're going to meet with a crushing defeat. I will admit that you caught me a little by surprise this afternoon. You had one bolt in your quiver and now you've shot that. When you get me back on the stand Monday morning, you ask me anything you want to know about the details of what happened and I'll be able to answer your questions in such a way that I'll crucify your client.''

''So what do you suggest?'' Mason asked.

''*I* have no suggestion,'' she told him, rising and smoothing her skirt.

''Very well,'' Mason said. ''Good night.''

''Good night.''

She walked over to give him her hand. For a moment she looked in his eyes. There was curiosity and a certain amount of admiration in them. There was no fear.

"Come back," she told him. "Any time."

Chapter 4

At 11:15 the following morning the unlisted telephone in Mason's apartment shrilled its summons.

The lawyer, who had been following his Saturday morning custom of reading the advance decisions, put down the printed pamphlet, picked up the telephone and said, "Hello."

"Don't be irritated, Chief," Della Street said, "but I have someone here you should talk with."

"Who is it?"

"Mary Brogan."

"Brogan, Brogan?" Mason said. "Isn't that the name of . . . why, yes, that's the name of our client in the holdup case."

"That's right."

"And who's Mary?"

"His niece from St. Louis. When she heard about him being in trouble she caught the first bus and never stopped until she arrived here this morning. I think you should see her."

"When? Where?"

"As soon as possible, either here or at the office."

"The office in an hour," Mason said.

"Could you make it half an hour?"

"That important?"

"I think it is. I think you'll want to do something about it. Have you checked with Paul Drake today?"

"No."

"He has something to tell you but he didn't want to disturb you."

"All right," Mason said. "The office in half an hour."

He slipped out of his sport shirt and slacks, put on a business suit and went to the office. Della was already there with a blue-eyed, blonde young woman who came forward to give the lawyer a firm handshake. Her candid eyes peered up into his with frank appraisal.

"This is Perry Mason, Mary," Della Street said. "Mary Brogan, Chief. She's been sitting up all night on a bus, arrived here this morning, and got in to see her uncle on a special visitor's permit."

"And she has some money," Mary Brogan added.

"How much?" Mason asked curiously.

"Three hundred and eighty-five dollars. At first I thought I'd just send Uncle Albert the money. Then I thought I'd better come and see what it was all about."

Mason nodded. "Won't you sit down?"

She seated herself in the client's chair. Mason sat at his desk. Della sat at her secretarial desk and flashed Mason a quick, significant glance.

"The money I have is cash," Mary Brogan went on. "I have a round-trip ticket on the bus, so I . . ."

"What do you do?" Mason asked, eyeing her curiously. "I take it that you work."

"I pound a typewriter," she said, "and, believe me, I pound it."

"Tell me something about your uncle . . . and about you, about your job."

"As far as the job is concerned, there isn't anything to tell, Mr. Mason. I get up to the office at eight-thirty in the morning, get the mail opened, put it on the boss's desk, take dictation, start in on the typewriter, dash out for lunch, come back, take more dictation, go back to the typewriter, always finish up in one terrific rush trying to get the letters on the boss's desk so he can sign them before he goes home. Then I stay and get the letters in the envelopes, put on the postage, file the carbon copies of what I've written, close up the office, go up to the apartment I share with another girl, have something to eat, wash out my stockings and undies, roll into bed, sleep, and get ready for another day."

"And you've managed to save money?" Mason asked, more by way of comment than question.

"Yes. I always try to invest in a vacation. I'll skimp on anything else just so I can get out somewhere for two weeks. We watch our expenses and cut corners wherever we can. We watch our figures and our grocery bill and we're doing all right.

"However, it's kind of a rat race at that. By the time a girl keeps herself looking good, pays her cleaning bills, keeps herself in sheer stockings so the boss can have a little scenic relief, pays rent on the apartment, pays income tax, social security tax, sales taxes and excise taxes, every time you put a buck in the piggy bank you feel you've wrested a hundred cents right out of the maw of Old Man Mammon."

Mason grinned.

Della Street caught his eye and winked significantly. "Mary has a very interesting background," she said, "She helped her uncle retire."

Mason nodded. "I imagine coming out here with enough money to offer me a fee must have meant quite a sacrifice, Miss Brogan."

"That's my hard luck," she said. "You've got yours. I bet by the time you pay the office rent, dig up for all these law books that keep coming in, meet your payroll twice a month, make contributions to all the various drives, and then get notices from the Bureau of Internal Revenue, you have plenty of headaches of your own."

"It isn't quite as bad as all that," Mason said, laughing.

"You're not kidding me. It's a run-around, but what's life for anyway? You have to keep busy and take things as they come."

"You must be rather attached to your uncle."

"I sure am. My parents are dead, and Uncle Albert helped put me through school. He was a salesman and he tried to get ahead by working days and driving nights. A drunk driver who had been making whoopee smashed into him at midnight one night, and by the time Uncle Albert healed up he'd lost just about all of his steam. They did the best they could but they can't seem to fit spare parts to a person the way they can to an automobile."

"So what did you do?"

"He started getting blue and despondent, and I pointed out there was no sense in it. He could get by on what he had coming in if he only found some place where he didn't have to spend everything out for rent and clothes. I told him to get himself a house trailer and go out and be happy."

"And you helped him some?"

"A little. I financed the trailer, not all of it, but my vacation money made the down payment."

"And now he's in trouble and has appealed to you?"

"No appeal to me. He didn't even write me. I certainly raked him over the coals for that."

"Why didn't he write?"

"He said that he knew I'd come barging out here and try to get some lawyer for him. He said he'd had a break—the court had appointed the best lawyer in the state to defend him. And you can say that again! I've stuck my ear to the ground and found out that you're *the* Perry Mason."

"You realize that when the court appoints a lawyer to defend a penniless man the lawyer is obligated to give his best services without any fee?"

"That's what Uncle Albert told me. Sounds cockeyed to me but that's the way it is, I guess."

"And yet you tell me you have money?"

"Sure. Why not? Lawyers aren't supposed to work for nothing except when the prisoner doesn't have a dime. Uncle Albert was holding out on you. He's got me, and he knows it. Of course, my little pile of dough isn't up in the class of your fees, Mr. Mason, but since you're already stuck with the case, what I can pay will help."

"But I was already handling the case. You didn't need to offer me anything."

Her eyes widened. "That would be a dirty trick on you. No, I don't play that way, Mr. Mason. As I go through life I try to play fair. If someone gives me a square deal I try to give him one. Uncle Albert tells me you've been fighting his case just the same as if there'd been a million-dollar fee."

"Are you going right back, now that you've seen your uncle?" Mason asked.

"No. I'm staying until the trial's over. I told the boss I was going to take my two weeks' vacation now, and he's arranged for temporary help in the office."

"You arrived this morning?"

"Yes. I couldn't find anyone at your office, but the elevator operator referred me to the Drake Detective Agency. Mr. Drake turned me over to Della Street, and here I am."

She opened her purse.

Mason waved his hand in a gesture of negation. "Let's not argue about the money right at the moment," Mason said. "I know you have something important to tell me, otherwise Della wouldn't have called me up. What is it?"

She said, "I went down to the jail to see Uncle Albert before I came up here. They let me see him without any fuss at all. Then a smooth-talking detective came along, took me off to one side and told me that if I wanted to get wise things could all be fixed up."

"In what way?"

"The charge against Uncle Albert would be reduced to something that would be just a misdemeanor, he could plead guilty to that and the judge would continue the case, then give Uncle Albert probation and everything would be all fixed up. There wouldn't be any need even to go into court any more, only just long enough for Uncle Albert to say that he'd plead guilty to a reduced charge, and that would be all there'd be to it."

"Who was this man?" Mason asked.

"Just a smooth-talking boy who seemed to know the ropes," she said. "I think he was somebody fairly high up. He seemed to know his way around and he told me that you were a fine lawyer, but that you asked too many questions, and that if you kept on doing that influential people were going to get mad at Uncle Albert and throw the book at him."

"And what did you tell him?"

"I told this smoothie that I'd come all the way from St. Louis, that I didn't know a thing about what had been going on in the case, but that I certainly appreciated his interest. I asked him why he hadn't told Uncle Albert about this before they slapped him in the puss with that information charging first-degree holdup."

"And what did Mr. Smoothie say to that?" Mason asked.

"Well, he squirmed around and said that the police had to handle it that way because of newspaper pressure, but that the evidence wasn't too strong against Uncle Albert, and that he himself thought perhaps there might have been a mistake. He said Uncle Albert was smart enough to have put the empty wallet and the woman's purse in the trash container of some other tenant in the trailer court, or thrown them into a vacant lot, or something like that. He said the fact they were in Uncle Albert's container made him believe it might have been a plant."

"Did he say anything about the identification?"

"No. He didn't talk much about the case. He was very big brotherly and sympathetic and he suggested that I go tell Uncle Albert to think it over."

"Did you?"

"I did nothing of the kind. I came up here."

"Why?"

She said, "I don't know much about law, Mr. Mason, but two girls don't share an apartment in St. Louis and try to make an honest living without learning a heck of a lot about men. I've found out that whenever a man gets that smooth-talking, purring note in his voice, he's getting ready to throw a forward pass that'll go right between the goal posts."

Mason laughed.

She went on, "There are different kinds of sugar in the world. Sometimes you can find heavy sugar if that's what you're looking for. It isn't smooth. That smooth sugar is only used to disguise the taste of some bitter pill you don't want to take."

Mason said, "Did you ever play poker, Miss Brogan?"

"Strip, stud or draw?"

"Any of them?"

"I have played all three."

"Then you understand the advantage of running a bluff?"

"Yes. Is that what you're going to do?"

Mason nodded. "Something has happened. These people are frightened. They don't want to dismiss the case and give your uncle a clean bill of health. They'd like to have him plead guilty to something. Then they'd give him probation."

"Why have him plead guily to anything?"

"So he can't sue for false arrest."

"So what do we do next?"

Mason said, "First, we serve a subpoena on a girl named Inez Kaylor. We couldn't subpoena her while she was out of the state, but now we can. Then if she doesn't attend court on Monday we can get an order forcing her to attend. We at least make her think we are going to put her on the witness stand, and we make Martha Lavina think we are going to put her on the witness stand. We also make Rodney Archer, the man who was held up, think we're going to recall him to the stand and cross-examine him about what happened with his cigarette lighter."

"But in the meantime they've had the entire week end to fix up a story."

"That's right."

"And they're clever?"

"Very clever."

"It doesn't sound too good. They'll fix up something!"

"Then we'll unfix it."

"Is there," she asked, "anything I can do?"

Mason nodded.

"What?"

"Paul Drake has had detectives shadowing Inez Kaylor. I think by this time he knows where she's stopping. You could get in touch with Inez Kaylor."

"What do I do when I get in touch with her?"

"Try to make her tell the truth."

"Will they claim I was trying to influence the testimony of a witness for the prosecution?"

"She'll be subpoenaed as a witness for the defense."

"Will you put her on the stand?"

"Not until I know what she's going to swear to," Mason said. "I don't dare to. Unfortunately I can't impeach my own witness. Technically I can show surprise and contradictory statements, but practically I don't dare to put her on the witness stand until I know that her testimony is going to be favorable."

"And you don't think it would be favorable if you put her on now?"

"I'm pretty certain it wouldn't," Mason said. "Something is bothering her. She may not dare to commit perjury. The other side may be bluffing too."

"So you want me to wade into the battle and smite the Philistines hip and thigh?"

"That's the general idea," Mason said.

"Get me the address," she told him. "I'll gird up my loins and start smiting."

"The address," Mason told her, "is something I'm going to pick up from my detective agency—at least I hope I am.

"You hold off your Philistine smiting until I go down the hall and see what Paul Drake knows."

Chapter 5

Paul Drake was in his office when Mason walked in.

"How do we stand on the Kaylor girl?" the lawyer asked.

"We know the place where she's living," Drake said. "We're waiting on you now. How did you get along with her last night?"

"She made passes at me. I rode along for a while then started to talk about the case. She clammed up and started crying. She pretended she was hurt because I wouldn't make passes. I couldn't tell how much of it was a stall and how much was fear."

"Find out anything?"

Mason said, "Those hostesses play a pretty slick racket. There's a gambling house over The Villa Lavina Number Three. Apparently it's located there permanently, but they make patrons think it's one of those floating gambling places that moves from place to place every night."

"In that way they couldn't have many regular customers," Drake said.

"They don't want regular customers," Mason told him. "They fleece 'em on a one-time basis. They're careful about who they take up there. Probably they have another setup and they can alternate back and forth between the two setups. I think every game in the place is as crooked as a crippled eel with St. Vitus's dance. When they really wanted to get rid of me I dropped two hundred bucks without even getting a smell of a win—not a number, not a color."

"They build it up as a transient game," Paul Drake mused.

"That's right. It gives you the impression of a game that

71

was moved in a light truck and set up an hour before you got there. You feel at any minute a bunch of men will come in, pick up the stuff and move it to the other end of town."

"Yet you think it's permanent?"

"That's my best guess."

"Why would they go to all that elaborate rigmarole to make the patron think it was a migratory setup?" Drake asked, frowning.

Mason grinned. "It saves the expense of putting Oriental carpets on the floor, pictures on the walls and all the swank that goes with it. Then *if* they're raided they only lose some cheap portable equipment."

"That's a thought," Drake admitted.

"And," Mason went on, "it also lulls the sucker into believing there's no payoff for protection. That keeps him from becoming indignant and informative."

"You think there is a payoff?"

"You've been around, Paul. You know that wherever there's organized gambling there's a payoff."

"Who gets it in this instance?"

"I've been wondering about that," Mason said. "Notice the strategic location of the various Villa Lavinas. There are three of them and each is located in a small suburban city."

Drake frowned. "Darned if they aren't. I never thought of that."

"Probably," Mason said, "Martha Lavina picks her locations with extreme care."

Drake nodded, then became thoughtfully silent.

"I'm interested in finding out what your shadows uncovered last night, Paul," Mason said after a few minutes.

Drake grinned. "You were riding on quite a merry-go-round, Perry."

"I know I was. I felt like reaching for the brass ring. Where did we go?"

"You drove up one street and down another, then along a

cross street, around a block, back on the same cross street, and finally wound up at the back door of The Villa Lavina. You and the hostess got out and went upstairs. When you came down you started back on a long runaround, then something happened, and all of a sudden the car streaked right back to the front door of The Villa Lavina.''

"That's where I missed my cue,'' Mason said.

"What was your cue? Were you supposed to make a pass, or were you supposed not to?''

"I'm darned if I know for sure,'' Mason said. "I don't know what the ordinary program was supposed to be, but in my case I was definitely supposed to make a pass—at least that was indicated.''

"Then what?''

"You can't tell. The car was wired so the driver could hear what went on. They might have tried to blackmail me. They might have claimed an assault. I was playing them pretty close to my chest.''

"What's the regular racket?''

"The girl gets a flat rate for bringing a sucker up to the gambling place and gets a percentage of his losses.''

"Suppose he wins?''

"I don't think he's supposed to win. They'll let the hostesses win, but I don't think she can cash in the chips and keep the money. If the sucker should win, the girl is in an enviable position. She can prolong the trip back as long as she wants to. The sucker is feeling exuberant, his pockets filled with easy cash and his mind imbued with the principle 'Easy come, easy go!'

"The hostess can control the situation at all times. The microphone keeps the driver posted on what's going on. If the hostess wants to kid the guy along she teases him until she decides the ride has gone far enough, then she uses some code word that's a signal, and the first thing the customer knows he's right back at the front steps of The Villa Lavina.''

"That,'' Drake said, "sounds like a hell of a fine racket.''

"It might be a *very* good racket," Mason agreed thoughtfully.

"Now that you have this information, Perry, there may be some uneasiness in certain circles."

"That," Mason said, "is something that bothers me. There's undoubtedly a lot of uneasiness in certain circles."

"What circles for instance?"

"Well," Mason said, "there's Martha Lavina. There's Rodney Archer. There's the Kaylor girl. And there are the law enforcement officers who are getting a payoff on letting the gambling place run. Then there are people whose jobs depend on having the gambling place remain in operation."

Drake frowned. "I don't like that, Perry. It makes for rather a formidable array of enemies you've drawn all at once."

Mason said, "I don't like enemies who aren't formidable, Paul. There's no fun in shooting sitting ducks."

"What do you want me to do?" Drake asked.

"I want you to serve a subpoena on that Kaylor girl ordering her to appear as a witness on behalf of the defense. I want you to start getting everything you can on Rodney Archer. I want you to find out in particular if there's any woman in his life who might not want people to know she was riding around in an automobile with him."

"Now look, Perry," Paul Drake said, "let me give you a little fatherly advice."

Mason grinned and shook his head. "I know what it is, Paul. I don't need it."

"Yes, you do," Paul said. "This man you're defending isn't worth all this gamble. If you go stirring up a hornets' nest you're apt to get stung."

"Thanks for the advice, Paul."

"Are you going to take it?"

"No."

"I figured you wouldn't. I don't like this, Perry. Things

have a way of happening to people who get in the way of some of these boys. They're pretty ruthless at times."

"I know."

"No you don't know. I've seen things happen, Perry. People get crowded off a road into the ditch. An automobile upsets. A man gets beaten up so bad he is never the same afterward. It's supposed to be a holdup, but he knows it isn't a holdup, and the police know it isn't a holdup, and the police become singularly unenthusiastic about finding out who did the job."

"Some of the police are on the square."

"I know, but the ones who are on the square are pretty badly handicapped when there's a fix."

"I'll take a chance on the beating."

"Here's something else that bothers me, Perry."

"What?"

"That Kaylor girl."

"What about her?"

"I picked her up in Las Vegas," Drake said. "I had a straight tip she'd been in Las Vegas for three or four months. She told me she had. She was living there in Las Vegas."

"Alone?" Mason asked.

Drake grinned. "She had a swell apartment. I didn't ask her where the dough came from or how many keys there were to the door, but she seemed like a nice kid."

"All right, so what?"

"Now then," Drake went on, "when we put our shadows on this Kaylor girl last night we find that she's keeping a little apartment here. When she ditched me she went right back to The Villa Lavina. That Kaylor girl is maintaining a double address. She's living a double life for some reason, and Martha Lavina knows what it is and can make her jump through hoops."

Mason said, "Slap a subpoena on her and we'll find out what it's all about. Where's she living, Paul?"

"The Windmore Arms Apartments. She has 321."

"Okay. Go ahead and serve her. As soon as the subpoena has been served I want to know about it. Do you have an operative watching the apartment, Paul?"

"I have three of them. Two are parked in cars. Of course, it's hard to tell just who goes up to the Kaylor girl's apartment because there are thirty-one apartments in the building, but fortunately we were able to rent a room directly across the street in the Keynote Hotel. The third operative, with powerful binoculars on a tripod, is in that hotel room watching the doorway of the Windmore Arms Apartments. Whenever a visitor presses the call button on an apartment, the watcher can usually tell which one it is."

"Good work," Mason said. "I may take a run out there about the time the subpoena is served on her. She'll probably call someone. That someone might call on her. Plan on keeping enough men on the job to take care of any emergencies."

"How do I contact this spotter with the binoculars, Paul?"

"The Keynote Hotel is right across the street from the apartment house. We have room 102. The man in there knows you. Go over any time. He'll be glad to see you. Knock once, wait three seconds, knock twice, wait three seconds and knock three times. He'll let you in."

"I'll take a look-see," Mason said. "In the meantime, Paul, you get all the dope you can on this Rodney Archer."

"Archer," Drake said, "is a widower, a big real estate operator, an investor, a sharpshooter in financial circles. He's all cluttered up with respectability."

"Get the low-down on him," Mason said. "After all he knows Martha Lavina."

"Sure he does. He's real estate. He sold her the leases on two of her places."

"The hell he did. Who picked the places?"

"He got the options."

"Then he must have picked the cities that had police officers who would listen to reason, Paul."

"If that's the case, the guy knows his way around."

"All right," Mason said. "Find out about him. Get his background. Rip into his past."

"All of this stuff is going to cost money, Perry."

"I didn't expect to get it for nothing."

"*You're* working for nothing."

"I'm working in the cause of justice."

"Has it ever occurred to you," Paul Drake inquired, "that while there might be a cover-up somewhere along the line, your client might really be guilty after all?"

Mason grinned, said, "Hell, no," and walked out.

Chapter 6

Perry Mason walked down the dingy corridor of the Hotel Keynote, found the door of 102, knocked once, waited three seconds, knocked twice, waited three more seconds, then knocked three times.

There was a moment of silence, then Mason heard the sound of steps in the room, a key twisted in the lock and the door opened slightly. A safety chain which was designed to keep the door from being pushed open held the opening to a narrow crack.

A pair of steel-gray eyes surveyed Mason, then silently a hand moved up to release the safety chain lock and the door opened.

Drake's detective nodded but was careful not to exchange any word of greeting until after Mason was in the room, the door had been closed and locked and the safety chain put into place.

"How are you, Mr. Mason? I didn't know you were coming up."

"Thought I'd look the setup over," Mason said. "How are things doing?"

"Pretty fair. The binoculars give us a good view."

Mason walked over to where a pair of large binoculars, clamped to a swivel on a tripod, were trained through the open window so that they gave a good view of the entrance to the apartment house across the street.

Mason looked through the binoculars. "You may have to move that right eyepiece a diopter," the detective said. "I have them adjusted for my eyes and . . ."

"It's all right," Mason told him. "I won't bother. I just wanted to see how much field of vision you have. . . . These are good enough for my eyes . . . I could probably sharpen them up a little, but it's good enough."

He could see the doorway across the street, the triple list of names printed on cards. He could even make out the name "Miss Kaylor, 321" and could quite plainly see the push button below the name.

"That one we want is in a good location," the detective said. "It's the upper right-hand corner. A person may stand in front of one of the other cards, but the Kaylor apartment is . . . there comes someone now. You want to take it, or shall I?"

Mason fitted his eyes to the binoculars, raised his thumb and forefinger and moved the focusing device on the right eyepiece a fraction of a turn.

"I'll take it," he said.

He saw a well-dressed young woman turn into the doorway, pause for a minute as though looking for the name she wanted, then press a gloved forefinger against a button.

Mason called over his shoulder to the detective, "She's ringing Apartment 409—I can't make out the name."

"I have the name," the detective told him. "James Darwin. We should take a look at the guy, Mr. Mason. I don't know what bait he's using but he has some mighty smart-looking gals go up there. They stay about half an hour and leave. Quite a procession of them. That's the fifth one today."

"That's on the fourth floor?" Mason asked.

"That's right."

"Well, she evidently got a prompt buzz signal on the door. She's going up."

The young woman pushed against the door, which swung open. She vanished into the dark interior of the apartment house.

Mason said, "One of our men is coming to serve a sub-

79

poena on Miss Kaylor. As soon as he leaves, a blonde young woman is going to put in a follow-up. That young woman is the niece of the man who's being tried for the stick-up. She's quite a character, a direct, straight-from-the-shoulder girl who just might be able to get that hostess to loosen up and tell us what really did happen.''

"Okay, I've got it. Anything else?"

"Yes," Mason said. "After the blonde leaves we'll keep a very careful watch. If the blonde, whose name, by the way, is Mary Brogan, gets to first base, she'll call Paul Drake and he'll relay the call through to me."

"He knows you're here?"

"That's right. I told him I was going to come up and take a look-see."

"Okay. Suppose she doesn't get to first base?"

"In that event," Mason said, "one of two things will happen. Either the Kaylor girl will go out to talk with someone and get instructions, or she'll telephone and someone will come to her apartment to give her instructions."

"You don't think the whole thing will be handled over the telephone?"

"It could be, but probably not. It's something they'd prefer to handle in personal contact. There'll be something to talk over."

"I take it that means a shadowing job."

"That means a double shadowing job," Mason said. "Paul will take his cue from Mary Brogan after she comes out. If she doesn't get anywhere he'll send out more men for the shadowing job and . . ."

"Here comes the process server now," the detective said.

"Okay," Mason said. "You're keeping a written record of visitors, with the times they arrive and depart?"

"That's right. I'm keeping a log book."

"Okay," Mason said, "you can clock this fellow in."

He stepped away from the binoculars, looked the hotel room over and said, "Rather a dump, isn't it?"

"Not high class. This is one of the better rooms in the place. That chair over there by the bed isn't too bad. It's more comfortable than it looks. Usually it's the other way around."

Mason went over and settled himself in a chair that was covered with cheap imitation leather, took out his cigarette case and selected a cigarette.

"Don't suppose there's any chance she'll open up with the process server, do you?" the detective asked.

"He's instructed not even to try. Just to go up and slap her with the subpoena and then walk out. As soon as he leaves, Mary Brogan will go in and pretend she doesn't know anything about the subpoena having been served. She'll put it right up to the hostess that her uncle is innocent, that she's a working girl herself, that it would be a lot better all around if the Kaylor girl were to tell exactly what happened."

"Well, the process server's on his way up," the detective said.

Mason held a match in his cupped hands and inhaled deeply from his cigarette. "She's on the third floor?"

"That's right, 321."

"Give him five minutes," Mason said. "That should do it. The Brogan girl is going in as soon as he leaves."

"She's wearing a light-colored jacket and skirt with a blue blouse?" the detective asked.

"That's right."

"Blonde, good-looking?"

"That's the one."

"She's down by the corner now, waiting."

Mason said. "They can't see you from the street, can they?"

"Not very well. Looking in from the street, it's dark up here. These binoculars have a lot of light-gathering power. They make faces so close and sharp you want to duck every time they look your way because you think they're looking you right in the eyes from a distance of three or four feet. Actually they can't see in here at all. The only thing we have

81

to be afraid of is that someone in an apartment across the street might happen to have a pair of binoculars and be using them. There's not much chance of that. You notice we keep the curtains up just far enough to let us see the entrance of that apartment house.''

Mason dropped ashes from his cigarette into an ash tray, said, ''You have to play poker in a case like this—if you don't put on pressure you can't get anywhere, and if you put on too much pressure they fight.''

''That subpoena should make her either fish or cut bait,'' the detective said. He waited a minute, then added, ''Here's our man coming out now. There's the Brogan girl pressing the button. Yes, she's going in.''

Mason pinched out the cigarette, moved slightly so as to get into a more comfortable position, and said, ''Well, we can tell a lot. If she's out inside of ten minutes she probably didn't get anywhere. If she's in there for half an hour, it's a pretty good sign.''

''She looks like a mighty competent young woman,'' the detective said.

''She's all right,'' Mason agreed. ''Poor kid had been saving money for her vacation, had almost four hundred dollars saved up, and she wanted to hold out fifty dollars for her expenses and give me all the rest of it.''

''This is an assigned case, isn't it?'' the detective asked.

''That's right.''

''That's what I read in the paper. Do they give you anything for expenses?''

''They give you nothing,'' Mason said. ''You donate your time, money, energy, everything.''

''You get many of those cases?''

''No. They usually give them to the younger attorneys who they feel need the experience and who have more time.''

''Well, you could go broke pretty fast on this kind of case,'' the detective said. ''We've clocked Mary Brogan in. We'll see how long she stays. You think this Kaylor girl has a story?''

''She must have. Paul Drake located her in Las Vegas, Nevada. She had an apartment there. He brought her back here. And now it seems she also has an apartment here just as snug and cosy as you please.''

''Leading a double life?''

''We don't know.''

''She has that Apartment 321 all by herself,'' the detective said.

''The one in Las Vegas was by herself, too. I gather it was a pretty swank place. That apartment house across the street doesn't seem to be very swank.''

''It isn't. It's a good, medium-priced apartment—as apartments go these days.''

Mason looked at his wrist watch, said, ''Well, it's a good even money bet either way.''

''You mean whether she stays more than ten minutes?''

''That's right.''

''What'll you do if she gets a story?''

''I'll go across and button it up,'' Mason said. ''I'll want you as a witness. That's why I'm here. I have a tape recorder down in my car. We'll sew it up tight, and, having her under subpoena, we'll fix it so there isn't any opportunity for things to go sour.''

''This Mary Brogan doesn't know you're here?''

''No. I felt she might inadvertently tip her hand if she knew it. I'm playing the cards close to my chest. She's to call Paul Drake as soon as she gets an answer and then Paul Drake will know what to do. He'll call me here if everything's okay. Otherwise, he'll concentrate on shadowing the Kaylor girl as she goes out, or anyone who calls on her.''

''I don't know this Kaylor girl when I see her,'' the detective said. ''One of the operatives down there does. There were two of them at the night club last night. She works there as a hostess. They tell me she's class.''

"A neat package," Mason said reminiscently.

"They tell me those girls at The Villa Lavina have to wear gowns that cling to them like the skin on sausage."

"That's right," Mason said. "It's quite a place. Did you ever hear anything about those Villas?"

"In what way?"

"Rackets, gambling? Anything of that sort?"

"Nope."

"They're night clubs, and there's some kind of an angle on the hostesses—a little different from the ordinary B girls. They're good scouts and good lookers."

"Uh-huh. I . . . oh-oh, here's your party," the detective said. "I guess she didn't get to first base."

Mason came up out of the chair.

"There she is just coming out, and she's sure excited," the detective went on.

Mason moved over toward the window.

Mary Brogan looked up and down the street, then plunged toward a little restaurant next door to the apartment house, went into the telephone booth and hurriedly dialed a number.

"Well," Mason said, "I guess that's it. She got a turn-down. She's calling Drake. Drake will call me here."

Mason stood by the window, standing far enough back so he was not readily visible, and watched Mary Brogan talking excitedly from the telephone booth. He saw her hang up, hurry out of the restaurant and walk rapidly down the street.

Mason frowned. "That's funny. I wanted her to stick around and keep in contact with Drake's operatives so she could . . ."

The phone in the room rang sharply.

"That'll be Paul now," the detective said.

Mason picked up the receiver and said cautiously, "Hello."

Drake's voice, edged with excitement, said, "That you, Perry?"

"Uh-huh."

"Just heard from Mary Brogan. You probably saw her come out."

"I did. What's happened?"

"This Kaylor girl put on quite an act. She'd just received the subpoena when Mary called. She listened to a few words of what Mary had to say and then ran into the bathroom. She came out with a bottle of sleeping tablets, dumped out a whole handful of them and started chewing them up; went to the faucet, got water and washed them down. Mary says there must have been two dozen of the sleeping tablets."

"Oh—oh!" Mason said.

"So what do we do?" Drake asked.

"Notify the police," Mason said.

"That may make a stink."

"Go ahead and notify them. It's the only thing we *can* do. They'll take her to a hospital, pump her stomach out and save her life."

"And ruin our chances of getting any story," Drake said. "I was wondering, Perry, if, under the circumstances, you couldn't get some doctor and . . ."

Mason said, "It might be too late. Suppose she refuses to let him treat her? We have to wait until after she becomes unconscious, and by that time . . . No, Paul, call the police. Tell them the story."

"How shall I tell it?"

"Tell it straight. Simply tell them that you're working on a case but don't say what one. Say that one of your operatives served a subpoena on the Kaylor girl at that address, and she grabbed a handful of sleeping tablets and is trying to commit suicide."

"Let the police think that the process server is the one who saw her doing it?"

"That's right. You don't need to answer detailed questions. Be in a hurry. Simply tell them you served the subpoena and that she grabbed the sleeping pills."

"Okay. I'll get on the job right away."

Mason hung up the telephone, turned to the detective and said, "I guess you got it from what I said over the telephone."

"She's trying to kill herself?"

"That's right."

"Just to keep from testifying?"

"That's the way it looks."

"This thing is really getting hot," the man said.

"Uh-huh. Paul's going to telephone the police."

They waited for a couple of anxious minutes. Mason lit another cigarette.

Suddenly a siren sounded, at first faint in the distance, then screaming to a high-pitched crescendo of urgency.

"Well," Mason said, "Paul sure got fast action. That must be a radio car coming now."

The detective, standing near the window where he could look down the street, said, "Nope, it's an ambulance. Red light going and all the rest of it."

The ambulance parked by the apartment house. Two white-clad attendants entered the door.

"I'm not certain I figure this one out," Mason said. "I thought the police would get here first and then phone for an ambulance."

"They're probably taking Drake's word for it and figure she has to go to a hospital."

"If police aren't there she may refuse to go and . . ."

"She may be groggy by this time."

"I don't think the stuff works that fast. She'll come out under her own power. Take a good look at her and then you'll know her when you see her again."

Mason moved toward the window. The detective fitted his eyes to the binoculars. A few moments later the two attendants come out supporting a young woman who was walking between them, but whose head was hanging limply.

The detective swore under his breath.

"What happened?" Mason asked.

"Can't get a look at her face. Her head's drooping. They're putting her in the ambulance now."

"Never mind. You have her picture, haven't you?"

"Yes. Drake gave me one, but I always like to look at their faces. Photographic identification is hard stuff."

"I know," Mason agreed. "She's droopy and they had to hold her up. That's why they kept getting in the way so we couldn't see. . . . There they go."

The ambulance took off up the street, moving at high speed, siren screaming for the right of way.

Mason picked up his hat, started for the door.

The detective said, "Another siren coming, Mr. Mason."

Mason turned back toward the window, stood by the side of the detective as a police radio car came down the street and slid to a stop in front of the apartment house. Two officers jumped out of the car. One of them pressed the bell button of Miss Kaylor's apartment. The other one talked with a group of bystanders that had rapidly gathered seemingly from nowhere.

After a moment the officers returned to the police car, communicated with headquarters and drove away.

"Well, I guess that's that," the detective said.

Mason said, "Dammit, the thing doesn't make sense. How did that ambulance manage to get here so quickly?"

"It was probably dispatched as an emergency by the radio dispatcher who took the call," the detective suggested.

"That's the only possible solution," Mason said, "but that police prowl car couldn't have been too far away. It also got the call over the radio—and the ambulance got here first."

"Don't worry about it," the detective said. "Those things happen. If she'd cut an artery and had been bleeding to death it would have taken the ambulance an hour to get here. They just happened to have an ambulance available and shot it out here on a quick emergency priority."

"I suppose so," Mason admitted.

"In any event," the detective told him, "she'll be all right

87

now. They'll pump her stomach out before the sleeping tablets have had much effect.''

Mason turned back toward the door. ''Well, I'm going back to my office. If Paul rings up tell him he can locate me there within ten or fifteen minutes.''

''No need to keep watching this apartment?'' the detective asked.

Mason hesitated, then said, ''Stay with it for a while. Paul can get in touch with you when we're ready to call it off. Get a description of anyone who presses the bell button. Get license numbers of any cars.''

''Thank heaven we got that subpoena served before she tried to make with the pills.''

''You probably won't be here very long. My plan's ruined now. I'll have to rely on the subpoena and make a play in court Monday morning.''

''That wasn't the way you wanted it?'' the detective asked.

''Hell, no!''

''But you served the subpoena telling her to be there.''

''That,'' Mason said, ''was dressing—and now someone's smashed the glass and walked off with the merchandise.''

Chapter 7

Mason pushed his way into Paul Drake's private office, said, "Paul, I've been thinking."

Drake looked up from the desk, grinned and said, "So have I."

"There's something fishy in connection with this case," Mason said.

"Are *you* telling *me*?"

Mason said, "That Kaylor girl—she must have been living a double life of some sort. She had her apartment in Las Vegas. Also she had an apartment here and she was working down at The Villa Lavina Number Three."

Drake nodded.

"Why *should* she do that, and how *could* she do that?"

"Were you out there when the ambulance came?" Drake asked.

Mason nodded.

"I had a good man on the job there," Drake said. "He tried to follow the ambulance, but, of course, that was out of the question. The ambulance had a siren and blasted its way through closed traffic signals and my man couldn't keep up. He might have done it if he'd plastered himself right behind the ambulance, but then they'd have known they were being followed. He tried to do the best he could, but, as was to have been expected, when the ambulance went through a red light a traffic officer on duty flagged my man down. Of course my man told the cop a great story about it being his wife who was in the ambulance and that they'd told him to

89

follow, and all of that stuff, and the officer waved him on, but by that time it was too late to catch up."

"Sure," Mason said. "I'm not bothering about that, Paul. It's the other thing that's bothering me."

"Well, wait until you've heard the rest of this and you'll have something else to be bothered about," Drake said.

"What's the rest of it?" Mason asked.

"My man was a darned good man. He took the precaution of getting the license number of the ambulance while it was parked out there. Then we tried to get busy and find what hospital the Kaylor girl had been taken to. Okay, here's the answer. She wasn't taken to *any* hospital."

"Where was she taken?"

"Now there's the point," Drake said.

"But your man got the license number of the ambulance. Let's call up and trace the ambulance and . . ."

"The license number isn't going to do you any good, Perry."

"Why not?"

"We have it, and it's unlisted."

"Unlisted? What do you mean?"

Drake said, "Every state knocks off a few licenses that are unlisted. They put those licenses on cars that are used for confidential investigative work. In that way it's impossible to trace them."

"But, good Lord, Paul, they don't put unlisted numbers on an ambulance, do they?"

"*Someone* put it on *this* ambulance," Drake said.

"No chance your man was mistaken in taking down the number?"

"None whatever."

"Where *did* that number come from, Paul?"

"It must have been stolen. It's a cinch it didn't belong on the ambulance."

"And that ambulance showed up suspiciously soon,"

Mason said. "I was commenting on that to your detective out there, and . . ."

"He told me about it," Drake interrupted. "After you left he began thinking over what you'd told him and the more he thought about it the less he liked it, so he called me up, and that's when I started making a search. I've been in touch with the receiving hospital and, when they knew nothing about it, with the private hospitals."

Mason looked at his watch. "Of course it's only been about half an hour, Paul. They could have . . ."

"They'd have shown up long before this," Drake said.

Mason frowned. "All right, I'll tell you what you do, Paul. I have a suspicion this thing all ties together into a picture."

"What's the picture?"

"How do we know this is the girl we want?"

"The Kaylor girl?" Drake asked. "Why, of course she's the girl we want. She's employed at The Villa Lavina and is a hostess. She has the name, the photograph checks and . . ."

Mason said, "You can't make a positive identification from a photograph."

"In this case they made a good enough identification to find her."

"How do you know they did?"

"Why, they did. She's working at The Villa Lavina, the name's the same, the description checks. Hell's bells! You saw her yourself. Didn't she match the picture?"

"She matched the picture, but not the personality."

"Probably putting on an act. Martha Lavina put on the screws and the Kaylor girl decided to be a good dog."

Mason said, "I'm not too certain there aren't *two* Kaylor girls, sisters with a strong family resemblance.

"Paul, I want you to have an operative get in Petty Kaylor's apartment. I want him to go through the place for clues and dust it for fingerprints. Get the fingerprints of the woman

91

who was living there. That shouldn't be hard to do. They'll be on the fixtures, on the back of . . ."

"You don't need to tell me how to get fingerprints," Drake said. "But tell me this, how are we going to get in?"

"Ever hear about passkeys, Paul?"

"Sure I've heard about them. I've also heard about illegal search and entry."

"I think it's worth taking a chance, Paul."

"I don't. I have a license at stake."

"Don't be so damn conservative. Now then, I want a man in Las Vegas to do the same thing in the apartment there. As soon as he gets the fingerprints I want him to hop a plane and come back here. Then we'll compare the fingerprints and see if we have duplicates."

Drake shook his head. "No dice."

"What do you mean, no dice?"

"It would take a woman to do it. I haven't any female operative that good."

"Why would it take a woman?"

"A man would be too conspicuous. It's going to take time. A woman might get in by posing as a relative—a man, no."

"Get a woman, then."

"I tell you I haven't any—not that good. What's more, I had a little trouble about my license. Someone has made a squawk that my methods are too irregular."

"Oh shucks! Go ahead. They wouldn't revoke your license over a deal of that sort. Besides, you aren't taking anything, just dusting."

"I tell you I haven't any girl who can do that. Moreover, I can't take the chances on just a wild hunch."

"It isn't just a hunch. It makes sense. Suppose there are two girls?"

"Who look alike?"

"Sisters."

"Of course," Drake said musingly. "I didn't see this girl at The Villa Lavina myself. My operative had a picture. He thought he recognized her from the picture, inquired about her name, and it was Kaylor, and that was as far as he went. He figured he'd struck pay dirt and called in with the report that I passed on to you.''

"Exactly," Mason said. "I went out there on the strength of the operative's identification. There could very well be two Kaylor sisters—perhaps twins for all we know.''

"If that's the case," Drake said, "we're up against something a lot bigger than appears on the surface.''

Mason nodded. "I'm going down to jail and have a talk with my client.''

"What do you want me to do?" Drake asked.

"Turn loose your dogs," Mason told him, "all of them. I want the dope on Archer. I want anything you can pick up. Start men running around here in circles the way bloodhounds do when they've lost a scent.

"And remember this, Paul, if my hunch is correct we've lost two women. They've disappeared. One of them was friendly to our side of the case.''

"That's on the assumption that there *are* two Kaylor girls both employed as hostesses.''

"That's right. Petty for one, and Inez for the other. Inez was waiting for you to call her in the law library. She was friendly. Apparently she was on the square. There was nothing to indicate she'd walk out on us, and yet she did. She vanished.

"Petty was so-so. We can't figure her. She was an enigma. We served a subpoena on her and she gulped down a whole mess of sleeping tablets. As soon as the call went in for the police an ambulance whizzed around the corner, picked her up and took her some place. Where?''

"Presumably where she could get some treatment for the sleeping pills," Drake said.

"Or," Mason said, "where she *couldn't* get treatment.''

"What do you mean by that?''

"Petty Kaylor had very conveniently taken enough sleep-

93

ing pills to kill her. Suppose that the parties who took her away in the ambulance wanted to take her where she couldn't get treatment."

"Wouldn't that be murder?"

"It might if we could prove it," Mason said, "but look at what we're up against."

"What?"

"A girl voluntarily takes an overdose of sleeping pills. A witness who is completely trustworthy sees her take those sleeping pills. It's a free and voluntary act. She wasn't forced by anyone. An ambulance comes to get her. They may make a wrong diagnosis."

Drake frowned. "Could be," he said. "Of course, it's only a hunch. The police would laugh at it."

Mason nodded.

"You're going to see your client?" Drake asked.

"I'm going to see Albert Brogan," Mason told him, "and then I'll be back at the office. If Mary Brogan shows up, tell her to wait. I'll tell Della Street to stick on the job and keep things lined up. I don't like the way things are breaking, Paul. Start getting something on Rodney Archer. Also look into the background of Martha Lavina. I'll be back in about an hour.

"Now here's something else, Paul. If Martha Lavina is stalling and really wasn't the woman in that car with Rodney Archer, *her* purse wasn't stolen. The purse that was taken was that of the other woman, the one who was really present at the holdup."

Drake nodded.

"So," Mason told him, "get to work on that purse, Paul. It's been introduced in evidence. It's Saturday, so you'll have to hire some deputy clerk to come down and open the office, but you can arrange that with a little dough.

"Dig up some leather novelty man who knows purses, find out who manufactured that particular purse, where it was sold, all the stuff you can possibly scrape together. You

94

can't tell, we *might* even find to whom that purse had been sold."

"We *might*," Drake agreed, "on a thousand to one shot."

"Odds never stop me," Mason told him.

"Damned if they do," Drake agreed mournfully.

Chapter 8

In the visitors' room at the jail Albert Brogan's anxious blue eyes looked through the coarse-meshed screen at Perry Mason.

There was a certain family resemblance to his niece, but where her blue eyes held a merry, almost impudent twinkle, her uncle's were more pale and netted with lines of worry.

A rather chunky man, partially bald, with deep creases drawn from the sides of his nose to the corners of his mouth, he showed the effects of the nervous breakdown brought on from overwork and the injuries sustained in the automobile accident.

"How's everything coming?" Mason asked.

"All right."

"Anyone been talking to you today?"

"They sure have. Lots of people . . . say, Mr. Mason, my niece came out here from St. Louis."

"I know. I've talked with her."

Brogan was decidedly ill at ease. "I . . . I guess I didn't play very fair with you, Mr. Mason. I knew that she had some money and that she'd send it to me if I'd asked for it.

"I suppose if I'd told the judge that I could raise money by sending a telegram you wouldn't have been appointed."

"That's all right," Mason said, grinning.

"You know, Mary has always tried to give me the breaks whenever she could. When I got smashed up in an automobile accident and was laid up for a while, it seemed as though everything hit me all at once. I was worried, and the first thing I knew I was in a regular nervous breakdown.

"The only way I knew to make a living was by selling stuff. I'd lost the job I had when I got smashed up. When I started back to work I took on a new product and somehow or other I just lost all my confidence. I couldn't seem to sell anything.

"At first I thought it was the product, so I changed and got another job, and then I suddenly realized it was me, and then I guess I really did go all to pieces. I certainly was in a mess. That was when Mary told me not to worry, that I didn't ever need to work any more. She said I could simply rest, that I didn't ever have to meet another person as long as I lived or try to sell another bill of goods."

Mason nodded sympathetically, said, "Don't let it bother you now. You've finished with that."

"Mary doesn't have any idea that I know the sacrifices she's made. She's put up money, she's pretended that it didn't mean a thing to her, and all that. And now she's out here coming to my rescue once more, and she'll be flat broke again and . . ."

"No, she won't," Mason said. "I've already told her that I don't want her money."

"But you have to be paid. I had no right to let the court think I was a pauper."

"Who owns your trailer?"

"The finance company. My equity wouldn't amount to a dime if I tried to sell it."

"And your car?"

"The same way."

"That's fine," Mason said. "You didn't misrepresent anything to the court. Quit worrying about it. What I want to know is, who's been talking with you today?"

"Well, first rattle out of the box, right after Mary left, a detective named Smith came and talked with me."

"What did he want?"

"He told me that you were a good lawyer, but you were always fighting, that you didn't know how to compromise.

He said that if I wanted to work out a deal that he thought he could fix it up for me. He said that if he could put it across they'd give me a chance to plead guilty to petty larceny. The case could be continued while I made an application for probation and he thought I could get probation."

"Then what?" Mason asked.

"Then something happened, I don't know what it was. One of the old-time, hard-boiled prisoners walked past my cell and said out of the corner of his mouth, 'Watch out, Brogan. They're turning on the heat.'

"Just a few minutes after that they took me out of my cell and took me out to the yard. An automobile was there. A tan Chevrolet with a busted right front fender. They asked me if I'd ever seen that car before and I told them I hadn't, but that I wasn't going to make any statement until I'd had a chance to talk with you.

"Then they made me get in and out of the car and sit behind the steering wheel."

"Then what?" Mason asked.

"Several people walked by. Then two plain-clothes men and a girl walked by. The girl opened the door of the car and started to get in with me, and one of the officers yelled, 'No, no. That's not the car.' She got out and smiled at me and said, 'I beg your pardon,' and I told her that was all right, so she got out.

"I was left there for two or three minutes and then they came and put me back here in my cell again, and their whole attitude seemed to change. They'd treated me all right before, but after that they got tough.

"Detective Smith came by, looking very busy, and I asked him how I went about fixing up this deal the way he'd explained it to me. He said, 'What deal?' and I told him, 'Why, the deal you were talking to me about,' and he shook his head and said, 'You're nuts. I didn't talk to you about any deal. You're being tried for armed robbery, and you're going to be convicted you son of a bitch.' And with that he walked away.''

Mason pushed back his chair. "Was this girl anyone you'd ever seen before?''

"No.''

"How old?''

"About twenty-seven or -eight.''

"You'd never seen that tan Chevrolet before?''

"Never.''

"Do you know where it came from?''

"No.''

Mason said, "That looks bad, Brogan. They've got some new witness who is going to put you at the scene of that crime. I've got to get out of here.''

Mason started for the door, conscious of the look of frozen dismay on Albert Brogan's features.

Just as he left the visiting room he saw Sergeant Holcomb of Homicide grab Brogan's arm.

Mason hurried to the phone booth, dialed Paul Drake's office, said to the detective's switchboard operator, "Put me through to Paul in a hurry, will you? . . . Paul, I'm down at the jail. They've put Albert Brogan in a tan Chevy with a crumpled right front fender. Some girl took a good look at him and trapped him into speaking.

"Just before that he was all set to get out on a reduced charge, a plea and probation. Now they're acting as if they had a fist full of trumps. Just a second ago I saw Sergeant Holcomb of Homicide make a pass at him. Do you have any idea . . . ?''

"Good Lord!'' Drake interrupted. "Do you suppose it's that Daphne Howell murder?''

"What gave you that idea, Paul?''

"There's just been a flash that they have the murderer of Daphne Howell under arrest.''

Mason frowned, said, "Get in touch with your newspaper friends, Paul. Get the low-down. I'm on my way up.''

The lawyer slammed up the phone, raced to the elevator and ten minutes later was in Paul Drake's office.

The detective was talking on the telephone and motioned Mason to silence as he continued the telephone conversation.

"What? . . . He is? . . . Are they sure? . . . Well, that, of course, is quite a break for the police. You don't suppose they tried to plan it that way, do you?"

Drake listened for a while, then said, "Okay, thanks a lot, Jim," and hung up.

The detective's face was gloomy as he looked up at the lawyer. "That's it, Perry. Your man has the Daphne Howell murder pinned on him as of now."

"Who identified him?" Mason asked.

"A girl named Janice Clubb. She was coming home from visiting a girl-friend. She got off the inter-urban and started walking toward her apartment. There had been a couple of molestation cases in the neighborhood, and this girl was easy on the eyes, so she was alert. She had about three blocks to go.

"She had walked about a block when she saw a tan-colored car pass her, going pretty fast. Because she was nervous she looked it over and saw it had a crumpled right front fender. She also knew it was a Chevrolet because her boy-friend drives the same model car although his is a darker color.

"The car turned and drove right up over the curb into a vacant lot about half a block ahead. She didn't think too much about that because sometimes people will deliberately drive over the six-inch curb in order to find parking space in the vacant lot if the street is full."

"Go ahead," Mason said. "What's all this leading up to?"

"That man had Daphne Howell's body in the trunk of the tan Chevy."

"How do you know?" Mason asked.

"I'm coming to that."

"Go ahead."

"He parked the car in the vacant lot and got out and was opening the trunk when he heard Janice Clubb's footsteps coming along the sidewalk. He stopped and jerked down the lid of the trunk, ran around and jumped in the automobile and sat there with the motor running and the lights on.

"She was frightened on account of the molestation cases, and she started running. She ran all the way to her apartment house.

"Next morning the body of Daphne Howell was discovered lying there in the lot. She'd been garroted. Police figured the murder had taken place somewhere else, and this lot had been used as a place to dump the body."

"Sex crime?" Mason asked.

"Nope. She hadn't been molested. Just strangled with a thin wire cord. A very smooth professional job."

"This Clubb girl reported what she'd seen to police?"

"Sure. As soon as the body was found the next morning and the case came out in the newspapers she went to the police."

"When was this, Paul?"

"September 13th, a little before midnight."

"Go ahead."

"Well, you know how things are. Homicide Squad handles things its own way, and nothing was ever thought about Brogan until in the testimony yesterday when it was mentioned that the holdup man was driving a tan Chevrolet with a crumpled fender. Sergeant Holcomb read the account in the morning newspaper and hit the ceiling. He dashed out and got Janice Clubb. They put Brogan in the tan Chevrolet and she identified him."

"Where did they get the tan Chevrolet?" Mason asked.

"The tan Chevy was stolen the night of the murder. It had been reported then but wasn't recovered for nearly two months. Someone had stuck it in the private garage of an unoccupied building, closed the door and left it. There's no question about it having been a bona fide theft because the owner, a young high school kid who needed the car to go to school in, had notified the police it had been stolen a couple of hours before the murder was committed. He'd been attending a glee club, had left the car parked there and somebody had swiped it. The police felt certain some other kid had taken it for a joy ride and didn't pay too much attention to the report of theft at first. Then after this Daphne Howell murder case with the description of the tan Chevrolet with the crumpled right fender, they really went to town trying to find the thing.''

"September 13th,'' Mason said. "That was the date of the holdup.''

Drake said, "The police figure that your man staged a holdup during the early part of the evening, then went on from there and picked up this Howell girl and garroted her.''

"But why?'' Mason asked.

"Robbery,'' Drake said. "They never did find her purse. She was supposed to have had several hundred dollars with her. She'd been doing some modeling work and evidently made a pretty good thing of it.''

"What have they found out about Daphne Howell's background?'' Mason asked.

"That's it, Perry. They can't find a thing. She had a little apartment and no one knows anything about her. She lived alone, did modeling work and never took anyone into her confidence. She'd only been here about three months.''

"Where did she come from?''

"Kansas City. She had a few friends there and they knew a little something about her background. She'd been married but the marriage had split up. She didn't write any letters. No one had heard a word from her after she left Kansas City, except one friend who got a picture postcard sent from Guatemala with a brief message written on it in Daphne Howell's handwriting.''

Mason pushed his hands down in his pockets. "How I hate to face Mary Brogan now!'' he groaned.

102

"Well," Drake said, "you don't have to defend him on anything except this stick-up case. I don't suppose they'll make any offer of compromise now."

"Compromise!" Mason exclaimed. "They'll move heaven and earth to get a conviction in this case, Paul. Then they'll try him on the murder case. If he doesn't deny Janice Clubb's identification he's licked. If he does, they'll wait until he takes the stand and then on cross-examination the D.A. will ask him sneeringly if it isn't true he's been convicted of a felony. He'll have to admit that he was, that a jury found him guilty of a holdup that was pulled off on the very night of the murder. Then they'll ask him about the holdup. The defense attorney will object. The D.A. will say he's going to connect it up and he'll ask him if the holdup wasn't committed in the same tan Chevrolet with the crumpled right fender that was used in the murder of Daphne Howell."

"That," Drake said, "gives him just about the same chance as the proverbial snowball in hell."

"About half that chance," Mason said. "By this time they've probably got Martha Lavina and Rodney Archer down looking at that tan Chevrolet. They'll identify it as being the car that Brogan was driving the night of the holdup."

Drake said, "Get out of it, Perry."

"I can't get out of it," Mason told him. "The man's my client. I'm representing him."

"Get out from under," Drake repeated. "You've got a hopeless case. What's more, this stuff is coming out in the newspaper, Perry."

"I know it," Mason said. "Of course, the jurors aren't *supposed* to read the papers, but out of twelve members on this jury you can gamble at least nine of them will have seen the thing about the Daphne Howell murder having been solved and about the fact that the man who perpetrated that crime is at present on trial in Judge Egan's court on a similar crime."

Drake said, "For the love of Mike, Perry, quit beating your head against a stone wall. Your man's guilty."

"The jury hasn't said so."

"Well, it will."

"Until it does, he's my client and I'm representing him. The law guarantees a man the right of trial by jury. If every lawyer would throw in the sponge just because circumstances looked black against a client, the client couldn't have a trial by jury."

"Well, you can't argue with this combination of facts," Drake said. "This guy's guilty as hell. He has to be."

"Somehow he doesn't look it," Mason said. "You look at him and you can see the picture of a man who burned himself out. He carried an impossible load, working day and night trying to build up success. Then he had this injury, and you can see in the back of his eyes the haunting fear of another breakdown."

"He'll have a haunting fear of something else now," Drake said callously. "That guy's headed for the death chamber on a one-way ticket. You're licked now, Perry."

"I'm not licked until the jury says I'm licked," Mason asserted, "and not then if I can find some way of setting aside the verdict."

Drake shrugged his shoulders. "Personally," he said, "I think you've put a hell of a lot of faith in a good personality, a pair of blue eyes and a turned-up nose."

"You have to put faith in something," Mason told him and walked out.

Chapter 9

As soon as Mason entered his private office, Della Street instantly detected something was wrong.

"What is it, Chief?" she asked apprehensively.

Mason pushed his hands down in his pockets, walked across the office and stood looking dejectedly out of the window.

She came to his side, circled his left arm with her hands, stood for a moment offering silent sympathy.

Mason took his left hand from his pocket, patted her shoulder.

"How bad is it?" she asked.

"Bad."

"Want to tell me?"

Mason turned away from the window, smiled down into her troubled eyes, then started pacing the office.

"More witnesses?" she asked.

"More witnesses," Mason said, "and terrible ones."

"Well, after all, Chief, you can't make the facts in a case. You can only be certain a client gets a fair trial."

"I know it," Mason said.

"Just what has happened now?"

"Police have the automobile that they think Brogan was driving at the time of the holdup. It was a stolen car. It had been stolen about a couple of hours before the stick-up."

"Is that all?" she asked.

"And that stolen car," Mason went on, "is the one that was used to transport the body of Daphne Howell to the vacant lot where she was found. And if you'll look up the

105

murder of Daphne Howell you'll find that while the body was found on the morning of September 14th the autopsy shows the murder was committed late at night on the 13th. The police now have a witness who can identify the automobile and has probably identified the driver."

"Identified the *driver*?" Della Street asked.

"Albert Brogan," Mason said.

"Oh, good Lord!" Della exclaimed, and dropped into a chair as though her knees had suddenly lost strength.

"Exactly," Mason said.

"And Mary Brogan is in the outer office, waiting to tell you all about what happened when she went to call on Petty Kaylor," Della Street said. "Poor kid, she'll . . . oh, Perry, I just hate to face her with this!"

"We'll have to tell her some of it," Mason said. "It's in the afternoon papers."

Della Street said sympathetically, "She's such a nice kid!"

Again there was a period of silence.

"Just how bad is it?" Della Street asked.

Mason, pacing the office floor, said, "It's a matter of identification. Of course, the police will have both Martha Lavina and Rodney Archer identify that tan Chevrolet automobile now. They'll have to do it. The police are closing in for the kill."

"Do you suppose it really was the same car?"

"I don't know," Mason said, "but it will be the same car by the time those two get done testifying. After all, Della, one automobile looks pretty much like another automobile. Martha Lavina was rather vague about it, but Rodney Archer's testimony fixed it as a tan Chevrolet, and he thought the right fender was crumpled. I didn't go after him on that on cross-examination, but I will now. From his position he could hardly have seen the right front fender."

"But the point is he *did* testify the right front fender was crumpled *before* his attention was called to this tan Chevrolet in the Daphne Howell case?"

Mason nodded.

"Oh, Chief," she said, "that's terrible! Do you really suppose he did . . . gosh, he must have!"

Mason said, "Things certainly look black, Della, but it's an attorney's duty to stay in there and fight to the last ditch."

"For a guilty man?"

"Not for a guilty man," Mason said, "but for the cause of justice."

She said, "I feel just as though someone had hit me on the head with a sledge hammer. I'm completely numb. It's like trying to wake up from a bad dream and finding you've wakened into the middle of a nightmare."

"Well," Mason said, "let's analyze it. Archer and Martha Lavina have identified the defendant as the stick-up man, but their identification of the automobile to my mind is far from convincing. Standing by itself you wouldn't pay very much attention to it."

"Yes, I suppose that's right."

"But the moment the witnesses state that the murderer of Daphne Howell was driving that same sort of an automobile, then the situation changes."

"But the witness also identified Albert Brogan as being the driver of the car."

"Perhaps I can clarify the situation by putting it this way," Mason said. "Archer and Martha Lavina identified the defendant personally and positively. The identification of the car is incidental. Janice Clubb identifies the automobile positively and the identification of the driver is incidental. Or, to put it another way, if the identification of the *car* by Martha Lavina and Rodney Archer is erroneous, and there's every possibility that it is, then the identification of Albert Brogan as the *driver* of the murder car by Janice Clubb is quite probably erroneous. She's influenced by the fact that Archer and Lavina have identified him as the driver."

"No matter how you explain it, it makes a disastrous combination," Della Street said.

Mason nodded. "It means that it's absolutely imperative we find out what it is Martha Lavina is trying to cover up. We simply *must* find out how it happened that Inez Kaylor walked out of the law library yesterday and completely reversed her position in the case."

"You think there are two sisters?"

"I don't know what to think, Della. I do know it's necessary to explore every possibility. If Albert Brogan is convicted in this case he doesn't stand a ghost of a chance in the murder case. In other words, he's fighting for his life right now."

"What do we tell Mary Brogan?"

"We'll try to break it to her easy," Mason said, "and we'll try to find out more about it before we give her too many details. Let's have her come in."

"She wants to tell you about what happened when she went up there to the Kaylor girl's apartment."

"All right," Mason said, "let's get her in."

Della Street passed the word on to Gertie in the outer office.

Mary Brogan, entering Mason's private office, was so completely absorbed with her recent experience that she completely failed to notice the atmosphere of tension and somber gloom which permeated the office.

"My gosh," she said, "of all the exciting things! I could only stand there with my mouth open feeling like a ninny!"

"Go ahead," Mason said. "Tell us what happened."

"Well," she said, "this woman came to the door when I knocked, and opened it a crack. There was a safety chain on the door. I told her I wanted to come in and talk with her. I said I didn't want anything except the truth, but I knew she was a human being, and I wanted . . ."

"Never mind what you said," Mason interrupted. "What did she say, what did she do?"

"She said, 'I'm tired of being hounded. You just stay right there and I'll show you what you're driving me to!' She left me standing there a minute, then came back with a brown bottle. She cupped her left hand and poured a lot of tablets out of the bottle. Gosh, there must have been two or three dozen of them! She just popped the whole handful into her mouth and started crunching away on them. I'll never forget the spectacle of that woman standing there—that look of wild desperation in her eyes, her cheeks puffed out because her mouth was so full of sleeping tablets, crunching away on them with little fluffs of white power coming from her lips. And then she ran back out of sight for a minute, returned with a glass of water and just gulped the water down, swallowing tablets and trying to say something about, 'See what you've done,' or something of that sort, but the words were rather indistinguishable. She still had a lot of the medicine in her mouth.''

"So you ran down and called Paul Drake?'' Mason asked.

"Yes, I didn't know what else to do. I was frantic. Mr. Drake told me it was all right, that he'd take care of it; that I'd better come on back and join Miss Street; that it wouldn't look good to have it appear that I had driven this girl to an attempt at suicide. Any publicity like that would have a bad effect on Uncle Albert's case.''

Mason nodded.

"And now,'' Mary Brogan said, "I understand that an ambulance came and got her and she just disappeared.''

"We haven't found the hospital where she was taken yet,'' Mason said.

"And what's this in the afternoon paper about Uncle Albert being wanted for murder?''

"That's the story,'' Mason admitted without elaboration.

"They're referring to Uncle Albert, without actually naming him. They say a witness has made a positive identification in this Daphne Howell murder case, and that the man she identified is now being tried for a holdup in Judge Egan's court before a jury; that his trial will resume Monday, and

109

that the authorities have decided to wait until after that trial before pressing the other charges against him.''

Mason nodded.

Mary Brogan said, ''If I were the crying kind, I'd sit down and bawl all over your desk. As it is, I'm fighting mad. I feel like cussing.''

''Go ahead and cuss then,'' Mason said. ''I feel that way myself.''

''That won't do any good. I know Uncle Albert never held anybody up in his life, and I know darn well he never even thought of committing a murder. He wouldn't hurt a fly. This is the most absolutely sickening, nauseating, asinine thing I have ever heard!''

''Go ahead,'' Mason said, ''get it off your chest.''

''It isn't what's on my chest that counts. It's the responsibility that's on your shoulders, Mr. Mason. I . . . I guess I never realized how important lawyers were before. Dammit, I *am* going to cry!''

She blinked her eyes, took a handkerchief from her purse, said, ''No, I'm darned if I am. I'm going to fight.''

''That's the spirit,'' Mason told her.

''But we haven't anything to fight with. We haven't any ammunition. The jurors will read about this in the papers and they'll think Uncle Albert is a desperate murderer. . . . Why didn't the judge have that jury locked up? They have no business reading the newspapers and . . .''

''They're not supposed to read the local news,'' Mason said, ''particularly crime news.''

''Pouf!'' she exclaimed. ''I know what *I'd* do if I were on a jury and I saw something in a newspaper that had a bearing on a case. I think anybody else would do the same thing.''

Mason said, ''I'm going to move for a mistrial Monday morning on the ground of this publicity.''

''Will the judge grant it?''

''Not Judge Egan. He'll give the prosecution a rap for letting the news get out, and then say the jurors were instructed not to read any crime news, or anything about the case, and let it go at that.''

"Well, we've got a little more than a day. Can't we do *something*?''

Mason nodded. "I'm beginning to suspect that there may be two Kaylor girls—perhaps sisters. I don't think the Kaylor girl that I talked with last night was the one who disappeared from the law library. I doubt very much if she was the one who lived in Las Vegas. Evidently there's a strong family resemblance—enough to confuse a detective who's trying to locate one of them by a photograph—but I just doubt if they're one and the same.''

"Is there any way of finding out?''

"I outlined a way to Paul Drake,'' Mason said, "but he says it's too risky. It would take a female detective to do it and get away with it. A man around the apartment would attract too much attention from the neighbors. A smart female detective could claim that she was Petty Kaylor's cousin or a nurse. She could say that Petty was in the hospital and had sent her to pick up some clothes and things. She could dust the place and pick up all the fingerprints she could find, and . . .''

"What's wrong with me doing that?'' Mary Brogan asked.

Mason looked her over, said, "Nothing.''

"Well, what's holding us back? Let's go.''

Mason picked up the telephone and dialed Paul Drake on his unlisted phone. He said, "Can you come down to my office, Paul. Bring some fingerprint equipment.''

"What are you going to do?'' Drake asked.

"You may be a lot happier if you didn't know,'' Mason told him. "You won't have any compunctions about teaching someone how to develop and collect latent fingerprints, will you?''

"No.''

"Come on down then.''

Mason hung up and said, "It sounds like a good idea right

111

at the moment, but there are a couple of angles I'll have to figure. I don't want you getting in trouble, Mary, and . . ."

"Why, I can put it across in a breeze," she told him optimistically. "If there's a superintendent or somebody I'd tell her I am from the hospital, that Petty is going to be all right, that she was just nervous and excited and annoyed, and she took too many sleeping pills. I'll say she's got to be in bed for two or three days, and she asked me to drop by and pick up some clothes for her. I'll go through that apartment with a fine-tooth comb. I'll get the fingerprints that you want, and if there's anything else in there that looks good I'll put that in a suitcase and bring it up here."

Mason frowned, got up from the chair at the office desk to walk over to the window and stand with his hands thrust deep into his trousers pockets.

"No," he said. "You won't take anything tangible, only fingerprints. Even then there's a certain element of risk involved."

"Well, there's a risk in everything. There's a risk in life."

Drake's knock sounded on the corridor door of Mason's private office. Della Street let him in.

"All right," Drake said, opening a brief case, "here's where the class in fingerprinting starts. I hope, Perry, you're not going to try to do something like this yourself. You have more at stake than I do and . . ."

"Never mind who's going to do what," Mason said. "You show us how to fingerprint."

Drake said, "Well, here are two different kinds of powder. They will take care of any fingerprints you may happen to run onto. All you do is determine the color that you want. Naturally you want a color for contrast. You dust the powder over the surface with this camel's-hair brush."

Drake walked over to the door, dipped the camel's-hair brush into a bottle of powder and dusted it up and down the door jamb. "Now I'm using a silver powder here because it gives me just the contrast I want and . . . Oh-oh, here's a print. Now see the way this latent has been developed?''

Della Street said, ''It looks like just a collection of concentric lines.''

''That's all they are,'' Drake told her, ''but there's enough here to identify a person.''

''You mean just that little number of lines?''

''That's right. Now watch. I have developed this latent fingerprint. I now take this piece of Scotch tape and place it right over this fingerprint. Then I smooth the tape into position by stroking it with my finger, like this. Then I lift the edge and peel the Scotch tape off.''

''And the print comes with it!'' Della Street exclaimed.

''Exactly,'' Drake said. ''That's what's known as 'lifting' a fingerprint. Now you see it's all stuck to this Scotch tape. So I take this black card—I'm using black because the powder was silver—and put this Scotch tape on top of the black card. Then I fasten down the ends of the Scotch tape, and you see I have this fingerprint so I can study it at any time I want to. It's all on there and it will keep almost indefinitely.''

''And that's all you have to do to get fingerprints?'' Mary Brogan asked.

''That's right. Just pick the places where there are fingerprints. Then when you have secured a lifted fingerprint, write on the back of the card the place where you secured the fingerprint. Make a little diagram if you have to. For instance, here I'd write on the card 'Door to private office of Perry Mason. Fingerprint taken four and a half feet from floor, two and one quarter inches from edge of door.' Now, you see, I can drop this in my brief case and go around picking up more fingerprints.''

''That shouldn't take very long,'' Mary Brogan said, glancing at Perry Mason.

''It doesn't take long if you have luck and know where the fingerprints are.''

Mary Brogan picked up the bottles of colored powder, the

brush, the Scotch tape, replaced them in the brief case which Drake had brought in. She said breezily, "Well, I'll see you folks later."

"Take it easy," Mason cautioned. "Don't take any chances. Feel your way, Mary."

"Leave it to me," she told him. "I'm on my way."

She squeezed Della Street's hand, flashed Mason and Drake a smile, and a moment later they heard her high heels click-clacking down the corridor, then the automatic door stop clicked the door shut and the three were left in silence.

"There goes a gal that has a lot of gumption," Paul Drake said at length. "She sure has a way with her, doesn't she?"

"What can most aptly be described," Mason said, "as 'get up and git.' "

Della Street said, "I feel a little uneasy about her somehow."

Mason nodded. "We can't take chances on having anything happen. Paul, you telephone your men who are watching the apartment out there that Mary Brogan is going out to the apartment house. Tell your man who is in the Keynote Hotel across the street to make a particularly careful check, and if there's anything that doesn't look right to him, have him stop Mary Brogan before she goes in."

"Okay," Drake said. "It's probably all right, Perry . . . hang it, I'm sorry I had to fall down on you. I just don't have any good woman operative I can absolutely trust. I have a couple who are pretty good at getting information, but they're too cautious about taking chances. One of them would be all right otherwise, but she's inclined to gab a little too much. I have too much at stake here. My license is apt to be suspended or revoked if I . . ."

"We understand," Mason interrupted. "I don't blame you, Paul. I know how you feel. But I want to get this information, and I'm going to have to have it before Monday morning."

"They'll throw everything at him Monday?"

"Everything in the law books," Mason said confidently. "They'll be gunning for a conviction. Once they get a conviction Albert Brogan is crucified. He doesn't dare to take the witness stand and deny the charges that will be filed against him in that murder case. If he does they'll show his conviction in the stick-up case and make him sound like a desperate criminal."

"And if he doesn't, they'll figure the same thing anyway," Drake said.

Mason nodded. "That's the worst of it, Paul. I simply have to keep Brogan from being convicted in this stick-up case. The man's life depends on what happens over the week end."

Drake said, "Well, I'll go down and get to work, Perry. If you want anything else just let me know."

When the door had closed behind the detective, Mason and Della Street sat in silence for several thoughtful seconds.

Della Street said at length, "There seems to be a singular lack of enthusiasm on the part of Paul Drake."

"There is," Mason agreed.

"Well, you can't blame him. If it weren't for Mary, I think I'd feel lower than the basement. Somehow you can't imagine a girl like that having an uncle who would commit a holdup, let alone a murder."

Mason said, "I've got to find some way of putting her on the witness stand. I have a hunch a jury will feel the same way you do, Della."

Again there was a period of silence. Mason and Della Street, each wrapped in thought, avoided one another's eyes.

Mason started pacing the floor. He broke off at the sound of a sharp, quick tapping on the outer door of the private office, and he glanced quizzically at Della Street.

"Just far enough to see who it is, Della," he warned.

Della went to the door, opened it just a crack, then stepped back in surprise and said, "Good heavens, Mary, what happened?"

Mary Brogan entered the room, put the little brief case

115

containing the fingerprint outfit on the table by the door, slipped out of her hat and coat and said, "Well, I guess I'm here to stay."

"What happened?"

"There's a very innocuous-looking individual down in the lobby," she said, "who took a most unusual interest in me and who seemed determined to follow me. He tried to be nice about it, but I just happened to catch his eye and something about the quickness with which he turned away made me wonder, and . . . well, anyway, I saw he was following me."

"What did you do?"

"Went down to the drugstore at the corner, bought a couple of packages of chewing gum and some handkerchief-sized tissues and some toothpaste, opened the brief case and popped them all in as though that was what I was carrying the brief case for, and came right back here without letting the man know that I knew I was being followed."

"The devil!" Mason said. "I wonder how it happened they had *you* spotted."

"I went to jail this morning to visit Uncle Albert."

"So you did," Mason said. "That's probably where they picked you up, but why they should be following you now is more than I know."

She said, "I have an idea they've decided to keep an eye on everyone connected with the case. They must want to convict Uncle Albert pretty bad now."

"They do," Mason said.

"So they can 'solve' that murder case?" she asked.

"Lots of reasons," Mason said. "They're sketching your Uncle Albert now as a vicious character. I'm glad you came back. It would have been suicidal if anything had gone wrong, and they had caught you in that apartment. You'd have had *your* name in the papers, which wouldn't have helped any at this time."

"That's what I thought. I came back for instructions."

Mason said, "I'll go down and countermand my instructions to Paul. I told him to telephone his men that you were on your way out to Petty Kaylor's apartment. He'll have to tell them we've changed our plans."

"What do we do next?" Della Street asked.

Mason said, "You girls go on out. Mary, you go first. See if that man follows you. If he does lead him a chase. When you've ditched him, go to Della's apartment. Della, you may as well go home. I'm going to remain here until they get a line on where that Kaylor girl was taken."

"I don't have anything to do this afternoon," Della said. "I can wait and . . ."

"It won't do any good," Mason told her. "There's nothing at the moment that anyone can do. We've got to wait until we get some new leads. I'm trying to get leads on Archer's love life, trying to get a background on the Kaylor girl—the Kaylor sisters is presumably more accurate—and I want some stuff on Martha Lavina. There's no use trying to formulate a plan of campaign until you know the disposition of the enemy forces. You girls run on. I'm going down to see Paul Drake."

Chapter 10

When Mason returned to his office he found the door locked. A note on his desk read:

> Mary and I have gone on. Ring my apartment if you want anything. DELLA.

Mason read the note, crumpled it, dropped it into the wastebasket, and seated himself at his desk. He remained there motionless for some thirty minutes, then he pushed back his chair and started pacing the floor, eyes fastened on the carpet, his mind turning over every factor in the case, studying the bits of the puzzle piece by piece.

Abruptly the unlisted telephone shrilled, and Mason crossed over and picked up the instrument.

Della Street's voice, high-pitched with excitement, said, "Chief, I'm in a jam."

"What kind of a jam?"

"I don't think I'd better tell you over the phone."

"Where are you?"

"I'm out at the apartment that you were talking about."

"You mean . . . ?"

"Yes. Where you wanted the fingerprints."

Mason, suddenly realizing what had happened, looked over to the table where Mary Brogan had left the fingerprint outfit and noticed it was missing.

"Is Mary with you?" he asked.

"No. That man was following her. I told her to ditch him, then go to my apartment and wait there."

118

"And what's happened?"

"I think you'd better get out here."

"I'm on my way," Mason said, and then added suddenly as he was about to hang up the phone, "You aren't in danger, are you?"

"Not that kind, but . . . I'm afraid I've led with my chin."

"I'll be right out," Mason promised. "Sit tight."

The lawyer sprinted for the elevator, made time across the lobby to the parking lot where he kept his car, and within little more than a matter of seconds was gliding through traffic, taking advantage of every opening he could find.

Less than fifteen minutes later he had pulled up in front of the Keynote Hotel, found a parking place, crossed the street, paused before the entrance of the apartment house, then pressed the call button at the apartment marked "Miss Kaylor."

Almost instantly there was an answering buzz and at the sound of the electric door release Mason pushed against the door and entered the apartment house.

He walked back down a narrow, poorly lighted corridor and took the automatic elevator to the third floor.

Della Street was waiting behind the door of the Kaylor apartment. As soon as Mason paused in front of the door she opened it, placed her finger to her lips in a sign for silence and let Mason into the apartment, closing and locking the door behind her.

"What is it?" Mason asked in a low voice.

She said, "I knew how much you wanted those fingerprints. Mary knew what I was going to do. She led the shadow a chase and wound up at my apartment. I took the dusting powder and came up here."

Mason patted her shoulder. "Good work, Della, but you shouldn't have done it. You could have . . . ."

"I know," she interposed, her excitement making her impatient. "I thought I'd get the prints and let Paul give them

119

to you without you knowing where they had come from. Now I'm in a mess and you're going to have to call the shots."

"What's happened?"

"Take a look in here," she said, and led the way through the door into a bedroom.

A still figure covered to the neck with a blanket was lying unconscious on the bed.

"What the devil!" Mason exclaimed.

Della Street said, "She was on the floor in the closet when I came here. I fooled around for five or ten minutes picking up fingerprints before I realized she was here. I opened the closet door and this girl was sitting on the floor with her head and shoulders propped up against the door. She fell out into the room. I had an awful time getting her up on the bed."

"Any clothes on?" Mason asked.

"Fully clothed. Shoes and everything. Who is she?"

Mason said, "Bring the light over here, Della. That's what I want to find out."

Mason pulled back the blanket, checked the figure for pulse, listened to the breathing.

Della Street snapped on a floor lamp and the illumination flooded the girl's pallid features.

Mason said, "There'd be a difference in the way this girl would look when she's animated and vivacious, particularly at night with her war paint on. However, I'm damned if I know whether she's the Petty Kaylor I was out with. I don't think she is. Do her clothes give any clue?"

"I haven't looked," Della Street said. "I telephoned you and then I managed to get her up here on the bed, dragging her across the floor, lifting her, first her shoulders and then her hips, using a low stool from the dressing table to help me."

"Did she have a purse, Della?"

"I didn't see one—and I looked all over the closet floor."

Mason turned down the blanket, ran his hands along the two pockets in the jacket the girl was wearing, brought out

120

a small leather key container with a single key. "This should mean something."

Mason went back to the living room, opened the door to the corridor, tried the key, then returned to the bedroom.

"Does it work?" Della Street asked.

Mason shook his head.

Della Street said, "While you were out there trying the key, I looked for labels in the clothes. There's one on the jacket . . . a store in Las Vegas, Nevada."

Mason said, "We're going to have to find out about this key. It may be a real clue."

Della Street said, "Gosh, I was afraid you'd say a 'key clue.' What do we do next? Do we call the police, or a doctor, or both?"

Mason said, "I think we'd better call a doctor."

"Then what? Can you just walk out?"

"How about both of us walking out?"

She shook her head. "You see, I had to tell a fib in order to get in here. A Swede janitor opened the door. I told him that Miss Kaylor, who was at the hospital, had asked me to come and get some clothes for her. I told him I was a nurse from the hospital. He dug up his passkey and opened the door."

"Suspicious?" Mason asked.

"Not a bit, but he did take a good look at me."

"Old or young?"

"About fifty. A Swede, with a heavy accent. But if the police start checking around he'll remember me and describe me and . . . well, that might not be so good. I'd better stay and face the music."

Mason crossed over to the telephone. "Look up Dr. Hanover's number, Della."

"Can we trust him?" she asked.

"We're going to have to," Mason said. "I think we can. We got him out of that scrape on the blackmail racket. What's his number?"

Della Street thumbed quickly through the pages of the book, gave Mason the number and he dialed it on the telephone.

When a feminine voice answered he said, "This is Perry Mason, the lawyer. I have to get Dr. Hanover right away on a matter of great emergency. . . . I know it's Saturday afternoon. I'm telling you this is an emergency. . . . All right, I'll hold the phone."

A moment later, Dr. Hanover's voice came on the line, and Mason gave him the address of the apartment. "You got that?" he asked.

"Yes."

Mason said, "There's a girl up here who has, I think, taken an overdose of sleeping pills. She has a shallow pulse, bad color, is completely unconscious. You'd better get here as fast as you can."

"I'll be right up," the doctor promised.

"And we want it kept completely under cover," Mason told him.

"You can trust my discretion," Dr. Hanover promised. "You should know that. I'll be right up."

Mason hung up the telephone and turned to regard Della Street.

"Can you unscramble it, Chief?" she asked.

"I can't unscramble it," Mason said. "I can't even start."

"But this girl was taken away in an ambulance, Chief. She . . ."

"How do you know she was?"

"Why, the ambulance drove up here and picked her up and took her away. Of course, we don't know where the ambulance went but she was taken away. Of course . . ."

"Go on," Mason said.

"No," she said. "I can't figure it so it makes sense."

"Go ahead," Mason said. "You had an idea and then you stopped."

"Well, it just didn't sound reasonable."

"Why not?"

"Well, because . . . what *was* the idea? I can't see what could be gained by it."

"Go ahead. What was your thought?"

"Well, apparently," Della Street said, "the men from the ambulance came up here and found Miss Kaylor just beginning to feel the effects of a big overdose of sleeping pills. She was able to leave under her own power. They put her in the ambulance and took her away. Naturally everyone would assume they were going to take her to a hospital."

"Go ahead," Mason said.

"But instead of that they must have brought her back here and left her to die."

"How did they get her back here?"

"They must have brought her in a back entrance."

Mason walked over to stand by the side of the bed, regarding the girl thoughtfully.

"The only thing is," Della Street said, "I don't see *why* they'd do that. *Why* did they take her in the first place if they intended to bring her back?"

Mason said, "It would make a most artistic murder, wouldn't it, Della?"

"What do you mean?"

Mason said, "Miss Kaylor voluntarily took the sleeping pills. Mary Brogan can testify to that. Mary Brogan reported to Paul Drake, and Paul Drake said he'd notify the police. Drake did notify the police. That puts Drake in the clear. It puts Mary Brogan in the clear."

"What are you getting at?" Della Street asked.

Mason said, "Then an ambulance with an unlisted number whizzes around the corner and two ambulance attendants dash into the building. They come out supporting a groggy-looking woman between them. No one gets a good look at that woman's face. They put her in the ambulance and drive away."

123

"You mean they didn't take her away and bring her back? You mean it was some other woman?"

"How do we know that they even went up to this apartment? They could have entered the house and found someone staggering down the corridor who said, 'I've taken an overdose of sleeping pills.' Naturally they'd assume it was the case that had been reported to them. Then the police came and the police didn't even bother to go in the apartment house. They found a crowd collected in front—people who had come out from the restaurant next door and the beauty shop across the street and just the ordinary hangers-on that appear from nowhere in times like that. One of them volunteered a statement to the police that they were too late, the ambulance had left just a few minutes ago. The police naturally would feel that the case was all disposed of, so they made out a report and went on their way. In the meantime, Miss Kaylor was lying up here in the apartment . . ."

"In the closet," Della Street interposed.

"Exactly," Mason said. "Although that probably makes but little difference. She probably decided to go out. She went to the closet to get a coat and hat. By that time she was feeling very groggy and probably a little dizzy. She slumped down on the closet floor and promptly went to sleep. Her sleep turned into coma and after a short time the coma would have turned into death."

"But that's murder," Della Street said.

"Prove it," Mason challenged. "She took the sleeping pills herself. Everything else that happened *could* have been a chain of coincidence."

"But what caused her to take the sleeping pills in the first place?"

"Perhaps a double took the sleeping pills, Della."

Della Street's eyes widened as she grasped the full implication of Mason's meaning. "But . . . but how do you know there's a double?"

"I don't, yet. It's a hypothesis that continues to hold more and more interest for me."

"Good Lord, Chief! That would be cold-blooded murder . . . that could never, never be proven!"

Mason said, "We'll tackle that later, Della. In the meantime, let's go to the kitchen, put on a kettle of water and bring it to a boil."

"I'll do it, Chief."

"Not too much water," Mason cautioned, "just two or three cupfuls. The doctor may want some sterile water for a hypodermic. And how about coffee, Della?"

"Coffee?" she asked.

"The caffeine. It's a stimulant. You might put a big pot of coffee on the stove. Make it heavy and black."

Mason followed Della Street out to the kitchen, watched her move about with swift competence, putting water in a kettle, finding coffee and a percolator.

"Don't bother with the percolator," Mason said. "Just put in lots of coffee and boil it. We'll get it good and strong."

"How long do you suppose it will take the doctor to get here?"

"Not very long," Mason said. "He realized that I wouldn't be calling him unless it was serious."

They stood by the stove watching the gas flames under the kettle and the coffee pot.

Mason went back to the bedroom, picked up the wrist of the unconscious girl, timed the pulse, then returned to stand by Della Street.

"How is she?" Della asked.

"Apparently just the same," Mason said. "The pulse is just about the same as it was and so is the respiration."

"Do you suppose that there's . . . that it will be all right?"

"I don't know. She must have taken a terrific dose of the drug."

"And it's already begun to be absorbed by her system?" Della Street asked.

Mason nodded.

"Then minutes are precious."

"Very much so," Mason said. "I'm hoping that the doctor will get here within the next few minutes. If he doesn't, as soon as that coffee is brewed I'm going to take it on myself to try and get some of it down her."

"Suppose she . . . I mean before the doctor gets here . . . ?"

"I've been thinking of that too," Mason said.

They were silent for a while, then Mason said, "I don't think there's much chance of it, Della. The poison from sleeping medicines takes a long while to produce death, as I remember it."

"But all the time more of the drug is being absorbed in her system. That makes it just that much *more* dangerous, doesn't it?"

"There's no question about that."

"Well, here's the kettle coming to a boil."

They watched as the spout of the kettle, after a few preliminary spurts, gave forth a steady stream of steam.

Della Street turned down the gas flame so as to hold the water at the boiling point.

"You think this is the same girl who came from Las Vegas with Paul Drake and who vanished from the law library?"

"I don't know," Mason said. "I keep thinking of the possibility of two sisters, perhaps even girls who don't have any family connection but who do have a similarity of appearance."

"Just because of the two apartments?"

"Partially that."

"But what would be the idea?"

"I don't know," Mason admitted.

"Of course, this girl could be traveling back and forth between here and Las Vegas for some reason."

"She could."

"Well," Della Street asked, "what's wrong with that idea?"

126

"Nothing at all," Mason said. "The reason I'm interested in exploring the theory of two separate individuals is that I just don't believe the hostess I was with last night is the young woman who came from Las Vegas with Paul Drake."

"But she has the same name, the same connections, the same . . ."

"I know," Mason interposed, "but there's a difference in character, a difference in mental reaction."

"And, of course, there are the two apartments," Della Street supplemented, her forehead puckered into a puzzled frown.

The coffee started to boil. Della Street made a dive for the control but was not in time to keep the coffee from boiling over.

The buzzer sounded.

Della Street, moving the coffee pot, said, "Well, I should have known that he'd get here at the exact moment when I had coffee spilled all over the stove and . . ."

"Where's the push button?" Mason asked.

"Right there by the telephone."

Mason pushed the button which released the catch on the street door of the apartment house, then went to stand by the corridor door of the apartment while Della Street mopped up the spilled coffee, pulled up the cover of the coffee pot, lit the fire on another burner and turned the flame as low as possible.

Mason heard the elevator door open, then close, and stepped out into the corridor.

Dr. Hanover, radiating professional competence, came striding down the hall, entered the apartment.

"What do we have here?" he asked.

Mason said, "Probably barbiturates, and I think she's pretty far gone. Take a look."

Dr. Hanover took off his hat, dropped it on the floor, put down his black medicine bag, pulled back the blanket, picked up the wrist of the unconscious girl, held it while he took the

127

pulse, then dropped the wrist, pulled open the girl's blouse, opened his bag, took out a stethoscope and listened to her heart action.

"Hot water?" he asked.

"We have it."

"Boiling?"

"It's boiling."

"A big spoon," the doctor said. "Hold the spoon over the fire until it's good and hot, then fill it with boiling water and bring it to me."

Della Street hurried to the kitchen.

"Let's get this jacket off and get an arm where we can get at it," Dr. Hanover said to Mason.

"What do you make of her?"

"I think she's going to make it all right. We've got things to do. Who is she? How long since she's taken the stuff?"

Mason shook his head. "We found her like this."

"How does it happen you're here?"

"Looking for evidence."

"Who let you in?"

Mason grinned and said, "Does that make any difference in the treatment?"

"Not in the treatment," Dr. Hanover said, "but it may come in damn handy if someone expects me to sign a death certificate."

"Think there's any chance?"

"I don't know yet."

Della Street brought in the big spoon with the hot water. Dr. Hanover opened a small bottle, dropped a tablet into the water, waited for it to dissolve, then took a hypodermic syringe from his bag and sucked the sterile water up into the hypodermic.

"Okay," he said to Della Street, "hold that arm for me—in this position."

He spilled alcohol onto cotton, washed the arm, inserted the hypodermic, then withdrew the needle and said to Mason, "In order to be on the safe side this girl has to go to a hospital."

"Take her," Mason said.

"What do I tell people in case they ask questions?"

"You listen," Mason said, "and then you'll know what to say."

"Listen to what?"

"To the telephone conversation."

"What telephone conversation?"

"This one."

Mason walked over to the telephone, dialed a number and then, with a heavy synthetic Swedish accent, said, "Ay call you much time ago for suicide case. Police coom and then they go avay. Ay tank this girl maybe she die."

"Who is this? Where are you talking from?" the man asked.

"This bane the yanitor," Mason said. "Ay bane yanitor for the Windmore Arms Apartment. That girl bane in Apartment 321."

Mason heard an exclamation at the other end of the line, and then the dispatcher said, "Why, what are you talking about? She was taken away from there around one-thirty. The police were out there, an ambulance was out there and . . ."

"She bane right here on bed," Mason said. "Ay got doctor. He say she going to die if she don't get to hospital. Your police bane crazy. They stop at street door, never go up."

Mason slammed up the telephone receiver.

Dr. Hanover, who had been listening to the conversation, said, "*Now* what am I supposed to do?"

Mason said, "You were called by a Swede janitor. You came here and this is what you found."

"Wait a minute," the doctor protested. "This janitor will say he never heard of me in his life."

"Exactly," Mason said, "but the girl goes to the hospital."

"And what am I going to tell the police when the janitor says he didn't get in touch with me?"

Mason grinned and said, "The same thing the police are going to say when the janitor claims he never got in touch with them."

"I get it," Dr. Hanover said, grinning. "On your way, you two. I haven't seen you for weeks."

Chapter 11

As they emerged from the apartment house, Della Street jumped into Mason's car, glanced apprehensively at the lawyer. "The police are going to be irritated."

"Definitely."

"So what do we do?" she asked.

"So," Mason said, getting in the driver's seat and slamming the door, "we are going to be hard to catch for a while."

"Out of circulation?"

"Quite definitely. On the lam. We take a powder. We run out. We're gone. They look for us in our accustomed haunts and we can't be found."

"But . . . we can't do that."

"Why not?"

"You'll have to be in court Monday morning."

"On Monday morning a lot of water will have run over the dam."

"And, if I remember the criminal law that was taught me by that eminent attorney, Mr. Perry Mason, evidence of flight can be used to establish guilt?"

Mason started the motor. "You are quite correct, Miss Street. You will undoubtedly receive a passing grade in your course."

"Therefore," she said, "since it is almost certain that the police are going to try to charge you with something, why are you going to play into their hands by resorting to flight?"

Mason eased the car away from the curb and around the corner. "In the first place," he said, "we are not going to

131

resort to flight. In the second place, we are not going to play into the hands of the police."

"But I thought you said you were going to take a powder, to get out and . . . ?"

"Oh, quite definitely," Mason said, "but we are not going to resort to flight. We are going to be searching for evidence."

"That," she said, "would be a story that would carry conviction only in case we looked for likely evidence in a likely place."

"Exactly."

"And, in order to suit our purpose, that place must be somewhere where the police would never think of looking for us."

"Splendid," Mason said. "You're doing fine, Della."

"*Will* you quit being so exasperating and tell me what we're going to do?"

Mason grinned. "Right now we're in a very vulnerable position. We're also sitting in a game where we have a fistful of cards which, at the moment, don't look very encouraging, but we are handicapped by not knowing what is trumps. We're going to have to start playing our hand on Monday morning at ten o'clock when court convenes and trial is resumed in the case of People versus Brogan. By that time it would be very, very advantageous for us to know what is trumps.

"The other side undoubtedly has some aces to play. In fact, they seem to have every ace in the deck. Our only hope of winning is to put a low trump on somebody's high ace."

"That sounds very reasonable," she said. "Will you tell me how you propose to go about doing it?"

"Let's use our heads and resort to logic," Mason said.

"Suits me. Where are you headed now?"

"Las Vegas."

"And just what good will that do?"

Mason said, "Figure it out, Della. I'm still toying with

the theory that there are two girls who look alike. For a time I thought they were sisters, perhaps twin sisters. Now I'm inclined to doubt that. There may be a complete diversity of interests, probably they don't even know each other, but they *do* look alike."

"Well?" she asked.

"One of them," Mason said, "flew in from Las Vegas, Nevada. The other one lives here. We wish to establish that there are two girls. So we do two things, first, we ask Paul Drake to go to the hospital and look at the girl who took the sleeping pills; second, we go to Las Vegas and investigate the background of the girl who lives there. What could be more logical than that?"

Della Street said, "It's logical when you put it that way. We go by plane?"

"Yes and no."

"What do you mean by that?"

"We don't dare to go on a regular flight. Police might start asking questions at the airport and they might get the answers. It would be very inconvenient to find ourselves picked up in Las Vegas for questioning before we had an opportunity to ask any questions of our own. In that way we would be forced to tip our hand. I don't want to have to give out any information before I have the information to give out."

"So what do we do?"

"We charter a plane."

"A private charter job?"

"A little inconspicuous single-motored private jalopy," Mason told her. "We will be flying over long stretches of barren desert with only one motor to depend on, and we trust that nothing happens to that motor."

"If anyone should start looking for us," Della Street said, "don't you suppose they'd cover the airports?"

"Probably."

"And wouldn't we stand out like a sore thumb? In other words, won't people . . . ?"

Mason shook his head. "Not if we play it right."

"What do you mean?"

"The laws in California providing for blood tests and red tape in connection with marriage drive dozens of romantic couples to Nevada and Arizona every week end. We'll pretend we're deeply in love."

She glanced at him quizzically. "When will we get back?"

"Tomorrow."

"Baggage?"

"You'll have to buy anything you need. I don't dare to drive by your apartment and stop long enough for you to pick up an overnight bag. Remember that Mary Brogan's there and there's a man shadowing Mary Brogan."

He stopped by a phone booth and called Paul Drake.

"Paul, there's a girl at the Windmore Arms Apartments who's taken an overdose of sleeping pills. Go to the hospital and see if . . ."

"Good Lord, Perry," the detective exclaimed irritably, "I've told you she wasn't taken to any hospital, and . . ."

"She will be," Mason interrupted. "The case is in charge of Dr. Pete Hanover."

And Mason hung up before Drake could say anything else.

He hurried back to the car, drove to the plane charter section of the airport, rented a plane, and less than forty minutes after they had left the Windmore Arms Apartments they were roaring up off the airstrip.

Mason circled Della Street's shoulders with his arm. She came over to put her head on his shoulder. The pilot glanced back out of the corner of his eye, then devoted his attention to piloting the machine.

The air was bumpy for the first ten or fifteen minutes, then it smoothed off, then became bumpy once more as they climbed up over the Cajon Pass.

Far down below them they could see the road twisting and turning, dotted with automobiles. The ribbons of steel rails were like penciled lines. A streamliner crawled slowly up the grade. Far ahead, a long freight train twisted onto a siding. Behind them and to the left was a tumbled sea of mountains. Over to the right the twin snow-capped peaks guarded the pass to the Imperial Valley. The Salton Sea showed as a flat blue splotch. Ahead was the plateau of elevated desert, interspersed with jagged ridges stretching out through Victorville to Barstow, then on to the entrance to Death Valley.

The motor purred a song of steady power. Della Street's hand nestled into Mason's left hand. His right arm held her shoulder.

From time to time the pilot pointed out bits of natural scenery, but when it became apparent that his passengers were paying no attention to him he lapsed into silence and devoted his attention entirely to piloting the plane.

It was nearing sunset and the mountains were making long splashes of purple shadows when they saw the buildings of Las Vegas ahead.

"I won't be going back until daylight tomorrow," the pilot said. "If you want to fly back with me we can fix it on a round-trip basis. Call me at the airport. You can leave word there. They'll know where to reach me. Here's one of my cards."

"We'll let you know," Mason said, and then added self-consciously, "we may want to stay here a few days."

"Okay by me. I can give you a good rate on a trip back tomorrow if you want to go."

"Thanks," Mason told him. "We'll let you know."

The plane slanted downward in a long incline. The buildings of Las Vegas took form. Huge motels and resorts with swimming pools and spacious grounds, then more congested districts, then finally they were gliding over the main street of Las Vegas. Even though it was barely sunset the street was ablaze with neon signs, a tribute to the cheap power from Hoover Dam.

There was another strip of desert, then the plane swung

135

into the airport and a few moments later skimmed to a smooth landing.

The pilot shook hands with both of his passengers. "I just want to wish you folks all the happiness in the world," he said. "Let me know if you want to go back tomorrow."

"We will," Mason told him, and helped Della Street to the ground.

A taxicab took them up to the center of the city.

"What are we going to do?" Della Street asked.

Mason raised his eyebrows.

"About going back?"

Mason said, "We go back on a train. We won't be conspicuous going back. I was afraid about getting away without arousing suspicion. We'll get off here at one of the casinos, gamble a few dollars, and then go to Inez Kaylor's apartment."

"Then what?"

"Then," Mason said, "we'll just have to trust to luck."

"Suppose we get caught in there?"

"That," Mason said, "would be very awkward."

"Suppose someone should be in there?"

"We'll take the precaution of ringing the bell before we use the key."

"And suppose the key you have doesn't fit the apartment?"

"We'll find some way of getting in," Mason said. "Having come this far we're going to get the evidence we want."

"And just what is that evidence?"

"We want to prove conclusively," Mason said, "that there are two Kaylor girls. That the Kaylor girl who is a resident of Las Vegas and who was a hostess in The Villa Lavina is not the same girl as the Petty Kaylor who now occupies the apartment in Los Angeles."

They paused briefly at the gambling casinos, and this time luck was with them. Both Mason and Della Street won consistently. It was nearly an hour later that they cashed in their
136

chips and walked along the lighted main stem of the desert city.

"Do we go in a cab?" she asked.

"No," Mason told her, "we walk. It's only four or five blocks."

"You know where it is?"

"Yes, I know the layout of the city fairly well."

They walked several blocks down a side street. The dry cool desert air was like wine. The steady stars overhead fought their way through the aura of light above the main street of the city.

Mason, consulting the address Paul Drake had given him, paused at a small, two-story apartment house.

"Here it is," he said.

He pressed the button opposite the name of Inez Kaylor, waited several seconds, pressed it again, and then waited again before giving the button a final push.

"Okay, Della," he said. "Here's where we make our gamble."

He tried the entrance door. It was locked. Mason tried the key he had taken from the unconscious girl. The lock clicked back. Mason pushed the door open.

"Gosh, Chief, I feel like a housebreaker," Della Street said. "I have a feeling in my bones something's going to happen."

"You have that fingerprint outfit?" Mason asked.

"Yes, in the brief case."

"Let's go," Mason said.

They ignored the elevator to climb the stairs.

There was a party going on in an apartment on the lower floor and in back. They could hear the sounds of laughter. There was no other sound in the house.

They found the apartment they wanted. Mason took the precaution of knocking gently on the door. When there was no answer he tried the key in the lock.

The door opened smoothly.

Mason stepped in and switched on the lights.

"Good heavens!" Della Street exclaimed in an undertone.

Mason pulled her into the apartment and kicked the door shut behind them.

The place was in complete disorder. Pictures had not only been pulled from the walls but had been ripped from the frames. The overstuffed upholstery had been ripped with a sharp knife. In the bedroom the mattress had been slashed open, pillows had been cut. In the kitchen a jar of flour had been dumped in the middle of the floor. A sugar receptacle had been emptied, and they could feel the crunch of sugar crystals beneath their feet on the linoleum as they gave the place a quick inventory.

"Well, someone certainly wanted something," Mason said, "and wasn't wasting any time about it. He evidently didn't have any time to waste. He wanted to make a thorough search and he had to make it in a short time."

"Good Lord, what wreckage," Della Street said. "Look at that closet. The girl's clothes have been taken out, the linings have been ripped out, and . . ."

"Exactly," Mason said. "It gives us a clue."

"What sort of a clue?"

"To the type of thing they were looking for."

"What do you mean?"

Mason said, "It was small, flat and valuable. We're going to do what we came here for and then we're going to get out. Give me that fingerprint powder, Della."

Della Street opened the brief case. Mason started dusting for fingerprints, found a couple and promptly imprisoned them with the lifting tape and lifted them from their surroundings.

"How do you know whether you're getting prints of the girls or prints of the person or the people who did all this?" Della Street asked.

"I don't know," Mason said. "Right at the moment I'm just making a collection of fingerprints. We'll sort them out

138

after a while. The prints on the upper surface of that drawer should have been made by someone who put fingertips against the drawer and was pushing it closed. The person or persons searching the apartment didn't bother to close the drawer. They just pulled it open and dumped everything out on the floor.''

"Yes, that's true," she admitted.

Mason examined the writing desk. "All the personal correspondence seems to have been taken," he said. "There are only three letters left here and they're routine business letters. One of them's from a magazine subscription company, one from the Aphrodite Model Agency and one from . . ."

He broke off abruptly as a buzzing sound emanated from the kitchen.

"What was that?" Della Street asked. "Do you suppose that's someone at the back door?"

"More apt to be the front door," Mason said.

"What do we do? We're trapped here. We . . ."

Mason shook his head. "No, we're not," he said in a low voice, "the door has a spring lock on it. The girl who lives here is three hundred miles away. All we have to do is sit tight."

Mason stood waiting, listening.

The buzzer did not sound again. After a few moments there was a tentative knock at the door.

Mason signaled for Della Street to remain motionless and maintain complete silence.

They waited what seemed an interminable interval, and then heard the sound of metal clicking against metal as a key was inserted in the lock. The latch snapped back, the door opened and a man stepped into the room, then jumped back and stood rigid with surprise as he saw two people standing in the lighted room.

"Well," Mason said, "you may as well come in."

The man hesitated, his face drained of color, his eyes shifting about. Then he stepped in and said in a voice which he tried to make assertive, "Who are you people, and what are you doing here?"

"I think," Mason said with ominous calm, "that you're the one to answer that question. Close the door please. There's no use letting everyone know what's going on. Now what do *you* know about all this?" and Mason included the wreckage of the apartment with a sweeping gesture of his hand.

The man was in his late forties or early fifties. His hair had started receding from his forehead. His eyes were a cold glacial blue. His mouth was deep-set, straight and grim. At the moment he was badly nonplussed.

"What do *you* know about this?" Mason repeated.

"I . . . I don't know anything about it," the man said.

"Do you know Inez Kaylor?"

"I . . . I know her sister."

"You don't know Inez?" Mason said, and glanced significantly at Della Street.

"Just her sister."

Della Street almost surreptitiously raised an eyebrow. Mason nodded.

"And will you kindly tell me," Della Street said with indignation, "how it happens that you invade *my* apartment, using a skeleton key, just because you happen to know my sister?"

"Gosh, Miss Kaylor, I'm sorry, I . . . I had no idea you were here. I thought . . . why, you're supposed to be gone. That's why I came here."

"Perhaps," Mason said, "you'd better sit down and give us the story, and, incidentally, tell us what you know about this wreckage."

"I . . . gosh, I . . . what are *you* doing? Taking fingerprints?"

"That's right," Mason said. "I am assisting Miss Kaylor in trying to find out who is responsible for this outrage."

"Oh, my gosh," the man said, "a detective! Now look, let's be reasonable about this thing. I can't afford to have my name get into this at all. I'm married, and this would completely ruin me. If my wife thought I even knew . . . oh, good Lord."

He abruptly sat down in one of the straight-backed dining chairs.

"All right, go on," Mason said, "tell us about it, and do it fast."

"If you can keep me out of it," the man said, "look, I'll make it worth your while. Now I don't want to be crude about this thing but I'm desperate. I can't . . ."

"Go on," Mason said. "Who are you? What's your name? Where do you come from?"

"Can't we leave my name out of it, officer?"

"Before you get out of here," Mason said, "you're going to tell me your name and I'm going to be sure it's your right name. I want to see your driving license. I want complete identification and I want some damn good explanation of what you're doing here with a key and what you're looking for."

"Oh, Lord," the man groaned.

"What's your name?" Mason asked.

"After all, is that necessary?"

"What's your name?"

"Gibbs."

"What's the first name?"

"Thomas."

"Where do you live?"

"Los Angeles."

"Let me see your driving license."

The man took a handkerchief from his pocket, mopped his forehead, then pulled out a wallet, extracted a driving license and handed it to Mason.

Mason checked the name, the residence and the description, said, "This gives the residence as being in San Diego."

"I know. That's where I live. I do business in Los Angeles. I was trying to keep you from getting my home address, but you *would* demand to see that driving license."

"All right," Mason said. "Now how do you happen to be here?"

"I was on the loose yesterday and I . . . well, I drifted into one of The Villa Lavinas. You know how it goes. I wasn't looking for anything in particular, but I was lonely and I'd heard there were hostesses there and . . . really, it was just curiosity . . . one thing led to another, and I started dancing. Before I left the place this girl and I took a little ride."

"Where did you go?"

"We went to a gambling place she knew."

"Go in your car?" Mason asked.

"No, in a limousine, a nice cosy limousine with the curtains drawn and . . ."

"How much did you lose?"

"More than I wanted to."

"How much?"

"About two hundred dollars."

"Then what?"

"Well, the girl was very sympathetic. She'd won about a hundred dollars and she insisted on splitting it with me. You see, I'd given her the chips to play with when we first went in, and . . . well, she was really a nice sport, a darned fine girl! I happened to mention that I was driving to Salt Lake and . . . well, we were just talking about it and . . ."

"And you asked her if she didn't want to go along," Mason said.

Gibbs avoided his eyes.

"Didn't you?" Mason asked.

"Yes," Gibbs blurted, shamefacedly.

"All right, then what happened?"

"She said she couldn't go, that she had to stay on there as hostess. She said she'd like to. She . . . she liked me."

142

"I know," Mason said. "She told you you were different."

The man jerked up to startled attention. "How did *you* know what she said?"

"Never mind," Mason said, "just go on telling us what happened, but remember we have ways of checking you."

Gibbs said, "Miss Kaylor, I'm sorry . . . there was no reason . . ."

"Well, go ahead with your story," Della Street said.

"She told me her sister had moved to Los Angeles, that she wanted to get some things out of her apartment here in Las Vegas and asked me if I'd go to the apartment, pack the things up and ship them."

"What did she want?" Mason asked.

"A suitcase with a Mexico City hotel label on it and some clothes out of the closet, a black and white check suit, a long coat with a fur collar and the things that were in the upper right-hand drawer in the bureau."

"Anything else?"

"That's all."

"What were you to do with them?"

"I was to pack them in the suitcase, lock the apartment, put the key to the apartment in one of the pockets on the inside of the suitcase and express the whole thing to The Villa Lavina."

"To Miss Kaylor?"

"No. To Martha Lavina, the owner."

Mason studied the description on the driving license.

"Here," Gibbs said, "I'll prove who I am. My right thumbprint is on that driving license. I'll duplicate it for you."

He took a piece of blotting paper from the desk, folded it into four thicknesses, poured ink on it from a bottle of fountain pen ink, pressed his thumb against this pad, then picked up one of the letters from the desk and made several impressions of his right thumbprint on the back of the letter.

"There," he said, handing the paper to Mason. "You'll find some of them good enough for a comparison, officer."

While Mason studied the thumbprints, comparing them with the print on the driver's license, Gibbs picked up one of the other letters, crumpled it, wiped his thumb on it, looked around for a wastebasket and, finding none, pushed the paper down in his side coat pocket.

"They are the same thumbprints, officer," he said.

Mason nodded, returned the driver's license, folded the paper with the thumbprints, put it in his pocket.

"Where are you staying here in town?" Mason asked.

"At the Arrapahoe Hotel."

"Registered under your right name?"

"Yes, of course."

"All right," Mason said, "we may call on you again. Now you can give Miss Kaylor that key you have and go."

Gibbs gave the key to Della. "I'll do anything," he said, "anything to keep my name out of this. I . . ."

"We understand," Mason told him.

"You can reach me at any time at that San Diego address. Only please be careful. Don't write, telephone on a person to person call. Make it collect. Say it's about a traffic violation. If my wife should have any idea . . ."

"Okay," Mason told him. "Get going."

Gibbs hurried out of the door like an animal released from a trap.

"Phew!" Della Street said after he had had time to get down the corridor. "You certainly did a great job of getting him on the defensive as soon as he came in. My knees were ready to buckle, and I was going to collapse right on the floor. What do we do now?"

"Now," Mason said, "we get out of here fast."

Della Street arched surprised eyebrows. "Why?"

"Because there's something off color about Gibbs. I'm not too certain he isn't telephoning the police right now."

"Gibbs?" Della Street asked in surprise. "Surely you

don't think he'd be doing that. He's scared to death. He's down in the nearest bar right now, ordering a double brandy, and his hand is shaking so he can hardly hold the drink. The man's scared to death, Chief.''

"That's just it," Mason said. "He's too scared."

"What do you mean?"

"It isn't natural for a cold-eyed man with a deep-set firm mouth to get that scared."

Della Street laughed. "He's a middle-aged Lothario having a fling and got caught. You can't judge how scared he is until you know what he's scared of. Perhaps if you could see Mrs. Thomas Gibbs that's all you'd need to know."

Mason grinned. "Nevertheless, Della, we get out of here."

Chapter 12

Mason and Della Street gravitated to a cocktail lounge in one of the quieter spots.

"Well," Della Street asked, "what do we do now?"

Mason said, "The Union Pacific's crack streamliner *The City of Los Angeles* comes through here a little after two o'clock in the morning. We'll see if we can get a couple of compartments. It gets into Los Angeles around nine in the morning. I'll get off at East Los Angeles and take a taxi."

"A great ending for a honeymoon," Della Street said.

Mason laughed. "The man who piloted us over in the plane would be rather surprised if he could see us now."

There was silence for a moment, then a radio over the bar which had been featuring dance music was turned up as the voice of an announcer said, "Your Las Vegas station brings you news of local significance about important visitors to Las Vegas, local weather conditions, and other pertinent information every hour on the hour.

"Your sponsor is the Silver Streak Cocktail Lounge, Bar, Casino and Café, catering to the wants of the most exclusive and sophisticated tourists, with a cuisine comparable in every way to that of the best restaurants in the largest cities. A casino that is fairly operated, a cocktail lounge serving only the best liquors . . ."

Mason made a gesture with his hand and said, "I suppose since these people sponsor the news items we'll have to . . ."

Della Street reached across the little table and grabbed his wrist. "Listen, Chief," she said.

The announcer said, "According to the Hollywood broadcast of one of the motion picture and celebrity commentators this evening, Perry Mason, the noted Los Angeles attorney, and his secretary, Miss Della Street, are in Las Vegas for the purpose of consummating a romance which has, according to friends, been in existence for several years. Mr. Mason and his charming secretary were recognized when they landed at an airport here in Las Vegas late this afternoon. A check with the pilot confirmed the fact that the couple were here to take advantage of Nevada's liberal marriage laws.

"Here's the weather forecast for Las Vegas and vicinity. Fair tonight and tomorrow. Clear, cloudless skies. Temperature varying from a low of forty-two degrees tonight to seventy-eight degrees tomorrow. Gentle northerly breeze."

There followed a few more items of general interest, then another commercial, and then the program swung into dance music.

Della Street raised her glass. "Well, Mr. Mason," she said, "may I wish you every happiness."

Mason raised his glass, smiled at her. "You wouldn't want to make a liar out of Louella Parsons would you, Della?"

They touched glasses, sipped their drinks. "It might have been Hedda Hopper," she said.

"Well, it's all over town, and you can't refuse to cooperate now. Why, the commentator could sue you for libel, and . . . good Lord!"

He put down his glass, grabbed a bill from his pocket, motioned for the waiter.

"What now?" Della Street asked.

"Gibbs!"

"And what about Gibbs?"

"I *thought* he was a little too glib about offering his thumbprint."

"What are you getting at?"

"And he did it right under our noses, too!"

"Chief, *will* you tell me what . . . ?"

147

The waiter appeared. Mason tossed him the bill. "Keep the change. We're on our way. Come on, Della."

She let him hurry her out of the cocktail lounge, down the street.

"What happened?"

"Gibbs. He went to that apartment because he wanted something—and he took it."

"No, Chief, he didn't take a thing from that apartment. I was watching him like a hawk."

"Think again, Della."

"No, he didn't. He didn't even touch anything, only that . . ."

"Go on."

"Why, just that circular letter he picked up to wipe his fingers with."

Mason said, "He wanted to get something off that desk, and by suggesting I take his thumbprint he saw a chance to get what he wanted."

"But, good heavens, Chief, just a circular letter? He wouldn't have gone to all that trouble to . . ."

"We're going to check on him and see," Mason told her.

"And where are we going now?" Della Street asked.

"Down to have a nice heart-to-heart talk with Mr. Gibbs."

"By this time he may have learned you're not an officer."

"Nevertheless, we'll just do a little checking on Mr. Gibbs."

They walked down the street, past a glittering array of lighted casinos thronged with people.

"The main street of Las Vegas reminds me of the business district of most any town on the day before Christmas," Della Street said.

Mason grinned. "It's just about the most active city in the world."

"Is it always crowded like this?"

"Every time I've been here."

"When does it let up?"

"It doesn't let up. It'll slack off a little bit toward morning, but almost any hour of the day or night you'll find business booming. Well, here we are, Della."

They turned in at the Arrapahoe Hotel, walked down to the desk where the room phones were located, and Mason picked up a phone, said, "I want to talk with Thomas Gibbs of Los Angeles."

"Mr. Gibbs checked out about fifteen minutes ago."

"Leave any forwarding address?"

"No."

"Thank you," Mason said, and hung up.

He glanced at Della Street. "Checked out."

"Now what?" Della asked.

Mason looked thoughtful for a moment, then walked over to the cashier's desk.

"Good evening," she said.

"Good evening," Mason said with cold formality. "I am a friend of Mr. Thomas Gibbs, who checked out here about fifteen minutes ago. Mr. Gibbs was in a hurry when he checked out and didn't look at his bill carefully. It wasn't until he met me that he realized he had been overcharged on some long-distance telephone calls."

The cashier shook her head. "Many times people talk longer than they think they have . . ."

"It's not that," Mason interrupted. "It's the fact that numbers were charged to his bill that he simply didn't call."

"On long-distance?"

"That's right. Los Angeles numbers."

The girl reached into a filing drawer, pulled out a carbon copy of a bill which had been marked "Paid," slid it over on the desk in front of Mason and said coldly, "There are three Los Angeles calls—all the same number. I'm absolutely certain that Mr. Gibbs put through those three calls."

Mason, looking at the bill, said, "Mr. Gibbs is quite certain he only talked twice."

"Well," the cashier said indignantly, "he talked three times. I'll check my reports, however, to make certain."

"Thank you," Mason said.

She turned away, walked over to another filing drawer, jerked it open and started checking accounts.

Mason made a note of the three long-distance charges, noted also that Gibbs had only been in the hotel for approximately four hours.

The cashier came back, said, "Those charges are absolutely correct. There were three separate calls. One shortly after Mr. Gibbs checked in at five o'clock this evening; one after six o'clock, and one just a few minutes before he checked out. I remember now that I asked Mr. Gibbs when he checked out if there had been any recent calls, and he told me himself that there had been a Los Angeles call just a few minutes before which might not have cleared through to get on the bill."

"Yes," Mason said, "that call and the first call are quite all right, but that middle one, I think, is the result of an error."

"There isn't any error," the cashier said.

Mason smiled. "Well, in any event, I told you about it. I promised my friend I would."

"Good night," she said, trying to control her anger.

"Good night," Mason responded coldly.

Mason and Della Street crossed the lobby of the Arrapahoe Hotel.

"Get that number?" Mason asked.

"I got it and looked it up in the directory while you were talking with her."

"You can't look up a number like that," Mason said. "You . . ."

"I looked up The Villa Lavina numbers," Della Street said. "That number he called was the number of The Villa Lavina Number Three."

"Good work!" Mason said. "Now let's start thinking. He

150

telephoned about six o'clock, and then he telephoned just before he checked out. Let's put two and two together.''

"Well,'' Della Street said, "the last call was undoubtedly to report that he had run into a girl who was claiming she was Inez Kaylor and a man who was supposed to be a detective . . .''

"Don't be too sure,'' Mason said.

"Why?'' she asked. "What do you think the last call was about?''

"The last call,'' Mason said, "was probably to report that Della Street, Perry Mason's charming secretary, was in the apartment posing as Inez Kaylor, and that Perry Mason was there taking fingerprints.''

"But, Chief, he couldn't have . . . why, he didn't show any signs of recognition. He was completely flabbergasted when he opened the door and . . .''

"Sure he was flabbergasted,'' Mason said. "He hadn't expected to find anyone there, and then when he found us there he was doubly flabbergasted, but I thought I was smart. I gave you the cue to act as Inez Kaylor, and I took the part of a detective. For a moment he was sparring for time, trying to find out how he could manage to get what he wanted.''

"You mean how he was going to extricate himself?''

"Not that,'' Mason said. "All he had to do was to turn around and walk out. He knew it. If we had tried to hold him he could have telephoned for the police and had them ask us what we were doing there. No, Della, he wanted something and he got it. Then he telephoned Martha Lavina and told her that he had it and . . .''

"Well, it had to be that circular letter. I don't know what a letter about a magazine subscription or . . .''

"We'll go take a look,'' Mason said. "Whatever it was that he took away with him in his pocket was the thing that he went back there to get.''

"Won't he telephone the police and give them at least an anonymous tip?'' she asked.

"He may."

"And yet you're going back and look around."

"That's right. We have to. Come on."

"Chief, it's dangerous."

"We'll look carefully before we go in," Mason said. "After that we'll get in and get out fast, but I simply have to find out what happened. *Three* calls to Martha Lavina!"

"I can't figure *three* calls," Della Street said.

Mason, walking rapidly, said, "Well, let's try this explanation, Della. Gibbs gets here to Las Vegas. He phones to make certain the coast is clear and gets the go-ahead sign.

"So he goes to the Kaylor apartment, gets in and tears things up trying to find what he wants. He goes out and phones again and tells Martha Lavina that he's gone through the place with a fine-tooth comb and hasn't got what he was looking for.

"Or perhaps he tells her he does have everything she wanted, and she asks him about letters, and he tells her there are only three circular letters left on the desk and describes them to her, and she says, 'You damn fool, you can't leave one of those letters. Go back and get it.'

"So he goes back, finds us there, and puts on an act. Then he gets out, rushes to the hotel, telephones Martha a tip-off that we are in the apartment, and triumphantly tells her that he got the letter she sent him back to get, whisked it right out from under my nose. Then he checks out of the hotel."

"Could be," Della Street said dubiously, "only that's an awful fuss over a routine letter."

"Well, we'll go see," Mason said. "There were three letters there. The magazine subscription letter I have in my pocket with his thumbprint. The other two were from a real estate outfit and a model agency.

"Here we are, Della . . . I think you'd better keep out of this."

"No, no, Chief. If you go up there, I want to go."

Mason said, "No. Walk across the street. If anything

should happen and I should be escorted out of that apartment by the police you can go down and put up a cash bail. If I should be escorted out by anyone else, try and get the license number of the automobile and a good look at the people in the car, and *then go to the police at once*."

"I don't like to have you up there alone and . . ."

"You can help me more this way."

"Okay," Della Street said.

Mason looked up and down the street. This time he didn't pause to ring the bell of the apartment. He simply fitted his key to the front door and ran up the stairs. He unlocked the door of Inez Kaylor's apartment.

It was as he had left it.

Mason walked over to the desk, paused only long enough to look at the form letter which remained there. It was from the real estate company. The one from the model agency was nowhere in evidence.

Mason didn't even bother to switch out the lights, but stepped back into the corridor, jerked the door shut behind him, ran down the stairs and out into the street.

Della Street, her face showing great relief, came across to him. "Gosh, Chief," she said, "I was scared. I . . . Listen!"

They heard the sound of a siren. A police car whipped around the corner, slid to a stop in front of the apartment house.

Two men burst from the car, ran up the steps to the porch, rang the bell.

"That," Mason observed, as he took Della's arm and piloted her around the corner of the first side street he encountered, "is how close it was."

"A tip from Gibbs?" she asked.

"An anonymous tip," he agreed. "Gibbs only waited until he had safely checked out and then phoned the police that there were prowlers in the Kaylor apartment."

They turned another corner.

"What did he take?" she asked.

"The circular letter from the model agency. Do you remember the name?"

"Gosh, no, Chief! It was something about Aphrodite Models."

"I think we can locate it," Mason said. "We'll go to the Apache Hotel. Get a telephone directory and comb through it for the name Aphrodite. In the meantime, I'll call Paul Drake."

They walked rapidly, reached the Apache Hotel.

From a phone booth Mason called Paul Drake.

"Well, well, well," Drake said. "Congratulations, Perry. So it finally happened! Well, I'm certainly glad to hear of it."

"Don't count your chickens before the coop is built," Mason told him. "Della and I are here on business."

"That's what *you* think," Drake told him. "The whole town is buzzing with the news. You might just as well get married now."

"Don't be silly, Paul."

"What's silly about it?"

Mason pulled the door of the booth shut. "Give me the dope, Paul. Never mind the ribbing."

"I've got some bad news for you," Drake told him.

"What is it?"

"You're on the wrong track."

"What do you mean?"

"Your client is guilty. In any event the scheme you had to defend him has blown up into a million pieces."

"How come?"

"That purse?"

"What about it?"

"It's Martha Lavina's purse."

"What!" Mason exclaimed.

"That's right."

"Paul, it can't be!"

"It is. I got the buyer of one of the leather novelty companies out there. He knows the whole background. That purse is made in Pasadena by a man who makes a specialty of manufacturing leather novelty goods to individual order. It's a handmade purse. It isn't sold through jobbers or retailers but is handled direct on a custom-made basis.

"Just in order to check, I went over and talked with the manufacturer. He was a little angry because I had to get him away from dinner on Saturday night, but he's apparently an honest old coot with a good reputation, and there's no question about the thing at all. He recognized the photographs. Martha Lavina bought this purse. She buys her purses there. The proprietor won't talk much. Says his client's business is confidential, but that he remembers making this particular purse and Martha Lavina bought it.

"As you know, it's a distinctive type of purse, with a mirror in the flap that comes down over the purse, keeping it closed. It's . . ."

"And he knows Martha Lavina? There can't be any mistake?"

"None whatever," Drake said. "I showed him a photograph of Martha Lavina. He says she pays for the leather goods she buys there with her personal check. He knows her name. He's sold her stuff from time to time."

"Well, I'll be damned!" Mason said. "I certainly would have bet a lot of money that she wasn't in the car with him and . . . gosh, Paul, maybe she loaned someone her purse and . . ."

"Sure," Drake said, "she *could* have, but it jerks the rug out from under your feet as far as your defense is concerned."

Mason said, "Keep working on things. What do you find out about Archer's girl-friends?"

"He doesn't have any. He's a widower. Stays pretty much to himself. If some other woman had been in the car with him the night of the stick-up, Perry, there's no reason on earth why he shouldn't have admitted it. He can go around with any woman he wants to. He's a rich widower with no children.''

"Unless it happened to have been a married woman," Mason said, "whose husband might . . .''

"Sure, you always have that angle, but in that case it had to be a married woman who had Martha Lavina's purse. I tell you, Perry, you're barking up the wrong tree. I think Martha Lavina's embarrassment and her failure to account for details of the holdup was probably due to some factor that we don't as yet know, some other reason that she didn't dare to trust herself to describe the details.''

"All right," Mason said wearily, "keep working at that end, Paul.''

"Look, Perry, I'm going to give you some advice. Call the whole thing off. This thing is terribly expensive. We're running around in circles just looking for a trail, and . . .''

"Keep going one more day at least," Mason said. "I'm going to have to be in court Monday morning with . . .''

"You take my advice and forget it," Drake told him. "This case has some element they don't want you to find out about, but it doesn't have anything to do with that holdup. Your client, Albert Brogan, pulled that stick-up. He'd been prowling around for two or three months. And he murdered Daphne Howell.''

"He's my client," Mason said.

"You're the boss," Drake told him. "But I think we should drop it. He isn't a regular client. He was wished off on you.''

"That doesn't alter the fact he's a client. Stay with it.'' Mason hung up.

Della Street regarded him questioningly as he emerged from the booth.

He shook his head.

"What's the matter?''

"The rug," Mason said, "has just been jerked out from under me.''

156

"Chief, what happened?"

He told her.

Della Street became thoughtfully silent.

"So what do we do now?" Della Street asked.

"What did you find out about the Aphrodite Model Agency?"

"It isn't listed."

"Nothing by that name?"

"Nothing."

"I'm almost certain that was the name on that letter. It was some model agency and the name Aphrodite was in it. I can't remember the full name but Aphrodite was part of it."

"I know," she said, "but they're not listed."

Mason frowned. "Let's get a Los Angeles paper," he said. "Start looking through the want ads. We've got lots of time to kill before that train comes. There's a place here that features newspapers from all over the country, and we can pick up a Sunday *Examiner* and a Sunday *Times*. We'll go through the classified ad section and see what we can find."

They located a newsstand which had out-of-town newspapers. Mason purchased several and he and Della Street went to the lobby of the Sal Sagev Hotel near the railroad station and sat down to read through the papers.

"What do we look under?" Della Street asked.

"Help wanted—female, business opportunities, personal, miscellaneous and anything else you can think of. You take the *Times* and I'll take the *Examiner*."

Within ten minutes Della Street had a lead. "Here's something," she said, opening her purse, taking out a pair of small manicure scissors, carefully clipping an ad from the paper.

"What is it?" Mason asked.

She read it to him:

"Attractive young women between 21 and 29 who are free to travel, with a liking for adventure, may be able to secure employment as models for foreign-owned steamships, plane lines and others wishing authentic American models for photography. Applicants should generally be average but attractive in appearance. Not too fat, not too thin, not too tall, not too short. Features not too distinctive but running to type of average good-looking American girl. Aphrodite Model Agency. Box 6791X.

"Does that get us anywhere?" Della Street asked.

"I don't know," Mason said. "I'm inclined to think that it will." He looked through the paper he had, said, "Here's a similar ad in the *Examiner*."

"She'd evidently answered the ad," Della Street said, "and received a letter by way of answer."

"That letter was important enough," Mason said, "so that Martha Lavina sent Thomas Gibbs back to that apartment to get it."

"You think so?"

"I'm damned near certain of it," he told her. "And I certainly wish I knew why."

Chapter 13

A grim-faced Perry Mason held a conference in his office shortly after his return on Sunday morning.

Paul Drake said, "I'm sorry, Perry. I have the feeling that we've washed out on you, but I think it's because you're following a wrong trail. There isn't any question in my mind but what Martha Lavina was in that automobile with Rodney Archer at the time of the holdup. It's her purse. There's no question about it."

"What about Thomas Gibbs?" Mason asked.

Drake said, "Gibbs is a phony, that's a cinch. But I haven't been able to find out much more than that. My first hurried check shows that his address in San Diego—the one that you gave me on the phone as being on his automobile driving license—has no existence. Undoubtedly that's a driving license he keeps for emergencies like that. He probably has another one in his own name that he uses when he knows he's going to be checked up."

"I need him," Mason said. "I want to find him."

Drake said irritably, "Well, you had him in your hands. If you had only reached me on the phone I could have contacted my Las Vegas correspondent and had Gibbs followed from the minute he left the hotel."

"You couldn't have acted that fast," Mason said, "and I couldn't. I'm not blaming you, Paul. I'm blaming the breaks. They're all against me. What have you found out about that box at the *Examiner*?"

"Anything that comes in is simply put in a big envelope and held for a messenger. A man comes in once every few

159

days. He's the one who pays for the ad. No one seems to know anything about him except that he convinced the Want Ad Department that is was a genuine business opportunity for the right kind of girl.

"I think the Better Business Bureau looked into it. In any event, it's on the up-and-up. He gave them names of two girls who had done some work for a Mexican plane company and a couple of resort hotels at Acapulco. He also furnished the names of some girls who had been to Cuba. He has a high percentage of rejects but the girls that can make the grade and meet the specifications get good jobs. They don't last long, but they get to travel, with all their expenses paid, and draw a salary while they're doing it. That's a soft touch for some of these girls who are on the loose and looking for contacts. Incidentally, he has an ad in both of today's morning papers."

Mason said, "Della Street is putting in her application, and so will Mary Brogan. I think Mary might stand a better chance. Mary, it's important that you stay away from court tomorrow."

"Why?"

"Because people will see you and recognize you. The newspapers will make a play about the niece of Albert Brogan coming to his aid, and want photographs. I don't want anyone to see your photographs and so know who you are. If you get a lead from that Aphrodite Model Agency, I want you to go there and try your darndest to land a job. I want to find out what it is."

"We haven't time for very much investigation," Drake said.

"Are you telling me?" Mason groaned. "Paul, get a couple of female detectives to answer these Aphrodite ads. I'd like to get a tumble on at least one application."

"Okay. I've got some girls who can handle that kind of an assignment okay. Now, what are your plans for tomorrow? What else do you need from me?"

160

"I don't know," Mason said. "I'm going in and kick the ball all over the lot. I'm going to take advantage of every loophole, of every legal technicality and of every opportunity I can find. When you come right down to it, that's all an attorney *can* do. He simply has to watch the case develop and look for a weak link in the chain of evidence."

"Of course," Drake said, glancing at Mary Brogan, "it's all right if the man's innocent, but the evidence points pretty conclusively to his guilt, Perry."

"I know it," Mason said. "It does now, but what I'm concerned with is what the situation will be when we get done tomorrow."

"Well," Drake warned, "you have a hostile judge who is noted for being opposed to any generalized fishing tactics. He wants everything reduced to a matter of evidence and proof. He doesn't want surmises or conjectures. He wants things to go through his courtroom clicking like clockwork."

"I know," Mason said.

"So what can you do?" Drake asked, throwing out his hands in a gesture of dismissal.

"I can go fishing," Mason said.

"I tell you, Judge Egan won't stand for it."

"The hell he won't," Mason said. "I'll go fishing in spite of him. I'll keep within the limits of the law and I'll fish, and believe me, Paul, if I get a strike I'll sink the hook so hard and so fast and so savagely it will surprise everyone."

"*If* you get a strike," Drake said.

"What about the Kaylor girl?" Mason asked.

"There again you're way off," Drake told him. "I went to the hospital and looked at her. She's Inez Kaylor, the one who came from Las Vegas with me."

"How's her condition, Paul?"

"Okay. She's recovered consciousness and improving. I understand she's okay now. Her husband showed up with his own doctor. They fired Dr. Hanover."

"Her what?" Mason asked.

"Her husband. And he fired Dr. Hanover."

"How could they do that?"

"Oh, keep your shirt on, Perry. There were no hard feelings. Her husband had letters from her. They were effecting a reconciliation. He had his own doctor, a personal friend, fellow by the name of Doyle. The girl's mother showed up and there was a lot of bawling."

"Where is she now?"

"The Restway—a private sanitarium. Dr. Hanover gave her emergency treatment, then the husband and the mother showed up. Of course, Doc Hanover was in a vulnerable position because he hadn't been retained by the patient or by any relative. He said the Swede janitor had called him. The janitor denied it. When the relatives took over, Hanover didn't have a leg to stand on. He had to bow out. He tried to contact you, but no one knew where you were. You should have told me where I could reach you.

"Then this report came over the radio about you and Della dashing to Las Vegas. I tried every hotel and prominent motel, but couldn't find you registered anywhere."

"What's the status now?" Mason asked.

"Dr. Doyle won't let her have any visitors. I understand she'll be too shaky to be in court tomorrow, but you won't want her, Perry. She sold us out."

Mason gave the matter frowning concentration.

"Hang it, Paul, I don't like it. If anything happens to that girl . . ."

"Forget it," Drake said. "Dr. Doyle is an ethical doctor with a good reputation. The girl's mother is with her and so is her husband."

"Any proof that they're her mother and husband?" Mason asked.

"Gosh, Perry," Drake said, "snap out of it! Hell, it's just a routine case. The gal took a swig of sleeping tablets. Mary Brogan here saw her take them."

162

"Then who was the girl who was taken in the ambulance?" Mason asked.

"Now there you've got me," Drake admitted. "It was probably some drunk who was staggering around the hall. I've found this out, the men from the ambulance never got up as far as the third floor. The girl they picked up was in the elevator."

"And what became of her?" Mason asked.

Drake shrugged his shoulders. "Have a heart, Perry. I only got on the job yesterday. Probably when the ambulance attendants found out they'd been duped by a drunk they let her out. Hell, I don't know, and the police don't know, but the police aren't too much interested.

"They're keeping an eye on Dr. Doyle's patient, I know that much."

"Where did you say she was, Paul?"

"She's at the Restway Sanitarium. That's a high-class place."

"And she's conscious?"

"Oh yes. I've got a line on the place. One of the nurses is a friend of one of my office girls. The kid's coming along okay, but is nervous. She doesn't want to be a witness for some reason or other.

"That's why she tried to black out. But there's no doubt about her, Perry. I tell you I *saw* the girl. She's Inez Kaylor."

Mason said, "Hang it, Paul, I still think there were two girls."

"Could be," Drake said, "but the one who's recovering from the pills is the real Inez. Her relatives identify her and so do I. And she's the one my man served the subpoena on. You've got nothing to worry about there.

"But you can't put her on the stand . . . not as *your* witness. She's sold us out."

Mason said, "Paul, put some shadows on that Restway Sanitarium. Be sure that girl doesn't leave there without being shadowed. Look up all you can find on Dr. Doyle."

Drake's expression showed how thoroughly he disagreed with the lawyer.

"Okay, if you say so. It's your case, Perry, and it's your money."

Chapter 14

From the moment when court convened at ten o'clock on Monday morning the effect of week-end developments became apparent.

The tight-lipped granite-hard hostility on the faces of the jurors showed that enough of them had read the newspaper accounts of the identification of Albert Brogan as the Daphne Howell murderer to communicate knowledge to the other jurors.

No longer was there any indication of open-minded tolerance. These jurors had their faces cast in the grim lines of executioners.

Mason caught the attention of the Court, arose and said, "Your Honor, I have a motion which I would like to make in the absence of the jury."

Judge Egan frowned, hesitated perceptibly, then said, "Very well. The jurors will be excused while a motion is made by counsel for the defense. The motion will be directed to a matter of law which has nothing to do with the deliberations of the jury. Therefore, the jury will remove themselves from the courtroom until they are called by the bailiff, during which time the jurors will remember the admonition of the Court in regard to conversing about the case, discussing it or permitting anyone to discuss it in their presence."

Judge Egan nodded. The jurors filed out.

When they had left the courtroom, Mason said, "If the Court please . . ."

"The Court is quite aware of what you have in mind, Mr.

165

Mason," Judge Egan said. "Please make the motion as brief as possible."

"I call Your Honor's attention," Mason said, "to the articles in the local press to the effect that the defendant in this case had been identified as the murderer of Daphne Howell."

"What about it?" Judge Egan asked coldly.

"Those articles certainly have a tendency to prejudice the jurors against the defendant in this case."

"How do you know they do?"

"It follows as a logical sequence, Your Honor."

"It might if you could prove that the jurors had read the article."

"You couldn't do that without asking them," Mason said, "and by asking them you would call their attention to the article and emphasize it—something, of course, which the defendant does not care to do."

"All right, what's your motion?"

"I move that the jury be dismissed, that this be declared a mistrial and that another jury be impaneled to try the defendant in this case, a jury which, under the circumstances, can be kept sequestered during the course of the trial."

Harry Fritch, the deputy D.A., leapt to his feet, said, "Just a moment, Your Honor."

Judge Egan motioned him to silence, said to Perry Mason, "Do you have any proof any member of the jury has read these articles you mention?"

"No proof, Your Honor, but they have been given wide dissemination in the press. I feel that if the Court would interrogate the jurors as to whether they had read the current newspapers there would be at least nine answers in the affirmative. We don't want that interrogation, but I venture that you'd get nine affirmative answers."

"The jury was instructed not to read any news which might have a bearing on this case," Judge Egan said.

"And naturally, not being mind readers, they'd have to

166

read articles in order to see whether or not they had a bearing on this case.''

"Not necessarily," Judge Egan said. "I cannot indulge in the presumption the jurors failed to heed the admonition of the Court.''

"May I say a word?" Harry Fritch asked.

"Not now," Judge Egan said. "I'm denying the motion. Now then, did you want to say anything, Mr. Deputy District Attorney?''

Fritch grinned and said, "Not under the circumstances, Your Honor.''

"Very well," Judge Egan said, "then the Court will say something to you, Mr. Deputy District Attorney. I don't know just how it happened this information was released to the press, but I do feel certain it wouldn't have been released and couldn't have been released if your office had taken the proper precautions. This Court wasn't born yesterday, and the Court practiced law for a long time before going on the bench. I feel that the release of this publicity was premature to say the least. I think it was unwise. I also think it was deliberate. It has brought up a point in this case which may find its way into the Appellate Tribunal. There is no reason on earth why that story couldn't have been held for release until after this case was terminated.''

"But, Your Honor," Harry Fritch protested, "we can't control news. Newspaper reporters have ways of getting news . . . ''

"Most of which are through tips coming from the county officers," Judge Egan interrupted. "If you had wanted to keep this matter out of the newspapers until tomorrow, the Court doesn't have the slightest doubt but what you could have done so. When I say 'you' I am, of course, referring to your office. Now, that's all. The motion is denied. Call the jury.''

Judge Egan glowered at Fritch and at Mason in turn, then

rapped his gavel in a peremptory gesture indicating that as far as he was concerned the subject was closed.

The bailiff called the jurors, who filed back into their seats in the jury box.

"Proceed!" Judge Egan snapped.

Mason arose and addressed the Court. "If the Court please," he said, "the defense would like to make absolutely certain that the witnesses understand they are under the rule and that no person who is to be a witness in this case is to remain in the courtroom."

Fritch said affably, "How about the witnesses who have already testified, Mr. Mason?"

"If you have absolute assurance that those witnesses are not going to be recalled to the stand under any circumstances, I have no objection, but if the witnesses remain in court I don't want them again called to the witness stand."

Fritch shrugged his shoulders. "Usually it's stipulated that after a witness has testified he may remain."

"There is no such stipulation in this case," Mason said. "I want the witnesses under the rule."

"Very well," Judge Egan ruled. "All persons who are going to be called as witnesses in this case are to be excluded from the courtroom. Now Mrs. Lavina was on the stand undergoing cross-examination when we adjourned on Friday."

"If the Court please," Harry Fritch said, "one matter was brought up on the cross-examination of Mrs. Lavina which I think might be confusing to the jury, and I think perhaps it might be confusing to Counsel. I would like to have the matter straightened out before we go further.

"I therefore ask the Court's permission to return Rodney Archer to the stand for just a few questions in order to get this one point straightened out. I ask the indulgence of Counsel. I feel that it will greatly facilitate trying the issues in the case, and will be of considerable assistance to the jury."

And Fritch made a little bow to the jurors as though to

168

indicate to them that he as least had their interests at heart and was anxious only to see that they had complete understanding of the facts in the case.

Judge Egan looked down at Perry Mason. "I think under the circumstances," he said, "I will be guided somewhat by Mr. Mason's position in the matter."

"No objection at all," Mason said. "We, too, would like to have the facts cleared up as we go along."

"Very well," Judge Egan ruled. "Mr. Archer will be returned to the witness stand, and you will remember, Mrs. Lavina, that as a witness you are under the rule. You are not to hear the testimony of Mr. Archer. You will retire to the witness room until the bailiff summons you, at which time, you may return."

Martha Lavina rose, smiled, said, "Certainly, Your Honor," and walked out of the courtroom, conscious of the fact that every masculine eye was watching her with the speculative appraisal that the predatory male reserves for a woman who he feels would be broad-minded enough to accept advances, and who is attractive enough to make them desirable.

A few moments later Rodney Archer, seething with suppressed indignation, entered the courtroom.

Archer's obviously expensive double-breasted suit had been so artfully designed that when he stood erect the coat hung in a perfect straight line. It was only when he sat down in the witness chair that the arms of the chair, pushing up on the sides of his coat, disclosed the padding and indicated the extent to which his paunchy figure had been subjected to the landscape gardening of an expensive tailor.

Apparently recognizing that fact, Archer tried to press his elbows to his sides and bring them within the line of the arms of the chair. Finding that this was too cramped to be comfortable, he brought his elbows out, rested them for a moment on the chair, then compromised by sitting partially sideways, raising one elbow to the arm of the chair, keeping the other one down by his side.

169

Fritch said, "Mr. Archer, I am going to ask you to recall the circumstances of the holdup."

"Yes, sir."

"Can you describe to the jurors *exactly* what you were doing at the time the door was jerked open and the holdup man pushed a gun into your face?"

"Yes, sir."

"Please tell the Court and the jury just what you were doing."

"I had just lit a cigarette," Archer said. "I was in the process of lighting that cigarette. I had pressed the electric lighter in the dashboard, and as soon as it popped out I had raised the lighter to the cigarette. It was at that moment that the defendant jerked open the door and ordered me to 'stick 'em up.' I raised both hands and the hot lighter fell from my hand."

"What happened to it then?"

"I don't know. I presume that it struck on the seat and burned the round hole in the upholstery which is shown in the photograph of the car."

"You are now referring to People's Exhibit Number Five," Fritch said, taking an 8 x 10 photograph from the pile and handing it to the witness.

"That's right, yes, sir."

"And later on did you have occasion to find that cigarette lighter and return it to the dashboard of the automobile?"

"I did. Yes, sir. I found the lighter on the floor of the car just before the police arrived. I picked it up and put it back in its proper place in the dash."

"Thank you," Fritch said, and then said to Judge Egan, "I simply wanted to get that matter cleared up in view of the possibility of a misunderstanding."

"You will reserve comments on the testimony of the witness until the time for arguing the case," Judge Egan said, quite plainly annoyed at the patness of the glib explanation which had the effect of rescuing Martha Lavina from the spot into which Mason's cross-examination of Friday afternoon had jockeyed her.

Archer got up to leave the stand.

"Just a moment," Mason said. "I have a few questions on cross-examination."

"Certainly," Fritch said, as though eager to grant defense counsel every concession.

Mason said sarcastically, "Thank you very much for permitting me to cross-examine a witness."

Fritch colored and Judge Egan banged his gavel. "Counsel will refrain from personalities," he said, but the tone of his voice indicated that he felt Fritch probably had this coming to him.

Mason turned to face Archer.

"You discussed this matter with someone over the weekend?" Mason asked.

Archer's glibness showed that this question had been anticipated and the answer carefully rehearsed.

"Mr. Fritch asked me to tell him exactly what had happened during the time of the holdup, and I described the matter to him."

"How did it happen you didn't tell us about this when you were on the witness stand Friday morning?" Mason asked.

"No one asked me."

"Perhaps I could refresh your recollection on that," Mason said. "Isn't it a fact that Mr. Fritch asked you to describe what happened when you stopped your car at the intersection?"

"Yes, sir."

"And didn't you then go on to describe . . . ?"

"Just a moment, Your Honor," Fritch said, jumping to his feet. "I object to any attempt to impeach the witness by this type of questioning. If Mr. Mason wishes to impeach the witness by calling his attention to the record, then he must produce the record and confront the witness with specific testimony and give the witness an opportunity to explain it.''

Fritch stood courteously awaiting the judge's ruling.

Mason, smiling affably, said, "And just in order to show Counsel that I have anticipated the situation, I have in my pocket the exact question and answer which has been transcribed by the court reporter and . . ."

"Your Honor, I object to Counsel's intimation that he anticipated that this situation would arise," Fritch said.

"Counsel will withhold comments until the case is argued to the jury," Judge Egan said. "Reframe your question, Mr. Mason."

Mason said, "Weren't you asked, Mr. Archer, here in court last Friday morning to describe what happened as you approached the intersection, and didn't you answer as follows:

"I slowed the car for the intersection and stopped. I was talking to the companion who sat on my right and for a moment did not notice the left-hand door. I had my eyes on the signal, however, waiting for it to change from red to green, and at that moment the door on the left was violently jerked open. I turned in order to see what had happened and found myself looking into a gun held in the hands of the defendant. The defendant ordered me to elevate my hands, which I promptly did. He immediately reached in my inside pocket, jerked out my wallet, grabbed a diamond stickpin from my tie, reached across my legs to grab the purse of the companion on my right, jumped back and kicked the door closed. He did it so rapidly that I hardly had an opportunity to know what was going on before it was all over.

"Question. Then what happened.

"Answer. I saw the defendant very distinctly running across the road to where he had a car parked at the curb.

This car was headed in the opposite direction, the lights were on, and apparently the motor had been left running because the defendant jumped in the car, slammed the car door and almost immediately took off at high speed.

"Question. Did you have an opportunity to notice the car that the defendant was driving?

"Answer. I did. It was a rather late model light-colored Chevrolet, and the right front fender had been crumpled somewhat."

Mason put down the paper. "Were you asked those questions and did you so testify?"

"Yes."

"Why didn't you tell us about the episode of lighting the cigarette?"

"I can only repeat that no one asked me."

"Weren't you asked to tell what happened as you approached the intersection?"

"Yes, sir."

"And did you understand that question?"

"I understood that question," the witness said glibly, "as calling for a statement as to what happened in connection with the holdup. I didn't think that it required me to state everything that I had done with my hands, every motion I had made, everything I had done. For instance, when I stopped the car, I put my foot on the brake and held it there, waiting for the signal to change. I had a hydromatic drive and did not need to shift gears. I neglected to mention putting my foot on the brake. I had assumed that it was not important, just as I had assumed that lighting the cigarette was not important."

Archer spoke with such assurance that it was quite plain he had carefully rehearsed his position in the matter.

"Now then," Mason said, "I am referring to the photograph, People's Exhibit Number Five, which you have identified."

"Yes, sir."

"This shows a round hole in the upholstery."

"Yes, sir."

"Do you know when that picture was taken?"

"I do not know, sir. It was taken by the police, but I don't know when."

"You surrendered the automobile to the police?"

"Yes, sir. They suggested that they should go over it for fingerprints, to see if they could find the fingerprints of the holdup man on the door of the car."

"When did you surrender the car to the police?"

"The morning after the holdup."

"When did you get it back?"

"The following evening."

"And you know that this hole had already been burned in the upholstery when you delivered the car to the police?"

"Yes, sir."

"Do you know *when* the hole was burned in the upholstery?"

"At the time of the holdup."

"And not before?"

"Certainly not."

"You're certain of that?"

"Definitely."

"When you took out your cigarette case, did you offer your companion one?"

"You mean Mrs. Lavina?"

"I mean your companion."

"That was Mrs. Lavina."

"Did you offer a cigarette?"

"I . . . I don't remember."

"It would have been the natural thing to have done, would it not?"

"Yes, definitely."

"She smokes?"

"Oh, yes."

"Then shall we say that your best recollection is that you offered her a cigarette?"

"Yes."

"And she took one?"

"Yes."

"Then," Mason said, extending an accusing forefinger, "you are mistaken about the cigarette lighter. You would have been holding it to *her* cigarette first."

"No . . . yes . . . come to think of it, I *am* mistaken. I did not offer her a cigarette. I had done that earlier in the evening and she had refused mine. I smoke Chesterfields. She prefers Luckies. She had her own cigarette case with her. She used her own cigarettes."

"But you did always light her cigarette?"

"No. Her case has a built-in lighter. She always uses that."

"Did you notice that case yourself, or did someone tell you about it?"

"I noticed it myself."

"That evening?"

"Yes."

"How many times?"

"Several."

"Half a dozen?"

"At least that."

"A dozen?"

"Possibly, I didn't count every cigarette she lit. At that time I didn't realize I was to be called on to tell every time she opened her purse to take out a cigarette."

"At least half a dozen?"

"I believe so, yes."

"You have stated that you noticed every detail of the defendant's face."

"Yes."

"Every detail?"

"Certainly. I was looking at the defendant."

"Right in the face?"

"Yes."

"For how long?"

"During the entire holdup, Mr. Mason."

"Which you state was executed very quickly."

"Yes, sir."

"How long did it take?"

"Only a matter of seconds."

"Thirty seconds?"

"No, not that long."

"Twenty seconds."

"No, a very few seconds."

"How many?"

"I would say perhaps five to ten seconds."

"Not more than ten seconds?"

"No."

"And you were looking at the defendant's face all during that time?"

"Yes, sir. That's the reason I didn't see what happened to the cigarette lighter, that it was burning a hole in the upholstery."

"The defendant reached into your inside coat pocket and pulled out your wallet?"

"Yes, sir."

"And put that in his pocket?"

"Yes, sir."

"Then he jerked your diamond pin from your tie?"

"Yes, sir."

"Then he reached across your lap and took the purse of your companion?"

"Mrs. Lavina—her purse."

"Exactly," Mason said. "Now, *you* carried your wallet in the right-hand inside breast pocket of your coat?"

"Yes, sir."

"That coat was open?"

"No, sir. It was buttoned. I habitually wear it buttoned."

"So in order to get that wallet the defendant had to reach through the opening in the coat at the top of the coat?"

"Yes, sir."

"And in order to do that, he must have lunged forward so that the top of his head was almost even with your jaw?"

"Yes, sir. He did."

"He was holding the gun in which hand? His left hand or his right hand?"

"I . . . let me think . . . in his right hand."

"So that the gun was then prodding against your left side and his left hand moved across your chest to bring out the wallet from your pocket?"

"Yes, sir."

"And when did he make this grab for the wallet?"

"Just as soon as he opened the door."

"Before he said 'Stick 'em up'?"

"No, just as he was saying, 'Stick 'em up.' "

"You raised your hands automatically as soon as he said, 'Stick 'em up'?"

"That's right."

"And the defendant was lunging for this wallet as soon as you had your hands raised?"

"I think even before."

"You elevated your hands promptly?"

"Yes, sir."

"How soon?"

"Immediately."

"Can you show the jury how quickly you put your hands up?"

The witness shot his hands up in the air with considerable alacrity.

"All right," Mason said, "while the defendant was taking your wallet from your pocket, if he was using his left hand he was reaching across your body, and all you could see was the top of his head. He had his hair pushed right up against your jaw. He would have had to have been in that position in order to have done what you claimed he did.''

''Well, I . . . yes, sir, that's right.''

''And while he was jerking the tiepin from your tie, he still had the gun in his right hand?''

''Yes, sir.''

''And was grabbing the tiepin with his left hand?''

''Yes, sir. He gave it a terrific jerk and tore it right out of the fabric of the cravat, a twenty-five-dollar hand-painted creation.''

''And while he was reaching across your lap to get the purse of the woman who was riding on your right . . . ?''

''Mrs. Lavina,'' the witness interrupted.

''Exactly,'' Mason said dryly. ''While he was reaching across to get the purse of Mrs. Lavina, all you could see was the back of his head. He *was* reaching across your lap at that time, was he not?''

''Yes, sir.''

''Now how long did it take him to get the purse, to reach across your lap and get the purse?''

''Oh, a matter not exceeding two seconds.''

''And you're certain of that?''

''Well, perhaps three seconds . . . let's say four seconds at the outside. I'll put it that way. From two to four seconds, Mr. Mason.''

''Now, your tiepin was anchored in your tie by some sort of a guard so as to protect it against loss?''

''Yes, sir.''

''And the defendant reached up and grabbed that tiepin and jerked it out?''

''Yes, sir.''

''Did it come readily?''

''The way he grabbed it, it did. He jerked the fabric right out.''

''And how long did that take?''

178

"I'll say the same thing—from two to four seconds."

"All right. Now, the defendant reached across and took the wallet out of your pocket. How long did that take?"

"I'll say the same thing—from two to four seconds."

"Then the defendant stepped back and slammed the door shut?"

"Yes, sir."

"Still holding the gun?"

"Yes, sir."

"Still in his right hand?"

"Yes, sir."

"How long did the closing of the door take?"

"Not more than two seconds. I'll say from one to two seconds."

"Then you weren't looking at the defendant's face *all* of the time during the holdup, were you?"

"Well, I . . . well, no, not every second of the time."

"You could only see the back of his head while he was reaching across your lap. You could only see the top of his head while he was reaching for your wallet. You could only see the top of his head while he was jerking out the tiepin, and you couldn't see his face while he was stepping back and slamming the door shut with his left hand. And you didn't see his face until after you heard him say, 'Stick 'em up,' because you testified that you were watching the traffic signal."

The witness squirmed uneasily.

"So," Mason said, "you only had a very brief glimpse of his face, not to exceed probably one second."

"I didn't say that."

"Figure up your time schedule for yourself," Mason said. "It took from two to four seconds for each of the operations you have described. You have stated that the entire holdup couldn't possibly have taken more than ten seconds, that it might have been completed in five, that there wasn't even time for the traffic signal to change while the holdup was in

179

progress. Now then, just turn to the jury, Mr. Archer, and tell them how long, in terms of seconds, you were studying every detail of the defendant's face.''

"Well, I . . .'' There was silence.

"Go ahead,'' Mason said.

"I can't answer that question.''

"Not much more than one second, was it?''

"Well, I . . . it all happened so fast, Mr. Mason, it's hard to determine.''

"Exactly,'' Mason said. "You had a fleeting, blurred glimpse of the face of some man who was holding you up. *Since* the holdup you have convinced yourself that it was the defendant.''

"That is not true at all. I recognized the defendant.''

"All right,'' Mason said. "Now let's go back to the night of the crime. You were holding the lighted cigarette lighter in your hand.''

"Yes, sir.''

"You were holding it up to the end of the cigarette?''

"Yes, sir.''

"Watching the traffic signal and at the same time guiding the red-hot cigarette lighter toward the tip of the cigarette?''

"I guess so, yes.''

"That's fine,'' Mason said. "Then were your eyes fastened on the red light of the signal or on the cigarette lighter?''

"On both—mainly on the lighted traffic signal.''

"That is a brilliant red light?''

"Fairly so. Yes, sir.''

"And you were also looking at the cigarette lighter which you held in your hand?''

"Yes, sir.''

"And directly beneath the traffic light there was a very brilliant neon sign advertising the drugstore across the street, was there not?''

"I . . . I believe so, yes, sir.''

"So your eyes were accustomed to rather brilliant light?"

"I assume that is the case."

"And the defendant was standing down on the street where it was relatively dark?"

"Well . . . yes, sir."

"And you saw him for not to exceed one second. That's the only time you ever saw his face?"

"I . . . well, have it your own way."

"You saw his face for one fleeting second," Mason said, emphasizing his words with repeated jabs of his pointed forefinger, "while that face was in the dark and after your eyes had been somewhat dazzled by looking at the bright lights of a neon sign, the red light of a traffic signal and the glowing end of a cigarette lighter?"

Archer shrugged his shoulders. "I guess so, if you say so."

"Don't guess, and don't let me or anyone else testify for you," Mason said. "Is that or is it not a fact?"

"Very well. It's a fact."

Archer's coat seemed suddenly to be much bigger than when he had settled himself on the witness stand with the arrogance of complete assurance.

"You say the defendant's car had a crumpled *right* fender?"

"Yes, sir."

"You were headed south?"

"Yes, sir."

"And the defendant's car was headed north?"

"Yes, sir."

"Parked across the street?"

"Yes, sir."

"At the opposite curb?"

"Yes, sir."

"And could you see the crumpled right fender through the hood of the car?"

"No, sir. I definitely saw the crumpled right front fender

after the defendant jumped in his car and pulled away from the curb. As he turned his car he swung it sharply to the left. I was looking at it to see if there were any distinguishing marks and I distinctly saw the crumpled right front fender. It was only a glimpse, but it was enough. I saw it."

"Have you seen that same car since then?"

"Yes, sir. I saw it at police headquarters yesterday."

"And identified it?"

"Yes, sir. It was the same car."

"But you didn't tell the police about that crumpled right fender the night of the holdup?"

"No, sir, not that night. I was excited. I believe I mentioned it the next day, however."

"That's all!" Mason said.

Harry Fritch said suavely, "I have one question and only one question on redirect examination, Mr. Archer. Regardless of the time in seconds, as I understand your testimony, you did see the defendant long enough to recognize him. Is that right?"

"Just a moment," Mason said. "I object to that question, Your Honor. It's leading and suggestive."

"Objection is sustained."

Fritch smiled triumphantly. "Who was the man who held you up?"

"The defendant."

"That's all," Fritch said.

Judge Egan frowned at Fritch. "The vice of a leading question," he warned, "consists in asking it. I think Counsel understands that as well as I do."

"I beg Your Honor's pardon," Fritch said. "I was merely trying to save time."

"Any further questions on cross-examination?" Judge Egan asked Mason.

"None, Your Honor," Mason said.

Archer left the stand.

"Now then," Judge Egan said, "Mrs. Lavina was being

cross-examined on Friday. Mr. Bailiff, call Mrs. Lavina back to the witness stand, and the defendant's cross-examination of the witness will continue.''

Martha Lavina re-entered the courtroom, walked to the witness chair, glanced at Judge Egan with just the trace of an arch smile, then threw a sidelong glance toward the jury box which seemed to include the jurors in the cosy intimacy of joint understanding.

Mason pushed back his chair from the counsel table, arose to his feet and walked around to the other end of the table to confront the witness.

"Since you were last on the stand, Mrs. Lavina," he said, "you have talked with Rodney Archer?"

"I have not talked with Mr. Archer," she said, smiling. "I realized that the witnesses were not supposed to discuss their testimony, and I have adhered strictly to the spirit as well as the letter of the Court's admonition."

"You have, however, discussed the case with Mr. Harry Fritch?"

"Mr. Fritch and I discussed certain aspects of my testimony."

"He asked you what you were going to testify to?"

"He asked me certain questions and I answered those questions."

"They related to your testimony?"

"They related to events."

"Oh, Your Honor," Harry Fritch said with easy affability, "I will readily admit that *I* talked with this witness. I am not a mind reader. I have to know what the testimony in a case is going to be in order to prepare my case."

"Mr. Mason is questioning the witness," Judge Egan said. "Do you wish to object?"

"Certainly not."

"Then sit down."

Fritch slowly resumed his seat.

Mason said, "Now, I would like to know a few details about the holdup, Mrs. Lavina."

"Yes, Mr. Mason."

"How long had you been with Mr. Archer that evening?"

"About an hour and a half. I had had dinner with Mr. Archer."

"Where?"

"At The Golden Lion."

"What did you eat? Do you remember?"

"It is some time ago, Mr. Mason, but as it happens I do remember. I had French fried prawns on the dinner. I remembered discussing the dish with Mr. Archer."

"And after you left the restaurant, do you remember what route you took to get to the scene of the holdup?"

"Certainly. We went down Harvey Boulevard to Murray Road, down Murray Road to Crestwell Boulevard, and along that to the scene of the holdup."

"Can you describe the holdup again?"

"Oh, Your Honor," Fritch said. "That's already been asked and answered. After all, a cross-examination should not be interminable."

"Objection overruled."

Martha Lavina smiled. "We stopped for a traffic signal. The signal went red just as we were pulling up to the intersection. Mr. Archer started to light a cigarette. Suddenly the door on the left-hand side of the automobile was jerked open. I saw the defendant standing there with a gun. He ordered Mr. Archer to put up his hands."

"Mr. Archer was on the point of lighting his cigarette at the time?" Mason asked.

"As to that I am not *entirely* certain, Mr. Mason. I am inclined to think that he was. I am forced to admit that I became somewhat excited."

"What did the defendant do?"

"He reached in and jerked the wallet out of Mr. Archer's inner pocket. He ripped loose a diamond tiepin, and he

184

grabbed my purse. Then he closed the door and sprinted back to his car and drove away.''

"Did you get a good look at the car?''

"Yes. But I can't be of much help in identifying that car, Mr. Mason. I am a woman, and I don't notice such things. I am not mechanically minded.''

"What was in your purse?'' Mason asked.

"About one hundred and twenty-five dollars in cash.''

"What else?'' Mason asked.

"Beside the money there were the usual things that a woman carries in her purse. Keys, lipstick, a small coin purse for loose change, a compact, a notebook and I suppose some odds and ends.''

"Now you have identified this purse,'' Mason said, picking up the purse which had been introduced in evidence, "as being your purse.''

"That's right.''

"The one you had with you that night?''

"That is quite correct, Mr. Mason.''

"When did you next see that purse after it was taken from you?''

"When the police showed it to me.''

"And when was that?''

"That was after I had identified the defendant in the line-up.''

"They showed you this purse and it was then in its present condition?''

"That is right. You will notice that the purse has a flap which folds down over the front which contains a mirror, so that in opening the purse the flap is folded back and discloses a mirror for emergency make-up.''

"Did you design that purse?''

"I didn't design it. It was manufactured to my specifications.''

"Your purses are all the same?''

"That is right.''

"How many of them are there?"

"I have several, of different designs. One black calf, one tan, one red alligator, one patent leather."

"You had these purses manufactured especially for you?"

"Does that make any difference?"

"I am simply trying to help you fix your identification."

"I don't think you're trying to *help* me, Mr. Mason," she said, smiling coldly. "I think you're trying to confuse me."

"I am trying to get at the facts," Mason insisted.

"I am quite certain that is my purse, Mr. Mason. If necessary, I can show you where I purchased it."

"And you never saw that purse from the time it left your possession at the time of the holdup until the police showed it to you?"

"That's right."

"Did you ever recover any of the contents of the purse?"

"No."

"That is rather a heavy mirror on the front flap of the purse?"

"It is a substantial mirror. I am somewhat superstitious. It is considered bad luck to break a mirror. I have, therefore, requested the manufacturer to insert a very heavy mirror on all of my purses. The mirror is backed with a thin plate of steel and is composed of heavy glass."

"Such as is the mirror on this purse?"

"That is correct," she said, "and the same is true of the mirror on the purse I am now carrying."

"And the contents of the purse on that night were about the same as the contents of the purse you are now carrying?"

"Generally the same, yes."

She snapped the catch on the purse, opened it, looked inside, then quite casually closed it.

"Do you smoke, Mrs. Lavina?"

"Yes."

"Do you have one particular brand of cigarettes to which you are very much attached?"

"I prefer Luckies."

"Do you know whether Mr. Archer smokes?"

"Certainly I do."

"Does he smoke?"

"Yes."

"Do you know his brand?"

"I . . . I am not certain."

Mason said, "I don't want to take any unfair advantage of you, Mrs. Lavina, but I asked Mr. Archer and he stated that while you smoked Luckies he smoked Chesterfields. Would you say that was correct?"

"I'm not entirely certain in my mind as to the brand Mr. Archer smokes. If he said that he smoked Chesterfields I certainly would assume that he knew."

"You had smoked on the evening you were out with Mr. Archer?"

"Naturally."

"You had had a cigarette before dinner?"

"Yes."

"One during dinner?"

"Yes."

"One after dinner?"

"Yes."

"Were you smoking at the time of the holdup?"

"I . . . I can't remember . . . I think not."

"However, you had smoked after dinner?"

"Yes."

"While you were in the automobile?"

"I believe so, yes."

"And since you preferred Luckies you used your own cig-arcttcs?"

"Yes."

"May I see them?"

"Oh," Fritch said, "I think this inquiry is going far afield. I think this cross-examination is getting out of hand, Your Honor."

"Are you objecting to the question?" Judge Egan asked.

"I object to it on the ground that it's not proper cross-examination, that it's incompetent, irrelevant and immaterial, that it does not cover any point on which the witness was examined in direct examination."

"I think, Your Honor, I can connect this matter up in a very few moments," Mason said.

"Objection is overruled," Judge Egan said.

"You carry cigarettes in your purse now?"

"Certainly."

"May I see them?"

She hesitated a moment, then, with considerable anger, threw up the flap of the purse, opened the purse and reached inside.

Mason moved up toward the witness chair. The witness abruptly swung around so that her back was to Mason, and then a moment later produced a silver cigarette case and handed it to him.

Mason snapped open the cigarette case, said, "This cigarette case is a silver cigarette case with a built-in lighter, containing Lucky Strike cigarettes. It has the initials 'M.L.' entwined in an oval on the front of the case."

Mason held the cigarette case so the jury could see it, turned to Mrs. Lavina and said, "You have had this cigarette case for some time? Apparently it is well worn. In fact, I notice there has been enough wear so that the engraved initials have become partially obliterated."

"I have had it for many years. It is a very treasured possession. It was given to me by a friend."

"It is with you constantly?"

"Yes."

"Then can you tell the jury," Mason said conversationally, "how it happens that if this cigarette case was in your purse on the night of the holdup and your purse was taken from you and you have never recovered any of the contents, this same cigarette case is now in your purse today?"

188

And Mason turned away from the witness, walked back to the counsel table and sat down.

Martha Lavina, on the witness stand, held the cigarette case in her hand. Her face might have been carved from plaster.

"Well," Mason said after a period of silence, "can you answer that question?"

"I didn't have this cigarette case with me on the night of the holdup. I didn't tell you that I did, Mr. Mason."

"You said that your purse contained knickknacks and cigarettes and . . ."

"Exactly," she said triumphantly. "I had forgotten to put my cigarette case in my purse. I remember about that now. I missed it as soon as I left my apartment, so I stopped and purchased a package of Lucky Strike cigarettes and a book of matches. I had them in my purse that night. I did not have the cigarette case in the purse."

Mason said, "Then when Mr. Archer stated positively that you had taken cigarettes from your silver cigarette case with the built-in lighter on that night, he is mistaken?"

She suddenly had the appearance of a trapped animal.

"Was he?" Mason asked.

"Oh, Your Honor," Fritch said, "I object to that question as argumentative."

"Sustained," Judge Egan said.

"You are now absolutely positive that you didn't have that cigarette case with you that night?"

"Positive," she said.

"And that you did have a package of Lucky Strike cigarettes which were not in a case, and that you lit those cigarettes with paper matches from a folding match container?"

Again there was a long period of silence.

"Can you answer that question?" Mason said.

"Yes . . . I am trying to recall certain matters."

"You were quite glib with your answer about it a minute ago," Mason said. "Has the intimation that Archer has testified about your cigarette case with the built-in lighter caused this hesitancy, Mrs. Lavina?"

"No," she snapped.

"You stated positively that you had remembered purchasing a package of Lucky Strike cigarettes and lighting them with paper matches from a book. Now is that correct, or wasn't it?"

"I . . . I think so . . . yes."

"Do you know?"

"Yes."

"You're positive?"

"Yes."

"Absolutely certain?"

"Yes."

"Just as certain as you are of any other testimony you have given?"

"Yes," she snapped.

"Just as certain that that is the case as that it was the defendant who held you up?"

"Yes."

"So if it should turn out you were mistaken in regard to the cigarettes, you might well be mistaken in regard to the identification of the defendant?"

"That question is argumentative," Fritch objected.

"I am merely calling on the witness to test her own recollection. She can best give us the standard by which we can test that accuracy."

"The objection is overruled," Egan said. "The witness will answer the question."

"Yes!" she snapped.

"Now there's no possibility of a mistake about this," Mason said, "if there should be any testimony in this case that you had on that night a silver cigarette case with you, that testimony would be erroneous. Is that right?"

"Well, of course, Mr. Mason," she said, "you were talking about one particular cigarette case."

"You may have thought I was," Mason said, "but I am now talking about any cigarette case. Is it true that if any testimony should enter in this case to the effect that you were carrying any silver cigarette case on that night, that testimony would necessarily be erroneous?"

"I . . . I'm trying to think."

"You do remember purchasing the Lucky Strike cigarettes in a package?"

"Yes."

"Would you have carried them in a package if you had had another silver cigarette case in your purse?"

"Sometimes I borrow a cigarette case from one of the girls."

"Why?"

"In case I . . . well . . . not very frequently. I have done it on one occasion."

"You have borrowed a cigarette case?"

"Oh, very occasionally."

"Give me the name of one of the girls, as you called them, from whom you have ever borrowed a cigarette case."

"Inez Kaylor."

"Inez Kaylor is the hostess who was employed by you at the time of the holdup?"

"Yes."

"And is still employed by you?"

"Yes."

"And has been in your employ ever since?"

"Yes."

"Where is she now, do you know?"

"Yes."

"Where?"

"She is under the care of a physician. She was hounded in this case to such a point that she . . ."

"That will do," Judge Egan interrupted. "You will simply state where this witness is."

"At a private nursing home."

"Do you know if she has an apartment in Las Vegas?"

"I understand she spends some time in Las Vegas."

"But she has been continually in your employ?"

"Well, yes and no."

"What do you mean by that?"

"She doesn't always work for me every single consecutive night. She can lay off whenever she wants to. My hostesses don't work . . . that is, they don't punch a time clock. They can have time to themselves if they wish."

"And Miss Kaylor wished enough time to herself so that she could remain in Las Vegas a large part of the time?"

"She loved to gamble."

"There aren't two girls by the name of Kaylor?"

"Who work for me?"

"Either who work for you or who didn't work for you?"

"Mr. Mason, I certainly can't tell you how many girls there are in the United States who are named Kaylor."

"How many do you know?"

"One."

"Only one?"

"Yes."

"That's all you have ever met?"

"Yes."

"Inez Kaylor doesn't have a sister?"

"No."

"Inez Kaylor is the same person who goes by the name of Petty Kaylor?"

"Petty is her professional name."

"There aren't two girls named Kaylor in your employ?"

"Why, Mr. Mason, I don't know what gave you that idea."

"Are there?"

"No."

"Have there ever been?"

"Well, now . . . I'm trying to think . . . of course, some of my hostesses I know better than others."

"Have there ever been two Kaylor girls in your employ?"

192

"I . . . I'd have to look at my books."

"Has there ever been a Kaylor girl in your employ other than the Inez Kaylor to whom you have referred?"

"I . . . well, now, Mr. Mason, that question is hardly fair. The hostesses who work for me assume professional names. Those names are hardly ever their real family names. The reasons for that are obvious."

"I am asking you," Mason said, "if you can recall any other girl by the name of Kaylor who was ever in your employ?"

"No."

"Any other girl who ever went by the name of Kaylor?"

"Well, now, of course, I . . . I seem to have a faint recollection, Mr. Mason, that . . . sometimes things like that will happen. A girl will take the name of another girl, particularly if they should happen to look alike. In that way one girl can pick up the good will of some predecessor who was popular."

"In other words, one girl moves out and another girl who looks like her moves in and begins to take over?"

"Well, not quite like that, but if there has been one girl who was rather popular, and she leaves, and . . . well, perhaps after an interval of several months or several weeks, some other girl would come in and possibly take the name of the other girl so that she wouldn't have to start out as a stranger. In a position of that sort the good will of the public is everything, and a girl wouldn't want to start in cold if she could avoid it. Word-of-mouth advertising, of course, means a great deal to a hostess. One person will hear about a girl and ask for her by name."

Martha Lavina had lost much of her calm assurance.

"So," Mason said, "do you now wish to state that it is customary for a girl who looks something like a girl who has previously been employed as hostess to take the name of the former hostess?"

The hesitation of the witness showed she was in trouble.

Harry Fritch jumped to his feet to come to the rescue. "Your Honor," he said, "I object to this. I have patiently refrained from objecting so long as Counsel limited his questions to the young woman who had given Mrs. Lavina a lift from the scene of the holdup. Let Counsel ask all the questions he wants about Miss Kaylor and whether she had a ringer or a double or anything about her, but when it comes to examining the private lives of some eighteen hostesses, I object. We will be here for the next six months if this examination is going to cover that much territory."

"The objection is sustained," Judge Egan said. "Counsel will limit his questions to the identity of the single individual who has been mentioned by the witness as having transported her from the scene of the holdup."

"And from whom she borrowed a cigarette case," Mason said.

"The Court understands," Egan said.

"I consider the borrowing of that cigarette case important, Your Honor, and . . . "

"There is no limitation as to questions concerning Miss Kaylor, Mr. Mason. Proceed with your cross-examination of the witness."

"Had you borrowed a silver cigarette case from Miss Kaylor that night, Mrs. Lavina, the night of the holdup?"

"I . . . I can't be absolutely positive."

"In other words, you may have had an empty cigarette case in your purse when you bought the package of Lucky Strikes?"

"Well . . . if it hadn't been empty I wouldn't have bought the package, would I?"

"I'm asking you."

"I . . . I might have had."

"Do you think you did have?"

"I would say that it was unlikely."

"But if you did have the empty cigarette case in your purse

you would have promptly filled it with Lucky Strike cigarettes from the package you had bought, would you not?"

"Yes."

"And if you did borrow a cigarette case that night you borrowed it from Inez Kaylor?"

"Yes, sir."

"Now you can't say whether you did or whether you didn't?"

"Well, I don't think I did on that particular night but I wouldn't know."

"Now then," Mason said, "do you have a friendly relationship with these hostesses who work for you?"

"I try to get along with them, yes."

"You are fair in your dealings with them?"

"I try to be."

"Do you keep them paid up, keep their wages paid?"

"Their compensation is hardly referred to as wages, Mr. Mason."

"Do you promptly pay them everything that you owe them?"

"Yes."

"Do you owe Miss Kaylor any money for anything at the present time?"

"I do not."

"She is fully paid up as far as you are concerned?"

"Yes."

"There's no relation of debtor and creditor between you?"

"No."

"You don't owe her a cent?"

"No."

"Did you ever pay her for a cigarette case?"

"For a cigarette case?"

"Yes."

"No."

"But," Mason said, "if her cigarette case, the one that you had borrowed from her, had been in your purse on the night of the holdup, you couldn't have returned the cigarette case to her, and therefore you would have had to compensate her for it, wouldn't you?''

"I . . . well, of course . . .''

"Yes or no?" Mason asked.

"Yes, I suppose I would.''

"And you didn't compensate her for a cigarette case?''

"I . . . no.''

"And you don't now owe her for a cigarette case?''

"No.''

"Therefore her cigarette case couldn't have been in your purse the night of the holdup?''

"No, I don't suppose it could.''

"Very well,'' Mason said. "I think that's all the questions I have about the cigarette case. Do you wish to return it to your purse, Mrs. Lavina?''

She swung around in the chair once more so that her body was between her and Mason as she opened the purse and put the cigarette case with the built-in lighter inside and snapped the purse shut. Then she turned to face Mason.

"Over the week end,'' Mason said, "you have remembered a great many details about the holdup which you couldn't recall Friday afternoon when you were on the stand.''

"Well, not a great many, but certain details.''

"And you haven't communicated with Mr. Archer about those details?''

"I have not talked with Mr. Archer, Mr. Mason. I want that definitely understood. I have not talked with Mr. Archer since early Friday morning, before this case started.''

Mason hesitated for a moment, then glanced at Judge Egan. "If I may have the indulgence of the Court for just one moment,'' he said, and, turning away from the witness, walked over to the rail which separates the space reserved for counsel from that occupied by the spectators. He caught Paul Drake's eye and beckoned to him.

Drake came up to the rail. The spectators watched with curiosity. Harry Fritch half closed his eyes in speculation, and Martha Lavina for the first time showed a certain amount of nervousness as she saw the person with whom Mason was having a whispered conference.

Judge Egan irritably looked at the clock, frowned at Mason.

Drake whispered, "What is it, Perry?"

"I don't know," Mason said. "I'm stalling."

"You're going to be penalized for too many times out," Drake said. "The old boy on the bench is restless."

"I know," Mason said. "Now look, Paul, this Martha Lavina has something in her purse, something that she forgot about until she came to court. She didn't remember it was in there until she opened the purse in order to take out that cigarette lighter. Now I caught a glimpse, just a fleeting glimpse of the interior of that purse. There was something yellow in there."

"What was it?"

Mason said, "I think it was a piece of paper that had been torn from one of the yellow pads of foolscap that are placed around here in the courtroom for the convenience of counsel. That *could* be something that had been passed on to her by Harry Fritch. It *could* have been something passed on to her by Rodney Archer. You notice that whenever I asked her questions about whether she had *communicated* with Rodney Archer she would state very indignantly, 'I have not *talked* with Rodney Archer since this trial started.'

"Now I don't think Martha Lavina would hesitate to tell a deliberate lie on the witness stand but I think she is getting a kick out of parrying my questions so that she can tell the literal truth and still leave me baffled. My best guess is that as soon as she leaves this courtroom she's going to try to get rid of whatever is in her purse that was bothering her. She may go to the women's rest room, or she may crumple it and dump it in one of the trash receptacles. I want you to have

197

operatives pick her up the minute she leaves this courtroom. I don't want her to be out of your sight for a second. You'll have to have some woman who can shadow her into the rest room. Of course, if she flushes it down the toilet there's not much we can do, but I'd like to stop it if I can. Now you're just going to have to use your imagination and . . ."

Judge Egan banged his gavel. "The Court is trying to give Counsel every indulgence," he said, "but we cannot have this trial unnecessarily delayed. I am going to ask Counsel to proceed with the trial."

"Very well, Your Honor," Mason said. He turned toward the judge, then suddenly turned back to ask one more question of Paul Drake.

Judge Egan's frown was ominous.

"How about the Aphrodite Model Agency, Paul?"

"I've had two woman operatives, including Mary Brogan, send in applications. The guy was supposed to be in to pick up replies to his ad this morning and . . ."

Judge Egan's gavel banged peremptorily. "I advised Counsel to continue with the case," he said. "The Court will brook no further delay."

"Yes, Your Honor," Mason said, and, turning back, announced, "I have no further questions of this witness, Your Honor."

"The prosecution rests," Harry Fritch announced unexpectedly.

"Call your first witness for the defense, Mr. Mason," Judge Egan ordered.

"Inez Kaylor," Mason said. "Will the bailiff please call Inez Kaylor?"

Martha Lavina, who was walking down from the witness chair, turned, walked back and whispered something to Harry Fritch.

Fritch jumped up. "Your Honor, I think I am probably more familiar with this aspect of the situation than anyone else. I may say at this time that the witness, Inez Kaylor, is going to be a witness on rebuttal for the prosecution as well as on direct for the defense, and we are just as anxious as Mr. Mason is to have this witness in court. However, I may state to the Court that owing to circumstances which I can discuss more freely in the absence of the jury it is impossible for the witness to be here at this time.''

"Why is it impossible?" Judge Egan asked.

"That is something that I would prefer to discuss in the absence of the jury so that neither party will be embarrassed.''

Judge Egan said, "We can't have the jury shuffling in and out of here. The jurors are busy people who are making a sacrifice of their time in order to get this case disposed of. I think it should be disposed of."

"Does the Court wish me to make this statement in the presence of the jury?" Fritch asked, an ominous gleam in his eyes.

"No, no," Judge Egan said. "Court will grant the request of Counsel. The jurors will leave the courtroom for another ten-minute period. The Court appreciates the inconvenience to which the jury is being placed in this matter, and the Court wants to state to Counsel that if any other matter is to be taken up in the absence of the jury it should be brought up while the jury is out of court at this time.''

Judge Egan waited while the jurors filed out of the courtroom, then said to Fritch, "Very well, proceed."

Fritch said, "What I am going to state to the Court is a matter which I am prepared to prove."

"Go right ahead," Judge Egan said. "Let's hear what it is.''

"Inez Kaylor has been hounded in this case. She has not only been hounded by detectives employed by the defense, but even Counsel for the defense, Mr. Perry Mason, not disclosing his identity and pretending to be merely a customer at the night club, engaged Miss Kaylor as a hostess.''

199

"Is there anything wrong with that?" Mason interposed. "The night club is open to the public."

"That will do, Mr. Mason," Judge Egan said. "Let Mr. Fritch complete his statement, then you can have your turn."

"I wish to repeat," Fritch said, "that this young woman has been hounded. On Saturday afternoon she was served with a subpoena, and the circumstances under which the subpoena was served were such as to leave her completely unnerved. Immediately after that a relative of the defendant tried to force her way into Miss Kaylor's apartment. Miss Kaylor attempted to commit suicide by taking a large dose of sleeping pills. She is now convalescing. In the opinion of her physician she should not be called on to give her testimony in this case at the present time."

"Why not?" Judge Egan asked.

"She is too nervous."

"Do you have a certificate of the physician?"

"Yes, sir. A Dr. Doyle."

"Dr. Hanover *was* her attending physician," Mason said.

"He was until her relatives arrived," Fritch said, "and then they called in her own doctor, Dr. Herkimer L. Doyle."

"Dr. Doyle has treated her before?" Mason asked.

"I don't know," Fritch said irritably. "I'm not putting in *my* time in the company of night club hostesses. I have other things to do."

"So it would seem," Mason said.

"Now there'll be no more repartee between Counsel," Judge Egan said. "What about Dr. Hanover? How does he fit into the picture?"

"Dr. Hanover was called by someone whom he cannot or will not identify. He furnished first-aid treatment and had the patient taken to a hospital for emergency treatment. The patient had never seen Dr. Hanover in her life before and naturally preferred a doctor of her own choosing."

"Had she ever seen Dr. Doyle before?" Mason asked.

"I tell you I don't know," Fritch retorted.

"Well, you know about her not having seen Dr. Hanover," Mason said. "How is it you don't know about Dr. Doyle?"

Fritch remained silent.

"It is my contention," Mason said, "that Dr. Hanover was dismissed and Dr. Doyle was brought in purely for the purpose of having Dr. Doyle make a certificate that this witness couldn't testify."

"I'm quite certain that's not the case," Fritch said with dignity.

"Didn't Mrs. Lavina employ Dr. Doyle?" Mason asked.

"I am certain I don't know who is paying Dr. Doyle. All I know is that I have a certificate from Dr. Doyle stating that this person should not come to court today, and I have talked with Dr. Doyle on the telephone."

Judge Egan said, "I don't want to subject this young woman to any undue nerve strain, but it seems to me that she should be able to come to court and testify. If every witness could get out of testifying simply by stating that she was nervous and that the giving of testimony would be an unwelcome ordeal, we would have very few witnesses in our lawsuits. The Court is only too well aware of the fact that it is quite frequently a disagreeable experience to come to court. However, this young woman took an overdose of sleeping pills on Saturday and . . . when did she recover consciousness, Mr. Fritch?"

"I don't know," Fritch said.

"When did she discharge Dr. Hanover and retain Dr. Doyle?"

"I don't know."

"Saturday?"

"I can't tell you, Your Honor."

"Well, it seems to me there are a lot of gaps that should be filled in here. It is quite plain that the witness is not available despite the fact that apparently she has been served by a subpoena. Now the Court's patience is wearing thin over

201

these repeated delays. I am going to continue this matter until two o'clock this afternoon. In the meantime the defense can go on with one of its other witnesses."

"The defense has no other witness," Mason said, "except the defendant, and the defense wishes to interrogate the witness Kaylor before putting the defendant on the stand. The defense feels that it is entitled to have the defendant the last witness to take the stand before the case goes to the jury."

Judge Egan frowned. "This is exceedingly annoying," he said. "We are complaining about our courts being congested. Jurors, witnesses and litigants are complaining about the delays, and here we have a situation where a court is asked to grant a continuance merely on the strength of a physician's certificate. The Court is going to take a ten-minute recess, during which time the Court will endeavor to get in touch with Dr. Doyle on the telephone. The Court is not going to take Dr. Doyle's certificate. We'll either have Dr. Doyle here or we'll have the witness here, unless, of course, certain matters can be clarified. Is it your contention, Mr. Mason, that Dr. Doyle is being paid by Martha Lavina?"

"It is my contention," Mason said, "that Dr. Doyle was retained purely for the purpose of seeing that this young woman did not come to court today. I think the Court will find that he is just as much a stranger to the patient as Dr. Hanover was."

"*I* don't want to be careless with *my* statements," Fritch retorted, "but it is my opinion that Dr. Hanover was selected by Mr. Perry Mason. I know that he is one of Mr. Mason's clients."

"Well, we'll try and get the thing straightened out in some way during the next ten minutes," Judge Egan said. "The Court is naturally impatient with a situation of this sort. I can appreciate Counsel's desire to have the defendant go on the stand just before the case goes to the jury, but the Court has other things to consider than the wishes of the defendant.

If it appears that Miss Kaylor is not going to be available, the Court will insist that the defense go on with its case, putting other witnesses on the stand. We can not be having one continuance after another in a matter of this sort. Court will take a ten-minute recess."

Judge Egan pushed back his chair, gathered his robes around him and stalked into chambers.

Mason stood up to look around the courtroom, saw Paul Drake pushing his way through the door, caught Drake's eye. Drake held up a finger and nodded.

Mason beckoned to him.

Fritch said to Mason, "I don't see why you're so obstinate about Inez Kaylor. She isn't going to do you any good."

"I want to examine her."

"Yes you do," Fritch said sarcastically. "I'm betting five to one right now that you don't dare to put her on the stand as your witness. You're only running a bluff."

"If you think I'm running a bluff," Mason said, "call me."

"That's what I'm going to do."

Mason said, "In the meantime, pardon me."

He stepped to one side. Drake came over to stand close to him.

"Well?" Mason asked.

Drake said, "You sure had it sized up right, Perry."

"What was it?" Mason asked.

"The yellow paper, folded," Drake said.

"Where is it?"

"I have it in my hand. Turn around to one side and I'll slip it in your pocket."

"Does she know you have it?"

"Gosh, no."

"How did you get it?"

Drake said, "I stuck my neck out a foot. I put a sign on the women's rest room—*TEMPORARILY OUT OF ORDER*. She came out of court and headed for the women's room, then she saw the sign and detoured, looked annoyed and finally slid up close to one of the covered trash boxes in the corridor. I saw her hand slip down and saw the cover of the trash box move, then she moved away.''

''What did you do?''

''I used a pocket flashlight to swing back the cover of the trash can, looked down and saw this folded yellow paper on top. I only had time to grab it and get the sign off the women's room before the Court took a recess and people came pouring out of the courtroom.''

''Does she know she was trapped? Did she see you take down the sign from the women's room?''

''I don't think so.''

Mason said, ''Okay, thanks. I think we're doing all right. Now, Paul, here's something I want to find out. When a postmortem was performed on the body of Daphne Howell was there a crescent-shaped mark anywhere on . . . ?''

''That's right, there was. On the left leg. About midway between the knee and the hip, on the outside of the leg.''

''About the size of a twenty-five-cent piece?'' Mason asked.

''Sort of a crescent mark,'' Drake said. ''The autopsy surgeon couldn't account for it, said it might have been . . .''

Judge Egan's secretary stepped to the door of chambers and said, ''Mr. Mason. Mr Fritch. Judge Egan wants both of you in chambers at once, please.''

''It's okay,'' Mason said to Drake. ''Everything's going to work out all right, Paul. Stick around. I may want you to testify about that paper. I'll be right out.''

Mason joined Fritch and stepped into Judge Egan's chambers.

Judge Egan was holding a telephone in his hand. He said, ''I have Dr. Doyle on the telephone, gentlemen. Dr. Doyle says it will be possible for Miss Kaylor to be in court at two o'clock this afternoon provided he can be there and watch her on the witness stand, and if she becomes unduly nervous or agitated he wants the privilege of withdrawing her."

"That certainly seems fair," Fritch said.

"I'd like to talk with Dr. Doyle," Mason said.

Judge Egan said, "Just a minute, Doctor. This is Mr. Perry Mason, attorney for the defense, the one who has subpoenaed the witness."

Mason picked up the telephone, said, "Hello, Doctor."

"Hello," Dr. Doyle said. "I think you understand the situation, Mr. Mason. This young woman has been subjected to a very serious nerve shock. There are, in fact, some symptoms of an incipient manic-depressive psychosis, which, of course, I'm trying to prevent from developing, with the corresponding periods of elation and depression, the suicidal tendencies and . . ."

"I'll ask you about that later," Mason said. "What I'm interested in right now is asking you what you know about the patient's past history?"

"Quite a bit. I . . ."

"You secured it after you were called in on the case?"

"Yes."

"When were you called in?"

"Saturday night, about seven o'clock."

"Who called you?"

"A friend of Miss Kaylor's."

"Had you ever attended Miss Kaylor before?"

"No."

"But you had attended this friend?"

"I had . . . may I ask what was the purpose of this question, Mr. Mason?"

"Was that friend Martha Lavina?" Mason asked.

"I don't think I care to answer that question."

"Try telling the judge about it then," Mason said, and extended the telephone to Judge Egan.

"Is that true?" Judge Egan asked. "Are you Martha Lavina's physician?"

The judge held the phone for a moment, frowned, then said, "I think I'm entitled to a better answer than that, Doctor. . . . Very well, Doctor, you have your patient in court at two o'clock this afternoon, and you be here. I'm going to ask you some questions in open court rather than over the telephone. . . . No, you can be here personally, Doctor. That was what you wanted to do. You wanted to be where you could watch the patient. Now you can come to court and answer questions in the courtroom. Good-by, Doctor."

Judge Egan slammed up the telephone, turned to the attorneys and said angrily, "I don't know just what's going on here. I don't like it. In the meantime, I'm going to have the jury come back and we're going to reconvene court. You can put some other witness on the stand, Mr. Mason. At two o'clock this afternoon we'll have Miss Kaylor here and she'll be on the stand, and we'll also have Dr. Doyle here. Now, gentlemen, we'll return to court and we'll try and discontinue the repartee which has been taking place between Counsel and get on with this trial in an orderly fashion."

Fritch said, "I am trying to keep within the bounds of decorum here, Judge, but I'm frank to state that I don't think Mr. Mason has the slightest intention of putting Inez Kaylor on the witness stand. I don't think he ever did intend to. I think he's running a bluff. I think Miss Kaylor is a hostile witness. I think her testimony would be opposed to the defendant's theory of the case, and I don't think the defense dares to be bound by her testimony by putting her on the stand."

Judge Egan frowned and said, "If that should turn out to be the case I would certainly be inclined to inquire into it. It is quite apparent that this young woman did take an overdose of sleeping tablets because a subpoena was served on her in this case. Counsel certainly realizes that it would be an abuse of discretion to subpoena a witness he did not intend to call, simply for the purpose of annoying or intimidating the witness."

206

"Counsel understands that perfectly," Mason said. "Mr. Fritch has offered to lay me a wager that I won't put Inez Kaylor on the stand. I'd like to have him repeat that offer. I'll take him up."

Judge Egan said, "You two can handle your own differences between yourselves. The Court isn't going to be party to any wager or become involved in any controversy, but I'll tell both of you gentlemen right now that from here on you're going to toe a chalk line, both of you, and the Court is going to be *very* interested in seeing whether or not you do put Inez Kaylor on the witness stand, Mr. Mason. Now, that's all."

Mason and Fritch filed out. Fritch said in an undertone, "I'd hate to be in your shoes at two o'clock this afternoon."

Mason grinned. "Your own shoes are going to become pretty hot long before that, Fritch."

"You think so?" Fritch asked.

"Stick around," Mason told him.

"I intend to," Fritch snapped.

The lawyers entered the courtroom and a moment later Judge Egan returned from chambers and rapped for order.

"Proceed with the case of People versus Brogan," he said.

Mason said, "Your Honor, it now appears that the witness I want will not be available until two o'clock this afternoon. As I have stated, I would much prefer to put the defendant on the stand just before the case goes to the jury."

"Well, your preference would ordinarily be considered," Judge Egan said, "because you would have it within your power to control the order of proof by calling your witnesses as you want them, but the matter is now out of your hands. Proceed with the case."

"Very well, Your Honor," Mason said, "but in view of those circumstances, I would like to cross-examine Martha Lavina once more. I would like to ask her two or three more questions."

"Your Honor," Fritch said, "the prosecution objects. The

207

prosecution has rested its case. Mr. Mason is attempting to kill time until the twelve o'clock adjournment. He . . ."

Judge Egan banged his gavel. "Just refrain from commenting about adverse counsel," he said. "Do you object?"

"I do."

"The Court sustains the objection. The request to call Martha Lavina for further cross-examination is denied."

"I would then like the privilege of calling Mr. Rodney Archer for further cross-examination."

"I object," Fritch said.

"Sustained," Judge Egan snapped.

"I will, then," Mason said, "call my first witness for the defense, Martha Lavina."

"As *your* witness?" Fritch exclaimed.

"As my witness," Mason said. "If I can't get her on the stand one way I will another."

"Call Martha Lavina," Judge Egan said to the bailiff.

A few moments later Martha Lavina entered the courtroom, smiling assuredly.

"You've already been sworn," Judge Egan said. "Take the stand. Mrs. Lavina is now being called as a witness for the defense. I trust you understand the position in which that places you, Mr. Mason."

"I think I do, Your Honor."

"Very well, proceed."

Mason said, "Mrs. Lavina, I have here a paper."

"Yes, Mr. Mason."

Mason took the folded yellow paper from his pocket. "There is writing on it," he said. "I am going to show you that paper and ask you if it is your handwriting."

Martha Lavina looked at the paper, then suddenly clutched her purse, lowered her eyes, raised them again, bit her lip, looked around the courtroom.

"Is that paper in your handwriting?" Mason asked.

"No, sir."

"Do you know whose handwriting it is?"

"I . . . I . . . I . . ."

"Just a minute," Fritch said. "Your Honor, I object. This is an attempt on the part of Counsel to cross-examine his own witness."

"The objection is overruled," Judge Egan said. "Answer the question."

"That is, I believe, in the handwriting of Rodney Archer."

"When did that paper come into your possession, Mrs. Lavina?"

"Just a moment, just a moment," Fritch shouted. "I object, Your Honor. There is no showing that the paper ever was in her possession. It is not shown that the paper is competent evidence in this case. It is incompetent, irrelevant, immaterial and an attempt on the part of defense to cross-examine his own witness."

"The objection is overruled. Answer the question," Judge Egan said.

"Can you answer that question?" Mason asked. "When did this paper come into your possession?"

"I . . . Saturday morning."

"Who gave you that paper?"

"Mr. Archer."

"Where?"

"In Mr. Fritch's office."

"Your Honor," Fritch said, "it is quite apparent that this entire examination is an attempt to embarrass and cross-examine this witness. I respectfully submit that the time for this cross-examination has passed. The prosecution has closed its case."

"There may be something to your objection," Judge Egan said, "although it is as yet too early to determine that matter, but I will state to Counsel that when the motion was first made to recall this witness for further cross-examination I felt certain that it was, as the prosecution claimed, an attempt to spar for time. It now appears that this is something else.

I'm going to ask you, Mr. Mason, whether this paper was in your possession before the last recess of court.''

"It was not, Your Honor.''

"It was not in your possession when the prosecution closed its case?''

"No, Your Honor.''

Judge Egan said, "I am going to suggest that you once more renew your motion, Mr. Mason, to recall this witness for cross-examination.''

"I object,'' Fritch shouted. "This is contrary to all established procedure. The prosecution has closed its case. Mr. Mason had every opportunity to cross-examine this witness. He exhausted every subject on cross-examination. He covered the entire field. Now, after the People have rested their case, Mr. Mason makes this motion which is manifestly ill-timed and out of order.''

"As I recall the law,'' Judge Egan said, "the matter is addressed purely to the discretion of the Court, which has a very great latitude in the matter of examining witnesses. The Court is going to grant the motion. The Court will also state, Mr. Fritch, that if you wish to put on additional evidence after this phase of the examination is completed the Court will permit you to reopen your case. Now then, Mr. Mason, you are interrogating this person not as your witness but as a hostile witness on cross-examination. Go ahead.''

Mason said, "The writing on this paper is in the handwriting of Mr. Rodney Archer. It was given to you in the office of Mr. Fritch on Saturday morning by Mr. Archer. Is that true?''

She hesitated a moment, then said, "Yes.''

Mason said, "You have read that paper?''

"Yes.''

"I call your attention to the words on that paper,'' Mason said.

"Your Honor, I object. I object to that paper being introduced in evidence or read in front of the jury," Fritch said. "It is not proper evidence in the case."

Mason saw Judge Egan hesitate.

"I think I'll look at the paper," Judge Egan said.

Mason handed it up to the judge. Judge Egan read it. His face became hard and stern.

"I am going to sustain the objection to the question in its present form," he said, "but Counsel is now at perfect liberty to cross-examine this witness. I think there should be a further identification before the paper can come in evidence, but it certainly can be used as a basis for cross-examination to impeach the testimony of this witness. Proceed, Mr. Mason."

Mason said, "Mrs. Lavina, you repeatedly stated that you had not communicated with Mr. Archer since court adjourned Friday afternoon, did you not?"

"I stated that I had not *talked* with Mr. Archer."

"You *had* communicated with him then?"

"Well . . . it depends on what you call a communication."

"He had communicated with you?"

"He had given me that piece of paper."

"Now then," Mason said, "I am going to ask you what you had for dinner on the night of the holdup."

"I had dinner with Mr. Archer. I had some French fried prawns on the dinner. We shared a bottle of red Chilean wine."

"And how did you get from the restaurant to the scene of the holdup?"

"We drove down Harvey Boulevard to Murry Road, down Murry Road to Crestwell Boulevard, and along Crestwell to the scene of the holdup."

"Now then," Mason said, "on Saturday morning you received from Mr. Archer a written memorandum stating in part," and Mason read:

"We dined at The Golden Lion. I had a filet mignon medium rare on the dinner. We had red Chilean wine. You don't remember the exact brand but you know it was from Chile. You ate French fried prawns on the dinner. From the restaurant we drove down Harvey Boulevard to Murray Road, down Murry Road to Crestwell Boulevard, and along Crestwell Boulevard to the scene of the holdup. I was about to light a cigarette when the holdup occurred, and the lighter fell from my hands to the seat of the car . . .

"There is much more on the statement, Mrs. Lavina, but I am asking you at the present time if that statement was not given to you and if you did not read it?"

She looked at Fritch desperately.

Fritch said, "Your Honor, I object to this form of interrogation. I object to this method of impeaching the witness. The paper should first be identified."

"Overruled," Judge Egan snapped. "Answer the question."

"Yes," she said.

"And you read this paper and used it as a basis for your testimony this morning, didn't you?"

"I . . ."

"Your Honor," Fritch said, "I dislike to be interposing objections, but I insist that there is no foundation for such a question, that it assumes facts not in the evidence, that it is not proper cross-examination. Just because Mr. Archer may have put something on a paper which he handed to this witness certainly does not indicate that this witness was not testifying entirely from her own recollection. Suppose, for instance, that Mr. Archer had merely written on the piece of paper, 'The defendant is the one who held me up.' It would certainly be improper to suggest that the entire testimony of this witness to that effect be thrown out simply because she had read a statement of that sort from another witness."

"Objection overruled," Judge Egan snapped.

"Well," Martha Lavina said, "I had read that before I testified, but I certainly didn't base my testimony on those statements. I based my testimony on my own recollection."

Mason said, "Now that Counsel has put the words in your mouth you're very glib at reciting them."

"Your Honor, I object!" Fritch shouted. "That is an insult to Counsel and to the Court."

"The Court makes no comment," Judge Egan said dryly. "Proceed with your examination, Mr. Mason."

"On Friday you couldn't remember these things, could you?"

"No."

"You remembered them this morning?"

"Yes."

"Because your recollection had been refreshed by this memorandum which had been given you by Mr. Archer?"

"There were certain details which were not as clear in my mind on Friday as they are now."

"Because of this memorandum?"

"No, because I have had a chance to think those things over. Your questions Friday caught me by surprise. I simply hadn't thought back and tried to remember those things. Since Friday I have done so."

"Assisted by this memorandum."

"That memorandum really had no significance, Mr. Mason. I knew all of the things that are on there."

"You remembered them?"

"I remembered them."

"You remembered the Chilean wine?"

"Very definitely."

"What brand was it?"

"I can't remember."

"Did you have coffee?"

"Yes, I had coffee."

"Did Mr. Archer have coffee?"

213

"I . . . I can't remember that."

"Perhaps you can remember that by tomorrow morning?"

"Perhaps."

"Just how did it happen that Mr. Archer gave you this memorandum?"

"Mr. Fritch requested us both to come to his office. He interrogated us one at a time, explaining that he did not want us to discuss our testimony with each other, but there were certain matters that he wanted to know about."

"So what happened?"

"So Mr. Archer was the first one to enter Mr. Fritch's private office. Mr. Archer was in there in conversation with Mr. Fritch for perhaps fifteen to twenty minutes and then he came out. He merely smiled and bowed at me and walked on out."

"But dropped this piece of paper into your lap," Mason said.

"Well, not quite like that."

"What did he do?"

"He paused to shake hands with me and slipped the folded paper into my hand."

"And you took it?"

"Yes."

"And read it?"

"Yes."

"Before you went into Mr. Fritch's office?"

"Mr. Fritch was standing right there in the door of the office."

"You read the paper before you went into Mr. Fritch's office?"

"No, afterwards."

"How long afterwards?"

"Shortly after I entered. I . . . I spread the paper out on my lap under the desk and read it. I wanted to see what was in it."

"And Mr. Fritch asked you certain questions?"

"Yes."

"Did you tell him about the dinner?"

"Yes."

"Did you tell him about the Chilean wine?"

"Yes."

"You told him you couldn't remember the brand?"

"Yes."

"But you did remember that it was Chilean wine?"

"Yes."

"You hadn't recalled that on Friday afternoon when you were on the witness stand?"

"No."

"But you knew it Saturday morning when you were in Mr. Fritch's office?"

"Yes."

"You knew it after you had received this memorandum from Mr. Archer?"

"That helped."

"How much did it help?"

"Some."

"It recalled the matter to your recollection?"

"Yes."

"As a matter of fact you hadn't had any recollection about that before, had you?"

"Certainly I had."

"You knew then by Saturday morning that Mr. Archer had ordered Chilean wine with the dinner?"

"I knew it on Friday night. The matter had returned quite vividly to my recollection."

"Thank you," Mason said. "I think that is all, Mrs. Lavina. If the Court please, I would like to ask some additional questions of Mr. Archer on cross-examination."

"Do you have any redirect of Mrs. Lavina?" Judge Egan asked Fritch.

"No, Your Honor."

"Very well, recall Mr. Archer to the stand for cross-examination."

There was tense silence in the courtroom as Mrs. Lavina left the witness stand, and a few moments later Archer entered the courtroom and again took his position on the witness stand.

"Mr. Archer," Mason said, "have you communicated with Mrs. Lavina since court adjourned Friday afternoon?"

"I said good morning to her this morning."

"Did you communicate with her about the case?"

"Certainly not."

"Now, just a moment, Your Honor," Fritch said. "I think in fairness to this witness, Counsel should advise him concerning the . . ."

"Sit down!" Judge Egan snapped. "The Court is very much interested in this phase of the case. Now I am going to ask Counsel for both sides to keep quiet and let the Court ask a question or two here. Mr. Archer, will you look up here, please?"

"Yes, Your Honor."

"Have you communicated with Mrs. Lavina about this case since Friday afternoon?"

"Why, no, Your Honor. I understood that Court had ordered us not to communicate."

"About any phase of her testimony?"

"No, Your Honor."

"About anything that happened on the night of the holdup?"

Archer paused to look at Fritch, at the courtroom, at the jury. He suddenly became conscious of the tension which gripped all of the spectators.

"Well, now, Your Honor, I don't know exactly what you mean by that question."

"Did you," Judge Egan asked, "communicate with Mrs. Lavina in any way about anything that took place on the evening of the holdup?"

"Why . . . yes."

"Oh, you did?" Judge Egan said.

"About some rather minor matters perhaps."

"Did you talk with her about them?"

"I . . . not exactly."

"Did you, perhaps, discuss what you had had for dinner the night of the crime with her?"

"If the Court please," Fritch said, "I . . ."

"I want Counsel to keep out of this," Judge Egan said.

"Nevertheless," Fritch said, "the prosecution certainly has a right to interpose an objection to the Court's questions."

"Well, what's wrong with my question?"

"I feel," Fritch said, "that it should be definitely understood by this witness whether the Court's question is such as to include a *written* communication."

Judge Egan settled back in his chair with an exclamation of disgust and said, "That's all the Court wanted to know, Mr. Fritch. You certainly were entitled to interpose an objection, but the manner in which you have worded that objection indicates to the Court . . . well, it indicates, I think, a rather significant fact. Go ahead with your cross-examination, Mr. Mason."

"Can you answer the Court's question, Mr. Archer?"

Archer said, "Well, on Saturday morning I had a session with Mr. Fritch in his office, and Mr. Fritch asked me certain questions that did not in any way pertain to the holdup, but were for the purpose of testing my recollection as to what had happened on the night of the crime. Since those matters did not have any bearing whatever on the case I saw no reason why I should not communicate a memo of the type of information that Mr. Fritch was interested in and pass that on to Mrs. Lavina, which I did."

"Telling Mrs. Lavina the kind of wine you had ordered with the dinner, what she had eaten, what you had eaten and things of that sort?" Mason asked.

"Yes."

"This is the memorandum?" Mason asked, producing the sheet of yellow paper.

"That is it," Archer said.

"It is in your handwriting?"

"That is right."

"And you prepared that memorandum so Mrs. Lavina would have a chance to familiarize herself with the things you had told Mr. Fritch so that she wouldn't contradict the statements you had just made to him. Isn't that right?"

"Oh, definitely not, Mr. Mason," Archer said. "I felt that perhaps Mrs. Lavina was unduly apprehensive at having been summoned to the office of the district attorney. I felt that she might be alarmed as to whether an attempt was to be made to examine her as to certain other matters . . . well . . . you understand that she is in business. She is operating a string of night clubs, and I felt that she might have been apprehensive, and I merely penciled this memo in order to indicate the type of question that had been asked so as to relieve her mind, that was all."

"Then," Mason said, "why didn't you simply write on the piece of paper, 'Mr. Fritch is only interested in finding out what happened that night and is not at all interested in the type of place you're running,' or something of that sort?"

"Dear me," Archer said. "It just never occurred to me, Mr. Mason! That *would* have been a more simple way of handling it, wouldn't it?"

"Indeed it would," Mason said sarcastically, "and that way never occurred to you?"

"To tell you the truth, Mr. Mason, it didn't. It certainly didn't."

"Now then," Mason said suddenly, "isn't it a fact that you did not have dinner with Martha Lavina on the night of the crime, but did have dinner with some other woman?"

"That is not a fact."

"Is it not a fact that Martha Lavina was not in the car with

218

you at the time of the holdup but that some other woman was?"

"That is not a fact."

"Isn't it a fact that when you went to the drugstore and before you telephoned to the police you made another call?"

The witness hesitated.

"Isn't it a fact?" Mason asked.

"I may have made another call. I . . . at this moment I can't remember."

"And wasn't that call that you made a call to Villa Lavina Number Two?"

"I . . . I can't remember."

"It may have been?"

"Well, I . . . I was very confused, Mr. Mason. I can't remember all of those details."

"You were confused?"

"Naturally. I don't have nerves of steel. At the time of this holdup I was . . . well, I was terribly frightened. I felt my life was in danger."

"What was there about the holdup that confused you?"

"Why, the whole thing."

"What was the most terrifying part of it?"

"The shock of having the door jerked open and this gun pushed in my face."

"And you were so confused that you can't now remember whether you went across to the drugstore and called Villa Lavina Number Two?"

"I . . . at the moment I can't recall."

"You were that confused?"

"I was that confused."

"You were at least that confused when you saw the business end of the gun pointed at you?"

"That was what confused me."

"And despite the fact you were so confused that you can't remember having placed a telephone call to Villa Lavina Number Two, you still want this jury to believe that you were able to identify this defendant from a one-second glance at his face?''

''I . . . I was not so confused but what I saw and recognized the defendant.''

''In a period of time that couldn't have been more than one second, during which you had a fleeting look at his face?''

''I can only state the defendant was the man I saw.''

''And you may have gone across to the drugstore and telephoned Villa Lavina Number Two before you called the police?''

''I may have. At that time I was very confused.''

''And when Villa Lavina answered the telephone did you ask to talk with Mrs. Lavina?''

''I may have . . . wait a minute, no.''

''Your first answer was that you might have.''

''I was confused.''

''So confused that you might have asked for Martha Lavina despite the fact that she was supposed to have been sitting in the car with you?''

''I mean I was confused when I answered the question the first time. No, the answer is that I definitely did not ask for Martha Lavina.''

''Then why did you call up The Villa Lavina?''

''I don't know that I did.''

''You don't know that you didn't?''

''No. If the records of the pay station, at the telephone booth, show that I put in a call for Villa Lavina, why, I would assume that I did so.''

''Thank you,'' Mason said. ''That's all.''

''Any questions on redirect?'' Judge Egan asked.

''As I understand it,'' Fritch said, ''you don't know at this time whether you called Villa Lavina or whether you did not? After all, that has been some time ago, and you simply adopt a position that you can't recall. Isn't that your position?''

''That is it exactly.''

"Thank you. That's all," Fritch said.

"Just one moment," Mason said, "just one more question. You can recall other events which happened on that night with startling clarity, can you not, Mr. Archer?"

"I can recall them."

"You can recall having had Chilean wine for dinner?"

"Yes."

"You know that it was Chilean wine?"

"Yes, sir."

"A red wine?"

"Yes, sir."

"You recall that perfectly?"

"Yes."

"You recall asking for Chilean wine?"

"Yes, sir."

"You recall that you had a steak?"

"Yes, sir."

"You recall how it was cooked?"

"Yes, sir. Medium rare."

"You recall that is the way you ordered it?"

"Yes, sir."

"But you cannot recall whether or not immediately after the holdup and before you telephoned the police you telephoned Villa Lavina?"

"No, sir."

"Thank you," Mason said, "that's all."

"That's all," Fritch said wearily.

Judge Egan said, "The Court is now going to take a recess until two o'clock this afternoon. During that time the jury will remember the admonition of the Court not to discuss this case or permit it to be discussed in your presence, nor to form or express any opinion as to the merits of the case, nor read anything in the newspapers concerning this case or concerning any crime news which in any way may have any bearing on this case. Court's adjourned until two o'clock."

Drake came pushing forward to grab Mason's hand and

shake it. "Gosh, Perry, it was wonderful," he said. "You've got them on the run! Everybody in this courtroom is now convinced that Martha Lavina and Rodney Archer are lying their heads off."

Archer, getting down from the witness stand, paused by Perry Mason. "You certainly do have a nasty manner about you," he said, half-joking, half in earnest.

"*Thank* you," Mason said, and turned away with Paul Drake.

Drake said, "Things have been happening, Perry. We got a line on this modeling agency. Now here's a peculiar thing. That modeling agency is in the Windmore Arms Apartment. The fellow that runs it is a man named James Darwin, who has apartment 409. My operative said that when you were up there he commented on the number of good-looking girls who went up there at about thirty-minute intervals."

"Yes, yes," Mason said. "How do you know where the address is?"

"Della Street got a tumble. She put in an application under the name Della Smith and left a telephone number. He called and asked her for an appointment."

"What time?" Mason asked.

Drake looked at his watch and said, "Now. She should be up there right now. We should know a lot more about it. The whole thing begins to look fishy, Perry."

Mason said, "Okay, I'll get back to the office. You have men watching that apartment?"

"Gosh, no, Perry, no longer, I . . ."

"Well, get some men out there," Mason said. "Dammit, I don't want Della out there without . . ."

"Oh, gosh," Drake said, "it's just some kind of a racket, Perry. She's all right."

"Well, let's make damn certain she's all right," Mason said.

Chapter 15

Perry Mason burst into his office, said to Gertie at the switchboard, "What have we heard from Della?"

"Nothing. She went out an hour ago and . . ." Gertie kept jerking her head toward the corner.

"Go ahead," Mason said impatiently.

"And Lieutenant Tragg's here," she blurted.

Lieutenant Tragg of Homicide eased himself up out of the chair in which he had been sitting and came across with hand outstretched. "Hello, Mason. How are you?"

"Hello, Lieutenant," Mason said. "What the devil are *you* doing here?"

"Came to pick up a little grist for my mill."

Mason hesitated for a moment, then said, "All right, come in. I have something to say to you."

Tragg followed the lawyer into Mason's private office.

Mason turned to face him. "Tragg, you're open-minded. You're not like Sergeant Holcomb. You're alert, intelligent and modern. Holcomb's an exponent of the old school of the blackjack, the heavy knuckles, the rubber hose and . . ."

"Now don't get Holcomb wrong," Tragg interrupted, laughing. "He's all right. His methods are a little more direct, that's all."

Mason said, "What do you know about this Albert Brogan case?"

"Not a thing. It's out of my line. The only thing I do know is that Albert Brogan has been identified as one of the murderers in the Daphne Howell case. That's right up my alley."

"All right, sit down. Keep your shirt on," Mason said.

"When Daphne Howell's body was examined they found that she had been garroted. Is that right?"

"Right."

"Grabbed suddenly from behind and a fine wire had been twisted around her neck?"

"That's right. It was a smooth professional job. We can't figure it."

"And on her left leg there was a small crescent about the size of a twenty-five-cent piece?"

"That's right. That may not have any significance, but, of course, in a case of that kind you have to appraise everything and . . ."

"I'll tell you what that was," Mason said. "That was a mark made by a lighted cigarette lighter taken from the dashboard of an automobile."

Tragg frowned thoughtfully. His eyes left Mason to regard the far wall of the office with thoughtful speculation. Abruptly his eyes swiveled back and he said, "You could be right at that."

"I am right."

"Well, it's a hell of an interesting theory. It might give us something to go on. Now perhaps you can go further and give us the name of the man who committed the murder."

"I can," Mason said. "The man's name is Rodney Archer. She was riding in his car when the holdup took place. But even then he was planning her death. He simply didn't dare to be seen with her. He was trying to keep things so no contact with him could ever be proven.

"So when the stick-up took place Archer was in a terrific predicament. He had to get Daphne Howell out of that car before the police arrived on the scene.

"Archer swears that Martha Lavina was in the car with him. The evidence all points to the fact that there was some other woman in the car with Rodney Archer. He spirited that woman out of the picture and Martha Lavina took her place.

"That puzzled me. I tried to find out why. I couldn't get

the answer. Rodney Archer was a rich widower. He could go out with anyone he wanted to. Of course, his companion might have been a married woman who was in the car with him and whom he was trying to protect. From all I can find out Archer doesn't go in for that kind of stuff. His name has never been connected with any woman since his wife died two years ago."

"Go on," Tragg said. "I'm listening, and believe me, that's all I'm doing. I'm not buying anything."

"You'd better buy it," Mason said, "because if you don't your face is going to be red."

"I've heard all that before."

"I know you have," Mason told him, "but you keep on listening and you'll buy this."

"Keep on talking."

"Archer is mixed up in some way with Martha Lavina, and Daphne Howell was in the thing. Daphne Howell had to be eliminated from the picture. The police tried to reconstruct Daphne Howell's past life and ran up against a blank. They knew that she had made a trip to Mexico City and that she'd made a trip to Guatemala. Apparently she went alone on each trip. They've never been able to find any relatives or . . ."

"You don't need to tell me all that stuff," Tragg said. "I know it by heart. It's one of the most baffling cases I've ever encountered. We can't go back over two years in the life of Daphne Howell, and we can't find anyone who can tell us very much about the last two years."

Mason said, "Before I get done collecting evidence in this case there's going to be a lot more information."

"I hope so," Tragg said. "You have some theories so far. That's all. You can imagine what would happen to me if I should come prancing into the department with a theory I'd picked up from you. They'd have me pounding pavements within forty-eight hours.

225

"I need facts and I won't budge until I get them. Now, what about the cigarette lighter?"

Mason said, "She was in Rodney Archer's car. He was lighting a cigarette. A guy popped open the door on the left side of his car, stuck a gun in his face and told him to put up his hands. He did.

"The red-hot lighter dropped to the seat. The holdup man grabbed Daphne Howell's purse. She turned slightly. Her bare leg hit the edge of the cigarette lighter and left a faint mark.

"When the police called for Archer's car because they wanted to go over it looking for evidence, they found the hole burned in the upholstery in the front seat. The hole didn't impress them as having any significance at the time, but they took photographs of the front of the car, and the photographs showed that round hole in the upholstery. No one thought very much about it, until I started asking questions on cross-examination, just fishing around trying to get some idea I could develop that would make a variance between the testimony of Martha Lavina and Rodney Archer. I realized that the burnt spot must have been made at some time or another by the red-hot tip of a dashboard lighter being pressed down on the upholstery. I asked a couple of questions and suddenly realized that I'd struck a jack pot. They began to be more concerned about that spot in the upholstery than any other phase of the case."

"Nice theory," Tragg commented dryly. "I'm not buying it, but I am looking it over."

"The purse that Daphne Howell was carrying with her was stolen at the time of the stick-up. Later on, after Daphne Howell's death, Martha Lavina swore *she* was the woman in the car. Naturally she had to swear it was her purse that was taken. It wasn't her purse because her combination cigarette case and lighter which was in her purse aren't missing. She forgot to cover up on that.

"Yet that purse was the exact replica of a purse carried by

226

Martha Lavina. It was made to her specifications. There's a novelty factory out here that makes those purses. They won't tell me how many Martha Lavina buys because I lack the official authority to make them come through with the information, but I have an idea those purses are manufactured in numbers."

"So what?" Tragg said. "Good Lord, Martha Lavina could give them away as good will gifts to women customers if she wanted to. They do that in some of the night clubs and . . ."

"But Martha doesn't do that," Mason said. "She was tempted to say she did when she was on the witness stand, but then she realized that I'd ask her for the names of people to whom she had presented these purses and she wouldn't be able to give me a name, so she shied away from that. No, I tell you, Tragg, those purses have some significance. Now you notice the purse that was recovered by the police in that stick-up job had been slashed, the leather had been cut and the lining had been torn away from the leather."

"Go ahead," Tragg said. "I keep wanting to listen. I don't know why. It's a fairy story. What about the tan Chevy your client was driving?"

"Don't you see?" Mason pleaded. "He wasn't driving it."

"Phooey! Two people saw him drive away in it," Tragg said, disgustedly.

"That's just it," Mason said. "These people were Rodney Archer and Martha Lavina. Don't you get it? That tan Chevy had been stolen. It was stolen to be used in connection with the murder of Daphne Howell. Then Archer and Martha Lavina decided to drag it into the holdup case. The man who really held them up wasn't driving any such car."

"Now you've left the realm of probability," Tragg said, "and have gone off on a cockeyed tangent that's lifted right out of a fairy story. I not only won't buy that, but I'm damned if I waste my time even considering any such . . ."

The phone on Mason's desk rang sharply.

Mason said, "That'll be Della Street." He scooped up the receiver and said, "Hello."

There was no sound at the other end of the line except a rhythmic tap . . . tap . . . thump.

"Hello," Mason said. "Hello!"

He could hear the singing of the open line and the steady slow taps but no other sound, then abruptly the receiver at the other end of the line was slammed up and the line went dead.

Mason stood for a moment looking at the telephone, then yelled to Tragg, "Come on, Tragg, hurry up, get started."

"Now what?"

Mason grabbed his hat from the desk, jerked the door open, said, "Come on, get going," and sprinted down the corridor.

Tragg hesitated, then got up from his chair and followed after Mason in a fast walk.

Mason all but tore the door of Paul Drake's office off the hinges. "Drake in?" he shouted at the surprised switchboard operator.

She nodded.

Mason pulled open the gate in the waist-high barrier, ran down the long runway, jerked open the door of Drake's private office and looked in on the startled detective.

"Did you call me?" he asked.

"When?"

"Just now."

"No."

Mason turned and dashed back down the runway, colliding with Tragg.

"Hey!" Tragg said. "What's the idea?"

"You got a police car down here?" Mason asked, dashing into the corridor and down to the elevators.

"Yes," Tragg said, following more slowly.

228

"With a siren?" Mason asked, jabbing at the "Down" button on the elevator signal.

"Yes."

Mason said, "Get out to the Windmore Arms Apartments. It's opposite the Keynote Hotel. I'll give you directions after we get started. Hurry, Tragg, it's life and death. The solution to the Daphne Howell murder case and the Rodney Archer holdup case are out there."

Tragg seemed dubious.

"Or," Mason said, "you can go to hell, I'll collect an assortment of traffic tickets and some other officer will solve the Howell murder."

With that he jumped into the elevator that had slid to a stop.

Tragg hesitated for only an imperceptible fraction of a second, then jumped in after him.

Mason said to the operator, "Drop us straight down to the lower floor! This is an emergency! Get going!"

The operator seemed dubious for a moment, then said, "Yes, Mr. Mason," and shot the elevator down to the lower floor.

Mason tore out of the door with Tragg right behind him. They ran across the lobby of the building and Mason said, "I suppose your car is parked right by the fireplug?"

"Sure," Tragg said.

Mason jumped into the police car. Tragg slid in behind the wheel, by this time imbued with a sense of urgency communicated to him by Mason's breathless haste.

"Hang on," Tragg said.

Tragg started the motor, took off the parking brake, slid the car out into traffic and started the siren as he screamed into a U-turn. Gathering speed, he tore down the street, burst through a red light signal at the intersection and rocketed into breakneck speed by the time he had reached the next intersection.

The siren screamed for the right of way. The red spotlight

sent its beam dazzling into the eyes of motorists coming from the opposite direction.

"Come on," Mason pleaded. "Get going!"

Tragg whipped the car around the left side of a street car, tore through another red light, skidded past a big truck which shot into the intersection from a side street, ignored a boulevard stop, and tore into a through boulevard.

"Get it going, get it going!" Mason yelled. "Good Lord, what are you waiting for?"

Tragg didn't even bother to reply. He was grimly concentrating now on the exigencies of driving in traffic at breakneck speed.

"Where do we turn?" he asked.

"Half a mile or so down here," Mason said. "I'll tell you where. It's on that boulevard . . . wait a minute, you're coming to it. It's down there where the signal is. Turn to the right."

Tragg swung wide to the left then whipped the car in a right turn, dodging in and out of cars, his tires sending up a crescendo scream that did more to freeze traffic in its tracks than the siren.

The car roared its way up the side street.

"Up at the next traffic signal and turn left," Mason said. "Now you'd better shut off your siren, Tragg. Keep the spotlight on. We don't want to alarm these people. We've got to get up there before anything happens."

"If you're doing all this on the strength of that phone call," Tragg said, "you'd better tell me what was said."

"Nothing was said," Mason told him. "That's the point. Only two people in the world have that unlisted number. Della Street and Paul Drake. Paul Drake didn't call."

"Oh Lord," Tragg said disgustedly, slowing down the car. "You're jittery, Mason. Good Lord, it was just somebody calling a wrong number. When he heard your voice he knew it was the wrong number and hung up, and you've led me on this wild goose chase . . ."

230

"He didn't hear my voice," Mason insisted. "Somebody picked up the receiver at the other end of the line and slammed it into place. The receiver was dangling at the end of the cord. I could hear it knocking against a table leg or something. I didn't know what it was at the time. Della Street couldn't talk, but she managed to dial that number and . . ."

"Oh my gosh," Tragg said, "and here I have been snarling up traffic all over the city."

"Well, keep going," Mason told him. "You're almost there now."

Tragg slowed the car to forty miles an hour. "No sense getting killed over a wrong number on a telephone," he protested.

"Park your car away from the apartment house, not right in front of it," Mason said. "There's a good place over there across the street. Slide in there. Come on, let's go."

Tragg said, "Now look, Mason, I don't know what you're . . ."

Mason threw the door open, gained the sidewalk in a leap, circled the back of the car and was halfway across the street before the grumbling police lieutenant had the door open on the driver's side.

At the Windmore Arms Apartments Mason started pressing buttons on the various apartments, being careful to ignore the number of James Darwin, but pushing other buttons at random until there was a buzz signifying the door was open.

Mason pushed open the door, hurried down the corridor, and into the automatic elevator. He whipped the door shut as soon as Tragg had entered and jabbed the button for the fourth floor.

"Now look," Tragg said, "I want to warn you, Mason, I'm not backing your play. I don't know what's up. You haven't a search warrant. You haven't . . ."

"All right," Mason said. "Stick in the background if you want. Just keep your eyes and ears open."

Mason hurried down the corridor, found that the apartment he wanted was at the front of the building. He knocked on the door.

"Just a moment," a man's voice said.

Mason heard a bolt snap on the other side of the door, then the door was flung open.

The man standing on the threshold looked at Mason with wide-eyed dismay.

"Well, Mr. Thomas Gibbs!" Mason said. "We seem to have had a little misunderstanding about the address on your automobile license, Mr. Gibbs."

Mason pushed his way past the startled Gibbs and into the apartment. Tragg followed.

"All right, you two," Gibbs said, "this is my apartment. I didn't invite you in. I don't know what you're trying to put over on me, but I don't want any of it. Now get out or I'll call the police."

"Which is it?" Mason asked. "James Darwin or Thomas Gibbs?"

"It's none of your business which it is."

Mason looked around the apartment, pushed Gibbs to one side, jerked open a door. It led to a kitchen.

"Here," Gibbs said. "Get out of that. Get away. Don't you touch that door."

Mason started for another door.

"Get away from it!" Gibbs yelled. "This is private property. What the hell do you think you're doing?"

He grabbed Mason's left arm and spun the lawyer around.

Mason's right fist lashed out in a sharp blow to the jaw that sent Gibbs staggering back.

Mason jerked the door open, entered a bedroom.

On the bed, Della Street, trussed up like a chicken, her mouth tied with a gag, made inarticulate noises.

Gibbs rushed in behind Mason, stopped for a moment, then turned and started out. The lawyer grabbed Gibbs by the coat, jerked him back into the room.

Tragg said, "What the hell's happening here?"

"Take a look," Mason invited.

Tragg saw Della Street on the bed.

"Get out of my way," Gibbs said, and tried to push past Tragg.

Tragg grabbed the man's necktie, slammed him back against the wall, said, "Just take it easy. This is the law."

Mason was tugging at the knots that tied Della Street. "You can't get away with this," Gibbs said. "I'll sue you for . . ."

"Shut up," Tragg said. "What's the pitch, Mason?"

Mason tugged at the knots, got the gag out of Della Street's mouth, untied her wrists.

Della Street made little tasting motions, trying to get moisture in her mouth so she could talk.

"Take it easy," Mason said. "Are you hurt?"

She shook her head.

"All right," Mason said. "What's the story?"

She said, "He recognized me as soon as I walked in and knew it was a trap. He pretended he hadn't recognized me, however, and invited me in. The next thing I knew there was a blow on my head. When I came to I was like this. He has a phone here and a phone in the other room. I think they're different lines. He was telephoning somebody, apparently asking for instructions. I managed to flop around on the bed until I could push the telephone off the stand onto the bed simply by butting with my head. My hands were tied behind me, but I rolled over on top of the telephone and dialed just by feeling, but, of course, I couldn't talk. I was hoping you would get the signal. The receiver was dangling on the end of the cord, hitting against the bed. He heard that knocking and came in to see what it was all about. He rolled me over and slammed the receiver back into place. I don't think he had any idea that I'd completed a call."

Gibbs said, "That's a lie. This woman came in here and tried to blackmail me. She . . ."

233

"Shut up," Tragg said, and slammed Gibbs down into a chair.

"Let's take a look around," Mason said.

"You can't search this place without a warrant," Gibbs told him.

Tragg looked at Mason dubiously.

"Maybe you can't, but *I* can," Mason said.

He opened a door, disclosed a closet filled with suits of clothes. He pulled out the hangers, throwing the clothes helter-skelter in a pile on the floor, then switched on the light in the closet, said, "Oh-oh, here's something, Tragg."

"Just a minute," Tragg said. "I'm going to put some bracelets on this boy so he won't make a run for it."

Gibbs said, "You don't have to put any bracelets on me, and I'm not going to make a run for it. You're the one that's going to run. I'm going to telephone my lawyer right now. I . . ."

"Shut up," Tragg said. "What have you found in there, Mason?"

Mason brought out a half dozen oblong mirrors.

"What are those?" Tragg asked.

Mason said, "Those are evidently mirrors of the kind that are put into the purses Martha Lavina has manufactured for her. There's a stack of them in there. Let's see what's in the things."

"How are they put together?" Tragg asked.

"Some trick screw or something. I haven't time to bother with it," Mason said. "This is supposed to be bad luck. Look out."

The lawyer brought the mirror down sharply on the corner of the stand by the head of the bed, cracking the glass. Then he put it over his knee and bent the steel support on the back of the mirror.

"Oh-oh," he said. "What's this, Tragg?"

Tragg strode over to take one look, then placed his thumb and forefinger in the opening back of the mirror, rubbed a

234

white powder together and said, "I'll be damned. It's Heroin."

Gibbs jumped up out of the chair, started to run. Tragg grabbed his coat collar, slammed him back against the wall.

Tragg said to Mason, "All right, Mason. There's more to this stuff. Come through with it. I'm buying now, and I want my purchase wrapped up."

Mason said, "When it comes to smuggling dope, it isn't much of a trick to do it once . . . provided the smuggler has a legitimate background. Gibbs here furnished the background. He'd hire girls to be models in foreign countries. They'd be smuggling dope, but they never knew it.

"There's a tie-in with Archer and Martha Lavina. Some of the models took over as hostesses in between times."

"Sounds screwy," Tragg said. "We've got this bird dead to rights, but we've got to go a hell of a long ways further to get anything on Archer and Lavina."

Mason said, "You find the real Inez Kaylor, the one who had the apartment in Las Vegas, and you'll have the proof."

"Where is she?" Tragg asked.

Mason pointed to Gibbs. "He's the one who can tell us, and unless he does tell us within the next ten minutes the probabilities are that her life won't be worth a snap of your fingers. Remember, Della Street said that he telephoned someone immediately after he tied her up."

Tragg looked at Gibbs.

Gibbs sneered, said, "Okay, wise guy, try and make *me* talk."

Tragg took off his coat, folded it carefully, dropped it over the foot of the bed, said, "Della, you'd better wait in the other room. Mason, there are times when Sergeant Holcomb's methods can't be improved on. Stand up, you scum. Now tell me where the hell that Kaylor girl is."

Gibbs shook his head.

Tragg's open hand hit him on the side of the jaw so hard the man staggered. Tragg grabbed him by the coat collar, spun him around, slapped him on the other side, then hit him full on the jaw.

He said, "If you want it the hard way, we'll do it the hard way."

Gibbs staggered back. There was panic in his eyes.

"Where is she?" Tragg asked, and hit him in the stomach.

Gibbs doubled over. Tragg jerked him upright, said, "If anything happens to that girl what the boys will do to you at headquarters isn't even funny. This isn't even a good sample."

Gibbs, gasping for breath, said, "All right, all right, I'll . . . I'll talk . . . I'll take you there."

"That's better," Tragg said. "Let's go. No funny stuff."

Tragg took handcuffs from his belt, said, "Stick out your wrists, punk."

Gibbs held out his wrists.

Tragg slapped on the handcuffs, then put on his coat, said to Mason, "All right, Mason. You and Della Street get a taxicab and go back to your office. I'll radio for a squad car to give me reinforcements. It'll be better if outsiders aren't in on this. You get me?"

"I get you," Mason said. "Now let me fill you in, Tragg. There are two girls who look a lot alike. When Inez Kaylor went to Las Vegas the other girl took on her name and her job as hostess.

"If it hadn't been for the holdup no one would ever have been the wiser. But we brought Inez Kaylor back here. They wanted her out of the way. The ringer, whom we'll call Petty, let herself be seen taking sleeping pills, then left the real Inez here to die!

"We saved her. So they showed up with trumped up relatives and fired our doctor, put in one of their own, moved Inez and then managed to switch girls in the process. The doctor may have been in on it or he may not.

"We want the real Inez."

Lieutenant Tragg jerked at the handcuffs, said to Mason, "All right, Mason, we'll get her."

He jerked Gibbs half off his feet. "Come on, punk, show us where she is, and do it fast."

Chapter 16

Mason, Della Street, Paul Drake, Mary Brogan and Albert Brogan sat in the lawyer's office.

Drake said, "I have to hand it to you, Perry, but how did you figure it out?"

"I went fishing," Mason grinned. "I got a little nibble and then finally I got a strike and hooked a fish."

"I'll say you hooked him. You say Inez Kaylor is on her way up here?"

"That's right. She completed a statement at the prosecutor's office, and Tragg says he's bringing her up. She wanted to talk with me and I sure want to talk with her."

Knuckles pounded on the door. Mason himself opened the door and said, "Hello, Tragg. Come on in."

Tragg said, "Folks, meet Inez Kaylor. This time it's the *real* Inez Kaylor."

The girl, standing directly behind Tragg, held back for a moment somewhat self-consciously, then entered the office.

Tragg introduced her all around. When he came to Paul Drake the girl smiled, said, "I know Paul Drake. We spent some time together."

Tragg said, "Sit down, Inez, and tell us your story."

She said, "I come from the East. I was married and it wasn't working out, so I came out here. It wasn't long before I got on my uppers. I started making a living the best way I could and making the best living I could. Then I saw this ad for the Aphrodite Model Agency. I went in there. They asked all sorts of personal questions, took measurements, photographs and told me to wait, that I'd hear from them later on.

"I didn't hear from them for almost a month, then they brought me in and told me I could have a job going to Mexico City and being photographed for an airplane company.

"I flew to Mexico City. They gave me a complete traveling outfit, suitcase, overnight bag and a purse. They impressed upon me that this was part of the property of the modeling agency and that they had to account for everything. They told me the value of the purse was one hundred dollars in case I lost it. I thought that was an absurdly high valuation, but I didn't intend to lose it.

"I flew down to Mexico City. They had an airplane down there, and some pictures were taken of me riding in the plane, getting in and getting out. Frankly, I began to suspect there was some sort of a racket connected with it. I didn't care. I was getting paid. I knew they could have picked up American girls down there to do the stuff I did and it wouldn't have cost them a tenth of the sum.

"After about ten days they shipped me back. I was paid off and my employment was terminated. I turned in the purse and all of the things I'd received. They kept in touch with me. About three days later they asked if I wanted to go to Havana. I went to Cuba. The same thing happened. I came back. Then they told me it might be another month before anything else opened up. In the meantime, if I wasn't too strait-laced there was a nice job open as hostess at Martha Lavina's club.

"I wasn't too strait-laced. I went in there for a month and then things began to tighten up. They weren't very agreeable and I left. Martha Lavina was rather catty to me. I thought she wanted to get rid of me. I went to Las Vegas. I think I had begun to ask too many questions about the tie-in between Martha Lavina's place and the model agency and just what we were supposed to be doing."

"Just what *were* you supposed to be doing?" Tragg asked.

She shrugged her shoulders and said, "Anything that Martha Lavina wanted us to. I wasn't too willing. I don't mind being pawed over, but I want to pick the people who do the pawing. I think I asked too many questions."

"I guess you've got the sketch now," Tragg said to Mason.

"How about the woman who acted as your double?" Mason asked.

"Apparently after I left, Martha Lavina put this other girl in Villa Lavina Number Three and had her take my name.

"When customers would ask for me they'd be informed I was at Number Three.

"Quite a few of them were fooled, I understand. I didn't care particularly. I was working in Las Vegas and I know what a hard job it is to start in as a hostess with no contacts. You see, Martha Lavina's hostesses don't hustle business, they wait for bids."

Mason turned to Inez Kaylor. "I'm interested in learning just what happened Friday afternoon in the law library."

She said, "Mr. Drake told me to wait until you sent for me. Then a good-looking man came in and asked if I was Inez Kaylor, and I said I was, and he said that he was Mr. Perry Mason's associate and that Mr. Mason wanted me to go to his office and make a statement before a notary public, that he had to have an affidavit from me in order to get a continuance of the case.

"I suppose I was dumb. I went down in the elevator with him, got in a car, and a woman was sitting in the car behind me. She was introduced to me as being Miss Della Street, Mr. Mason's secretary, and then I felt something jab in my back. The girl was terribly apologetic, telling me that she had accidentally struck me with a pin that she was going to use in fastening a corsage on me. She said that Mr. Mason wanted me to wear this corsage so I could be identified, and then all of a sudden everything just went black to me, and when I came to I was in a bedroom of what seemed to be an apartment. They kept me there and, I'm satisfied, intended to kill me if they found they could get away with it."

Tragg said, "I can fill in a lot there, Mason.

"They took Inez to the Windmore Arms Apartment where Petty lived. They felt certain you'd subpoena Petty. They'd have let Petty go on the stand and perjure herself, but Paul Drake had seen Inez and they were afraid.

"So it was all fixed for Petty to take a big shot of plain sugar pills in front of the process server and claim they were sleeping pills. The trouble was the process server didn't wait long enough for Petty to put on her act. Then Mary Brogan showed up and Petty did her stuff.

"They had a private ambulance waiting for a signal and as soon as they got the signal the ambulance went to the apartment house and spirited Petty away. The police learned the ambulance had been there so they didn't investigate.

"Inez was in the closet, out cold. They were keeping her under with hypodermics. Someone called Dr. Hanover. He notified police. Inez was taken to a hospital. Your friend Gibbs showed up with letters he'd stolen from her Las Vegas apartment, claiming to be her husband. He had a woman who posed as Inez' mother.

"They fired Doc Hanover and got Martha Lavina's doctor on the job and arranged to move Inez to a private sanitarium. They stopped the ambulance . . . their own ambulance again . . . made a switch and Petty took Inez' place."

"How about the Daphne Howell murder?" Mason asked.

Tragg said, "Figure that one out, Mason. It's a dilly."

"I'm asking you," Mason said.

"Well, it's like this," Tragg told him. "Daphne Howell had been one of the models. She smelled a rat. She was returning from Cuba when she decided to get smart. She found the combination by which she could take the back off the mirror and realized she had about twenty thousand dollars' worth of pure uncut Heroin. So Daphne Howell wanted to negotiate.

"Rodney Archer was driving her to a conference at The Villa Lavina Number Two when this holdup happened out of a clear sky. Archer felt it would be bad business to ever let it be known he was with Daphne Howell, particularly if they couldn't make some satisfactory arrangements with her. So he called Martha Lavina. Martha Lavina dashed out, grabbed Daphne out of the car and took her to The Villa Lavina Number Two.

"Now when Gibbs made dope deliveries he'd steal a car, and, as you know, he'd already arranged for a fake driving license so that if anything happened and he got caught he could never be traced to the name James Darwin and the Aphrodite Model Agency. That night he'd stolen a tan Chevy with a crumpled fender, and Archer knew it. So when the police called on Archer to describe the car in which the stick-up man had made his getaway, Archer had to think fast to describe a car that was unlike the stick-up car. So he described a tan Chevy with a crumpled fender. He did that because under no circumstances did they want the holdup man captured. It wasn't an ordinary holdup. It was a deliberate hijacking. The stick-up man had taken Archer's money but he'd also grabbed Daphne Howell's purse, and at the time he did it he made some remark to the effect that he needed the dope for his own use, that he wasn't going to sell it.

"Well, Daphne Howell proved to be difficult to deal with. She knew too much and she wanted too big a cut. Gibbs was the big shot in the dope racket. Archer and Martha Lavina wanted Gibbs to pay off Daphne Howell and get rid of her. Gibbs pretended he was going to. He took Daphne in the stolen tan Chevy, made her think he was going to pay off, but instead insured her permanent silence with a loop of wire.

"Archer and Lavina were shocked when they heard what had happened but there was nothing they could do except keep quiet. Then the worst thing of all happened. The police picked up Brogan here and charged him with the stick-up.

"Archer and Lavina knew, of course, that Brogan wasn't the stick-up man, but they wanted to get that holdup off the books so the police would quit investigating, so they pinned it on Brogan. Then one of those peculiar coincidences entered into the picture. Brogan's general appearance is very similar to that of Tom Gibbs. When Sergeant Holcomb read in the paper about the tan Chevy with the crumpled right fender being used in the stick-up, he suddenly put two and two together, so he grabbed Brogan and put him in the tan Chevy and the witness to the body dumping, Janice Clubb, seeing Brogan in the tan Chevy made a positive identification."

"I take it," Mason said, "somebody is trying to turn State's evidence or you wouldn't have all of this information."

"Your friend Gibbs," Tragg said, grinning. "I softened him up and once he started to sing he trilled like a canary. He's trying to get life and save his dirty neck. Naturally, he's trying to pin the blame on the other two. They're pinning it right back on Gibbs. It's a sweet situation."

Tragg turned to Brogan. "I don't know whether you realize how lucky *you* are," he said. "The way the breaks came in this case you didn't stand one chance in a thousand. You'd have been convicted of the stick-up and then you'd have been convicted of the murder. You've got about a million dollars' worth of legal services free. There are a lot of lawyers who would have thrown up their hands and quit. Perry Mason fought every step of the way and the fighting paid off."

"I fully appreciate that," Brogan said. "I only wish I could compensate him."

"You can say that again," Mary Brogan answered. "And here I was coming out here with the idea that I was going to dump my three hundred and eighty-five dollars in a lawyer's lap and pay him for defending my uncle. How dumb can a girl get? There isn't enough money in my whole family to pay Mr. Mason for even the expenses he's put out on this thing."

Mason grinned. "I think you're overlooking one thing."

243

"What?"

"There's a lot more money in your family than you realize."

"How come?"

Mason said, "Rodney Archer and Martha Lavina deliberately planned to get your uncle convicted. Fortunately, Archer is a very wealthy man."

"And Martha Lavina has a wad of dough, too. Don't forget that," Paul Drake said.

Mary Brogan's face lit up. "You mean we're going to sue them?" she said.

Mason nodded.

"And you'll take our case on a percentage basis?"

"I think," Mason said, "I'd like to cross-examine Martha Lavina and Rodney Archer once more, this time under a little more favorable circumstances."

"That," Mary Brogan announced, "is going to be something worth seeing."

She hesitated a moment, thought things over, then suddenly jumped up and threw her arms around her Uncle Albert's neck.

"My gosh," she said, "do you know what this means, Uncle Albert? We're rich! Rich, I tell you. By the time Mr. Mason gets done with that pair they'll be picked clean."

"And the State," Lieutenant Tragg said, "will move in and singe off whatever pinfeathers they have left."